SURVIVOR SKILLS

PROJECT GLIESE 581G BOOK 3

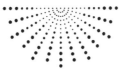

S.E. SMITH

CONTENTS

ACKNOWLEDGMENTS

I would like to thank my husband Steve for believing in me and being proud enough of me to give me the courage to follow my dream. I would also like to give a special thank you to my sister and best friend, Linda, who not only encouraged me to write, but who also read the manuscript. Also to my other friends who believe in me: Julie, Jackie, Christel, Sally, Jolanda, Lisa, Laurelle, Debbie, and Narelle. The girls that keep me going!

And a special thanks to Paul Heitsch, David Brenin, Samantha Cook, Suzanne Elise Freeman, and PJ Ochlan—the awesome voices behind my audiobooks!
—S.E. Smith

Science Fiction Romance
Survivor Skills: Project Gliese Book 3
Copyright © 2018 by S.E. Smith
First E-Book\print Published May 2018
Cover Design by Melody Simmons

Summary: A member of the Project Gliese 581g wakes on an alien
world and joins forces with a rebel fighter to locate other missing
crew members.

ISBN (paperback) 978-1944125189
ISBN (eBook) 978-1-942562-76-4

Published in the United States by Montana Publishing.

{1. Science Fiction Romance – Fiction. 2. Space Opera – Fiction. 3.
Action/Adventure – Fiction. 4. Suspense – Fiction. 5. Romance –
Fiction.}

www.montanapublishinghouse.com

SYNOPSIS

Two warriors—one mission: Survival....

Sergi Lazaroff is a weapons expert and a member of the Russian FSB, also known as the Federal Security Service Bureau—a nice term for his true profession as a spy. Assigned to the Project Gliese 581g exploration team, his job was supposed to be simple—find out what was in space, retrieve the technology, and return home with it, if possible. When he wakes up on an alien planet, Sergi knows the last part of his mission will be impossible. Instead, he must use his military training and skills to survive in a world where he doesn't know the rules.

La'Rue Gant's search for the mysterious occupant of the pod that landed on the assassins' planet of Turbinta quickly turns into a game of predator versus prey. She found what she was looking for—and discovers that the ancient legends may be true when the tables are unexpectedly turned, and she becomes the hunted. What she doesn't expect is the powerful reaction she has to this man from another world.

When word reaches them that another member of the Gliese's crew was found, Sergi and La'Rue embark on a mission to save that crew member at any cost. Caught in the middle of an alien civil war, two fighters from vastly different backgrounds must come together to fight for the survival of the Knights of the Gallant Order, even as the Legion forces close in around them. Can they slip through the traps set up to snare them, or will the Legion Director finally capture not one, but two of the prophesied ancient Knights of the Gallant Order?

CHARACTER REFERENCE:

Members of the Gliese 581g Exploration Team:

Commander Joshua Manson

American Mission Leader
Background: Navy

Commander Ashton Haze

American Pilot
Background: Army

Sergi Lazaroff

Russian Mission Specialist
Spy for the FSB
Background: Mechanical engineering, Payload, and Weapons

Julia Marksdale

American Navigator and Contact Support
Daughter of the professor who discovered the object
Mission Specialist
Background: Astronomy and Physics

Mei Li Hú

Chinese Mission Specialist
Spy for the Ministry of State Security
Background: Computer science, Biology, Environmental Systems

Landing Sites

Josh: Tesla Terra

Partnered with Cassa de Rola

Ash: Torrian

Partnered with Kella Ta'Qui

Sergi: Turbinta

Partnered with La'Rue Gant

Mei: Cryon II 5469220

Julia: Plateau

Other Characters

La'Rue Gant:

Freighter Captain
Daughter of a Knight of the Gallant
Home world: Tesla Terra

HL-9:

Spider-like service robot belonging to La'Rue
Nickname: H

General Hutu Gomerant:

Legendary Knight of the Gallant Order
Son of Kubo
Torrian
Home world: Torrian

General Kubo Gomerant:

Crafty Knight of the Gallant Order
Keeper of The Ancient City of Torrian
Father of Hutu
Home World: Torrian

Bantu aka Squeals:

Member of the Legion for 10 years
Agent for the Gallant Order
Home World: Tesla Terra

Slate:

La'Rue's ex-lover and ex-crew member on the *Star Runner*
Home World: Jeslean

Tallei:

One-eyed Master Turbintan Assassin
Kella's master
Home World: Flora Terra

Zoak:

Pupil of Tallei
Gailock species;
Raised as a Turbintan
Home world: Gaul

Andri Andronikos:

Director of the Legion
Half-brother to Coleridge
Uncle to Roan
Home world: Jeslean

Coleridge Landais aka Count Landais:

General of the Legion
Andri's half brother
Father of Roan
Home world: Jeslean

Nia:

Deceased wife of General Coleridge Landais
Mother of Roan Landais
Home world: Plateau

Roan Landais:

General of the Legion
Son of Coleridge Landais

Nephew of Andri Andronikos
Home world: Plateau – raised on Jeslean

Roanna:

Roan's grandmother on his mother's side
Home world: Plateau

Calstar:

Roan's grandfather on his mother's side
Home world: Plateau

Dorane LeGaugh:

Wealthy businessman
Home world: Cryon

Crock:

Freight Captain
Owns fleet of freighters
Home world: Torrian

PROLOGUE

Gliese 581
Eighteen months, twenty-three days, four hours:
928,081,020 km/6.2 Astronomical Units (AU) from Earth.

"*T*wo minutes," Sergi Lazaroff confirmed into the microphone in his helmet, responding to the warning he had been given.

He reached out and gripped the side of a long panel. While his spacesuit was bulky, he moved with ease in the zero gravity within the complex alien machine. He had attached a string of magnetic lights at regular intervals, and there were additional lights mounted to his helmet – but outside of their limited range, the interior was pitch black. Josh waited in the large gap created by whatever had struck the gateway, ready in case Sergi needed help.

A feeling of awe still struck him when he allowed himself to think about the fact that he was inside an alien machine that had been abandoned who knew how long ago. The results of the carbon dating they'd done on the metal were inconsistent, much to the disgust of Mei and Julia.

A smile curved his lips as he thought about Dr. Mei Li Hú's frustrated determination to extrapolate a plausible history of the object. Of course she would be better off waiting to theorize until they'd gotten more information, but some people were just too impatient.

Mei was one of the five crew members on this mission to investigate the unusual object discovered more than ten years ago by Dr. Harry Marksdale, a University of Arizona professor and amateur astronomer. Mei had ostensibly come to the mission at the behest of the Chinese space agency, and Sergi suspected the others were unaware of her secret objectives.

Her private mission was similar enough to his own that it had been relatively easy to recognize. She was a spy for the Ministry of State Security, the Chinese equivalent of Russia's Federal Security Service Bureau. Mei's father, owner of one of China's largest technology manufacturing and research companies, had been a major contributor to Project Gliese 581g, which had made it easy for Mei to become a crew member of the mission.

Mei was one of two Mission Specialists aboard the spaceship. Her background in computer science, biology, and environmental systems was an invaluable asset to the expedition. The other three members of the crew were Americans.

Lieutenant Commander Joshua Manson was a career Navy man. He commanded the Gliese 581g mission with military precision and attention to detail. Along with Lieutenant Commander Ashton 'Ash' Haze, the pilot for this operation, he had been brought on after a helicopter accident killed the first crew chosen for this highly classified international suicide mission.

The last member of the team was the only member without any military training. Dr. Julia Marksdale, Harry Marksdale's daughter, was there purely for her scientific expertise. Julia was in charge of navigation, medical, and contact support.

This project had been the brainchild of Harry and Julia. Sadly, Harry, along with the initial and backup teams, had been killed while returning to Houston. Sergi suspected the fatal mechanical failures of the helicopters had been contrived to ensure that he and Mei were added to the new list of recruits. Unfortunately, there had not been enough time to find out whether it had been his government's doing or that of Mei's.

His specialty was in mechanical engineering, payload, and weaponry. Sergi's mission was straightforward: find out what was out in space, retrieve as much data as he could, and return home alive to share it with his handlers. Unfortunately, there was no way to transmit the data without everyone involved with the Gliese 581g mission realizing that he was a spy. The only way to pass on the information covertly was to make it back home in one piece and do so personally.

Of course, this mission came with greater risks than any other he had been assigned before. After all, if things went south, there was no one to extricate him – not that anyone would have come for him on any of his other missions either.

"Sergi, you need to monitor your oxygen level. You are down to eighty percent while Josh is still at eighty-nine," Mei quietly said.

"Are you worrying about me, Mei?" he quipped.

The sound of an inelegant snort whooshed in his ear. "Dead people tend to soil themselves. I don't want you to ruin a perfectly good spacesuit because you hooked up the hoses incorrectly," she retorted.

"That is downright disgusting, Mei," Ash dryly added his opinion.

"But true," Julia responded. "The gas produced within a body after death combined with the incapacitation of the region of the brain that would normally control the muscles holding the sphincter closed would result in soiling. There are a lot of processes that begin after death that manifest in unfortunate ways because not all parts of a body die at the same time. Death creates more of a domino effect. As different types of muscles die, they can loosen, or they can contract, causing twitches and spasms *after* death. Plus, the blood still contains the nutrients it had before the heart stopped beating, and a person's death causes the membranes of blood cells to become more permeable to calcium as they, too, begin to die, so for certain muscle cells, like those in a penis, that are activated by calcium ions—"

"I don't think I like where this is going," Ash piped in.

Sergi shook his head inside the helmet. He didn't know if it was the growing familiarity with the two women during the voyage or if he was getting soft, but both of them amused the hell out of him. If he stopped to think about it, the lighthearted affection and protective instincts he had toward the two women were actually brand-new experiences in his life. While his relationship, if he could even call it that, with Mei had always been like two tigers circling each other looking for a weak point, what he had with Julia was different. She was a quiet, intelligent, yet strangely innocent and naïve, scientist, and he sometimes silently compared her to a delicate flower so rare that he'd thought it extinct – because she was genuine, and she was compassionate, and she was single-handedly giving him hope that there might be more like her somewhere in the world.

Josh and Ash were good men to have with you in a storm. He admired Josh's attention to detail and his ability to process information quickly and piece it together to form a larger picture. Ash, on the other hand, had a quick wit, easy smile, and impressive piloting skills.

As he listened to his team's chatter, Sergi turned the cameras embedded in his helmet and suit toward the circuit in front of him, making sure they would record his every movement. The 'unusual object' appeared to be an alien gateway of some sort, and inside the mechanism was a treasure trove of technology unlike anything he had ever seen before. He wanted as much documentation of it as he could get. After over eighteen months in space on an experimental spaceship, he was still trying to wrap his head around the fact that they had proof that humans were not alone in the universe – or at least that they hadn't been at one time.

He refitted the fourth of five panels he had repaired, and pushed off, floating nearly a half meter before he twisted and grabbed a bar to stop his upward momentum. He joked with Mei as he turned the cameras toward the damaged circuit in front of him. From the pouch attached to his utility belt, he pulled out the last circuit board he had reverse-engineered from the damaged alien boards. He hoped the components were a close enough match to work. When he had applied minimal power to it, the board had lit up the entire workroom.

Mei murmured that he was now down to sixty-nine percent, so he had better stop giving all the oxygen to his... *head*. Sergei smirked, imagining the pointed look she would be giving him if they were in the same room. He chuckled when he heard Julia's voice falter in confusion. Julia was extremely smart, but sometimes suggestive jokes went right over her head.

"Ah, Julia," Ash interjected with a laugh. "I think Mei was inferring that Sergi was feeding oxygen to his other head."

There was a pause as Julia switched mental gears, and he chuckled when she groaned.

"Well, damn. I missed the real meaning of the conversation again," she muttered.

"That's okay, Julia. It's just all that heavy breathing that gets to Mei," Sergi teased.

As if on cue, he heard Mei's exasperated hiss. "I believe your brain is definitely suffering from hypoxia, Sergi. I know men like to let their balls breathe, but really!" Mei retorted.

The sounds of Julia, Josh, and Ash's muffled laughter made him grin. He knew which buttons to push to get a predictable reaction out of his impossibly easy to ruffle counterpart. His smile faded as the depth of his deception hit him. This small group had become more than comrades on a mission to do the impossible – they had become a family.

"Sergi, how much longer do you need?" Josh asked from near the entrance, breaking into his train of thought.

"This should complete the final connection. Whether these things have a built-in power supply that is still working is another matter. I've gone through this one, and it looks like it's linked to the one before it and the next one, but I never found an actual power source," Sergi replied, inserting the circuit board into the empty slot.

"We'll deal with that when we get to it," Josh instructed.

"Roger that," Sergi replied, carefully adjusting the panel and feeling it click into place.

He pulled himself to the side. All the damaged panels that he could see had been repaired. Whether Earth materials and alien technology were compatible was another question, but the preliminary testing in the lab had shown a closed circuit. There was one more thing to do and that was to reconnect the line cable that he had noticed as he was entering. He wasn't sure how he had missed it during his space walks.

He turned slightly and in the glow of the lights they'd brought he could see Josh watching him intently. Returning his focus to the cable, he pulled the end around and aligned it with the port. He blinked when a flash of red light illuminated the interior of the gateway.

"What the...?! Sergi, we need to get out of here," Josh warned.

"Just a minute," Sergi responded.

He twisted and pulled his body upward to a long bar where he had strapped one of his tool bags. His fingers fumbled with the clip when the gateway shuddered, then roughly vibrated. A soft curse escaped him when his thickly gloved hands slipped off the clip.

"Leave them. We need to get out of here now," Josh ordered.

Sergi felt Josh tug on his foot. At the same time, he realized that the bag of tools, along with himself and Josh, were beginning to move. It took him a moment to comprehend that it was the walls that were beginning to spin, not them.

He twisted and nodded to Josh. With a wave of his hand, he motioned for Josh to go through the opening first since he was closer. Reaching down, he used the railing to follow Josh down to the gap in the outer wall. Josh braced his feet on a long crossbar and kicked off. A moment later, Sergi did the same and followed Josh through the gaping hole in the side of the gateway, his hand moved to unhook his tether to the mechanism. His hand stilled when he looked down the long line of circular gates and saw the other sections lighting up. He reached out and grabbed Josh's arm.

"Josh, look!" Sergi exclaimed, lifting his arm toward the lights.

He heard the alarmed communications of his team, but he was more focused on what could only be described as a miracle. Each of the six gateways was coming online. The long rows of cables connecting them began to glow. Sergi watched in fascination as each gate slowly began to spin – and open. It took a moment to register in his brain that Josh was urgently ordering him to use his jet pack. When it did, he realized that they were in extreme danger.

"Hurry up, Sergi. We need to get back to the Gliese," Josh said.

Struggling to unhook the tether, he grunted when the clasp refused to release. "I won't argue with you on that," Sergi muttered before he heard Josh's repeated urgent warning in his headset.

Sergi released a long string of curses in his native Russian when he was jerked backwards away from Josh. His fingers slipped from the clasp as he spun violently. Fighting to twist around so he could grab the tether, he clenched his jaw when the line was jerked out of his hand.

"I can't get the tether undone," Sergi growled in frustration.

He looked in the direction he had last seen Josh. The other man was leaning forward, his determined expression visible behind the glass of his helmet.

"Hold on, I'm coming," Josh replied.

Sergi released a nervous chuckle. "I don't think I'll be going anywhere. Though, I would appreciate it if you could hurry," he reflected, seeing the other gateways beginning to spin even more rapidly.

Sergi's breath caught in his throat when Josh struggled to grab him and missed. The tension on the tether was increasing and he knew he was seconds away from death. If Josh didn't leave him, they would both be dead, and the mission would be in dire jeopardy. He reached out and gripped Josh's shoulders when the other man was finally able to grab him.

Ash's tense warning sounded in their headphones. "Josh, you need to get a move on," Ash stated.

"I am," Josh replied.

Sergi shook his head. He kept his gaze on Josh as they both rotated at an increasingly dizzying speed.

"Josh... Commander, leave me," Sergi ordered in a quiet tone.

Josh ignored him and continued to work on the metal clasp. Sergi gritted his teeth and prepared to forcibly push Josh away when the tether finally broke free. Josh cursed before he warned Sergei to 'Brace for impact'.

Sergi grunted when his back hit the spinning ring of the gateway, and his momentum sent him spiraling toward the glowing cable. For a moment he wondered if being crushed to death or electrocuted would be better. Unable to stop his trajectory, all he could do was hope that a second miracle would occur, and he would just be cast out into space.

He knew his luck had run out the moment he connected with the cable. The powerful surge of electricity flashed through his suit. For a brief second, he stiffened and thought his heart would explode, but it just stuttered and stopped. A brilliant flash of white light shot through his mind. He wondered if he had been given a glimpse of heaven to add to his misery.

Sergi wasn't a religious man, but if there really were only two afterlife options – heaven or hell – he could see why a supreme being might give him a glimpse of what he could never have. It would make his eternity in hell all the more bitter. That was his last thought before his mind shut down.

CHAPTER ONE

One Earth week later:

*T*he alarms pulled Sergi back to consciousness, and he was suddenly aware of a steady downpour, making the world outside the pod look distorted and dismal. He looked at the digital readings. Oxygen was dangerously low. The system was showing a leak in one of the tanks. He lifted his head, and noticed the small portable tank with a mask attached. He read the oxygen level.

Thirty percent....

He had less than five percent in the capsule and thirty percent on the portable tank. He laid his head back and stared through the glass covering. At least the capsule didn't completely feel like a casket – if only for the moment.

Above him, Sergi could see the remains of the parachute that would have deployed once the capsule broke through the atmosphere. It was tangled in a large tree.

Four things registered in his brain. First, he hurt like hell, so that confirmed he was alive. Second, he was no longer on the Gliese 581. Third, wherever in the hell he had landed, there had to be some type of atmosphere if there was rain and trees – preferably the kind that wouldn't melt the flesh off of his bones. The last was the one that concerned him the most. He wondered if any of the others had made it out alive.

Sergi grabbed the mask, held it up to his face, and slammed his palm against the emergency release lever. Nothing happened.

"Open, dammit," Sergi ordered in Russian, violently working the lever again.

"Warning, current oxygen levels are critical. The system diagnostic has detected a leak in the main oxygen tank. Please replace the tank," the computer voice stated.

"You think I don't know that my oxygen is almost depleted? If you would open this casket, I would gladly remove myself," Sergi growled in profanity laced Russian.

He clenched his jaw in determination. Grabbing the release handle, he pulled on it again. This time, the very noticeable click of the lock releasing swept through the interior of the pod. With his free hand, he pushed against the hatch until he had enough room to sit up.

He shivered in the icy rain as he cautiously looked around. At least the parachute gave him a small measure of protection from the downpour. Barren trees surrounded him. The area was desolate: there was no life – and no other escape pods to be seen. He slowly pulled the mask away from his face, and gingerly took a deep breath. A slight cough escaped him as the swirling mist swept through his nose and down his throat. The air felt heavy, but he could breathe.

He dropped the mask to the side. His gloved hands gripped the side of the capsule and he rolled over the edge. A silent curse filtered through his brain when his booted feet sank into the dark gray mud.

"This feels like home," he muttered under his breath, taking in the freezing rain, thick fog, disgusting mud, and dreary landscape.

Unsure of where he was or how he had gotten there, his first focus was on getting out of the bulky spacesuit and into something that he could move in. He bent over, parted the fabric of the headrest, and withdrew the military-grade NRS-2 Scouting knife that he had stored in the foam cushion.

Sergi used the knife to gut the interior of the capsule. He had been very careful to modify the interior after it had been stored aboard the Gliese 581. He pulled out camouflage clothing, weapons, the portable oxygen tank that came standard with each pod, and a survival pack with a limited number of rations, medical supplies, and the essentials for the most dangerous covert operation.

Sliding the blade along the edge of the fabric of the bedding, he retrieved his SR-1 9mm pistol along with several clips. He did the same along the bottom, removing the parts for the VSK-94 Special Purpose Silent Sniper rifle. The rifle was perfect for Urban Warfare if he needed to strike without being seen. While he had never expected to need any of the items he had stored in the capsule, his training and experience had drilled into him the necessity to be prepared for any event – including a trip into space.

Within minutes, he had stripped himself of the bulky spacesuit and dressed to blend in with the environment around him. He quickly packed everything into the camouflaged grey and tan backpack, remembering at the last minute to remove the video camera that was recording his every move, and slid the straps over his shoulders. He tucked the pistol into the waistband of his pants against his lower back, making sure he could easily reach it.

He reached up and closed the lid of the capsule, then turned to face the gloomy forest. He had no map of the area or knowledge of his environment, which meant that, for now, he had to classify everything as hostile.

Sergi held the rifle ready as he left the shelter of the parachute and moved into the freezing downpour. His hat protected his head from the cold rain while the high-tech goggles gave him the ability to search for any heat signatures. He moved like a wraith through the woods, searching for evidence that he wasn't alone.

∼

La'Rue Gant flipped up the visor of her welding helmet, looked at the circuit panel for a moment, then took off the helmet and turned toward the storage unit. In the background, loud music played. While it might not be the smartest thing in the world to do at the moment, La'Rue had never really cared what anyone else thought. She lived by one rule – hers.

"Which isn't such a bad idea, La'Rue darling," she muttered to herself, "considering you are on a planet of assassins. Why *not* go to a place where the residents would love to slit your throat just for the fun of watching you bleed out? But, hey, it might be more profitable for them to hand me over to Bog. My face is probably plastered on every screen in the galaxy. Fuck Slate and his fucking thirty thousand credits owed."

She wouldn't be in this mess if she had listened to her head instead of her gut. Yeah, it was way messed up and should have been the other way around. Her gut was what had kept her alive this long, but this time she swore her internal warning system was fried.

"You just *had* to listen in on a secure transmission. You should have ignored it, La'Rue. People who cross the Legion end up dead. If anyone knows that, it should be you. Then, being the really smart person that you are, you decide you need to follow one of the signals that they were talking about – to Turbinta! Who the hell lands their escape pod on a planet full of assassins? I'll tell you who, the same kind of dumbass who lands their freighter and burns up their front shields in the process, that's who," she muttered.

For the past two years she had been monitoring both the rebel groups and the Legion. Lifting a hand, she wiped her nose on her long sleeve. Even with the environmental system working, she could still feel the chill in the air.

"The rebels have to be on to something this time," she said as she replaced the helmet and welder in the storage unit. She paused with her hand on a wrench and glanced at the circuit panel, a frown creasing her brow. "They have to be, otherwise why would the Legion be going crazy? Andronikos's prize Commander wouldn't have come here himself if he wasn't worried."

La'Rue shook her head and moved back to the circuit board, wrench in hand. She replaced the panel and tightened the bolts. Twirling the wrench in her hand, her lips twisted as she looked around the small but nimble freighter. It was the last of her heritage, a gift from her father. Sure, it hadn't worked when he'd given it to her, but it did now thanks to years of hard work, more daring cargo runs than she would admit, and a few high-stakes wins at the gaming tables.

Unfortunately, she might have pissed off a few of her lenders when she had turned out to be a little savvier than they'd been expecting and had actually paid them off with her winnings. Her goal was to never have to borrow credits again, and one way to do that was to earn a lot – by cashing in on what the Legion wanted. If she could find even one of the strange pods the Legion was talking about, she could live off the reward for a couple of years. She could ditch the lower end freighter runs, upgrade the *Star Runner,* and kiss Slate and his band of despicable, thieving pirates goodbye once and for all.

Her eyes darkened with anger and determination. She wasn't about to lose her only way of making a living because Slate had decided to put up *her* ship as collateral for *his* bad decisions. She had argued that the debt wasn't hers, but unfortunately, Bog didn't want to listen. Slate had used her thumb imprint to guarantee the loan.

She grumbled to herself as she stowed the wrench in the storage unit, then strode through the freighter, ducking her head under a low hanging conduit. HL-9 followed her. She turned at the end of the corridor and bent to open a hatch. Pulling it back, she waited for the ladder to rise before she slid down. HL-9 gripped the ladder with four of his legs on each side, and slid down behind her.

"I don't know when I'll be back, H. However long it takes, I guess. You have the position of the signal, right?" La'Rue asked. She glanced at the eight-legged bot before she turned and pulled open a storage compartment. "Where is the long barrel? Argh, I bet Slate took it. I have only two of the short barrels left and one of them doesn't work," she groaned, letting her head fall back to stare up at the ceiling in frustration.

La'Rue ground her teeth together before she looked down and made a face at HL-9. Slate had a lot to answer for and she planned on making sure that he did – if she survived this crazy quest of hers.

Opening the second cabinet, she pulled out the holster and the blaster that had belonged to her dad. Pursing her lips together, she swung the holster belt around her waist and tightened it. She pulled out the broken blaster and tossed it to the service bot.

"See if you can fix this while I'm gone," she said as she turned and pulled out a waterproof slicker and cap. "Let's hope I don't run into anyone. One lousy blaster meant for shooting field rodents isn't going to do me much good against a well-trained assassin."

La'Rue pulled on the slicker, sealing it over her black pants and shirt. Her matching black boots went almost to her knees and would protect her feet. Tucking the loose strands of her red hair into the cap, she pulled the padded strap tight under her chin. She grabbed the goggles and a stun rod last.

"I look like I'm ready to go out to harvest fields instead of hunting for a mysterious pod on a planet full of assassins. I swear if a Turbintan sees me dressed like this, they'll die from laughter," La'Rue grumbled to her only companion. "Don't let anything happen to my freighter, H."

The small bot flashed its multiple eyes at her to let her know that it understood her order. La'Rue released a long, loud sigh before she stepped into the circle on the floor and reached up to press the green button on the control panel attached to one of the support brackets. Within seconds, the platform she was standing on descended under the freighter.

La'Rue jumped off the round platform and landed on the soggy ground, wincing at the splat sound. She pressed the remote on her wrist cuff, scanning the area as she pulled her goggles down. There was nothing out there – she hoped.

"H, show me the best path to the signal," La'Rue softly ordered.

The display inside her goggles flickered, and a second later a map appeared. Gripping the stun rod in her hand, La'Rue left the safety of her freighter and headed out into the pounding rain on a mission to find one of the mysterious pods the Legion was so interested in locating.

CHAPTER TWO

*T*he distinctive hum of an aircraft alerted Sergi to the fact that he wasn't alone. He moved under the protective cover of a fallen tree trunk, and saw an alien transport soar over the trees.

A curse slipped from his lips when he realized what they might be looking for – his emergency pod. There was the possibility it had been sighted or had registered on some type of radar, but more than likely the emergency beacon was emitting a signal.

His gaze moved back toward the direction he had come. He was less than a kilometer from the capsule. Looking up at the sky again, he debated whether he should go back. With a muttered curse, he moved out from under the tree and retraced his steps.

Less than twenty minutes later, a long line of expletives was silently slipping through Sergi's mind as he crouched behind a thick log and studied the alien walking around his abandoned capsule, apparently scanning it with a device in his right hand. The alien was thankfully humanoid: one head, two legs, two feet, two arms and hands of typically human proportions, roughly average height, and a slender build. Sergi could see the gun in the alien's gloved left hand, but he couldn't see the alien's face. The person's head was covered with a dark brown and black hat with a wide brim. Goggles and a thick scarf covered the alien's eyes, nose, and mouth. A long, mud-splattered coat covered the alien from neck to knees. High, black boots, coated in mud, protected both feet.

Sergi quickly scanned the area, but he didn't see an alien transport nearby. The alien stopped near the top left corner of the pod where the instrument panel and the emergency beacon were located, stashed his device in his pocket, and pulled something from a pouch at his waist. Within seconds, the alien had opened the panel and disconnected the emergency beacon. An appreciative grin curved Sergi's lips when he saw the man expertly twirl the tool in his hand before replacing it in the pouch.

Sergi intently watched as the alien raised his wrist to his covered mouth and spoke. He was too far away for him to understand what the alien was saying, but Sergi would bet the man was calling for assistance. The alien moved his hand along the top of the pod. The sound of a loud click followed by the hatch opening made him grimace. It was going to be obvious that someone had been in the capsule and escaped.

He took advantage of the alien's distraction to back away. In seconds, he had left the capsule and the alien behind him. He would move out at a rapid pace until there was enough distance between them, then worry about covering his tracks while he circled around and tried to determine where the alien had come from. Once Sergi knew a little more about where he was, he would plan a course of action. At the moment, his main concern was disappearing.

One thing is for sure, he thought as he broke into a steady jog, *this is going to take every ounce of my training to survive.*

～

La'Rue gripped the side of the capsule as she looked inside. A shiver ran through her, and she looked over her shoulder. There was no denying that someone had been in the capsule and whoever it had been was now gone.

She reached inside and pulled out the bulky suit. There were colorful patches on the front and one arm of the suit. Slinging it over her shoulder, she decided she would take it back with her to get a closer look then. Her gaze swept the interior. Bending forward, she ran her fingers along the ripped material. Whoever had been in here had cut up the inside pretty good.

She pulled back a section and saw the indentations in the soft material underneath. Running her hand along the rips, she thoroughly checked each of them. One after another, she could tell that there had been items stored under the fabric. A wave of unease swept through her. She needed to get back to the freighter and grab one of the equipment skiffs she had on board. There was no way she could pull this thing through the woods without a heavy duty piece of equipment to help her.

Looking up, she saw the silver cloth tangled in the trees above. She wouldn't have much time to retrieve the capsule. At least one scouting transport had flown over this area. Disabling the signal the capsule had been sending out would only give her a short reprieve. She was positive there would be others looking for the thing – and whoever had been inside.

She started to close the lid when a glint of silver caught her eye. She ran her hand along the seam. Her fingers tangled in a metal chain. She tugged it free and lifted the chain so she could study the metal tags. At the end of the chain were two, small rectangular metal plates with an indecipherable inscription on them.

She pocketed the chain and reached up to pull the lid down. A quick glance at her wrist showed that another transport was coming. She really hoped that her freighter's digital paint camouflaged the ship enough for it to go unnoticed, because if not, HL-9 was going to have company. The last thing La'Rue wanted was to be stuck on this shit-hole of a planet with only an antiquated pistol and a rodent stunner.

"H, did you get the video feed I sent of the capsule?" La'Rue asked in a soft voice as she stepped away from the metal box.

A single light glowed on and off several times on the communicator on her wrist. The lights were HL-9's way of telling her that the video feed transmission had been successful. La'Rue adjusted the bulky suit on her shoulder and began her return trip to the freighter. Now, if she could just get the capsule back to her ship and get off this planet before dark, she could be on her way to kissing Slate and the debt collector goodbye once and for all.

CHAPTER THREE

*I*t didn't take long for Sergi to find the tracks the alien had left. Cutting between trees, he maintained a parallel path to the tracks, and slowed his pace when he saw a break in the trees up ahead. So far, except for the alien and the spaceship that had flown overhead earlier, he hadn't seen any signs of life. The ground varied from hard rock to slushy mud. The trees were all the same dark ash color and devoid of leaves. He didn't know if they were alive or dead. The driving rain was just as intense as it had been when he'd left the pod an hour and a half before. The sky was a blanket of dark clouds in every direction. He wondered if it ever stopped raining in this place.

The terrain was dotted with large boulders, and he had found a few places where he could create a temporary shelter if it became necessary. He wouldn't, of course. He needed to distance himself from the capsule before he could think of seeking shelter.

Sergi peered around a wet tree trunk to scan the small clearing in the trees. He frowned. Something was off. He bent his head, reached into his pocket, and pulled out a cloth to clean the water from his goggles. Replacing the cloth, he studied the area in front of him once more.

The clearing looked empty, but there was a difference between what his eyes and brain were telling him and what his gut was saying. It took him a few seconds to realize what was wrong. Amidst the rain, there were mini waterfalls flowing down – from thin air.

Curious, Sergi slowly squatted. His eyes widened when he saw the black underside of a spaceship. He rose to his feet, keeping his gaze trained on the spot where the water was falling. Appreciation swept through him at the cleverness of the paint. It had a reflective surface, making it almost invisible to the naked eye unless you saw something unusual – like small waterfalls flowing from out of the air.

He turned when he heard footsteps in the mud behind him. Crouching down once again, he kept his eyes on the alien who had discovered his capsule. He scowled when he saw his spacesuit draped over the alien's shoulder.

Sergi turned to keep the alien in sight as the slender man walked by him, ducked under the spaceship, and walked to the center of the clearing. He pressed a control on his wrist, and Sergi watched as a round platform descended from beneath the spaceship. A minute later, the man stepped on the platform, which rose until the alien had disappeared inside the vessel.

Sergi contemplated what he should do next. Without any knowledge of the area or the people, he was at a huge disadvantage. He needed to find a way onto the spaceship, and it would be nice if he didn't find out the hard way that the alien had companions in there.

The sound of a hydraulic door opening drew his attention. His eyes narrowed when he saw a large hatch lowering from the back of the spaceship, and he smiled when he saw the man emerge on a hovering forklift.

Sergi knew at that moment exactly where the alien was going – back to the capsule. He maneuvered the machine out of the large bay and down the ramp, pausing at the bottom. Sergi peered through a gap in the trees as the man turned and called out to someone behind him in the spacecraft.

So he is not alone, Sergi thought with a disgruntled frown.

He had two choices. He could return to his capsule and overpower the man there to discover some information, or, he could remain here and wait for the man to return, which would require moving out into the open to overpower the alien while he was preoccupied with loading the capsule on the ship. The problem with that was it would leave him exposed to whoever was inside the transport.

Deciding his first choice might be better, considering that he had no idea how many people were on board, he rose and turned to follow the alien. Even hovering, the large machine would have to move slowly through the forest, picking out a path between fallen trees and boulders. That slow movement would make it easy for Sergi to keep up with him.

Sergi followed almost a kilometer behind the hovering forklift. They were half way to the capsule when a dark shape rose from a group of boulders and fired on the alien he'd been following. Sergi instinctively crouched down as the slender man tumbled off the forklift and fell to the ground.

He cautiously scanned the area for any others. The alien on the rock jumped off and landed on the far side of the forklift. He didn't have any difficulty seeing the facial features of this alien. He had dark green, leathery skin with long scars etched into the side of his face, and his mouth was full of sharp, jagged teeth. The alien had thick, muscular arms, torso, and legs. His upper body was devoid of clothing while his lower half was covered in dark brown, leather pants and boots. A leather harness filled with weapons crisscrossed his torso. From this vantage point, Sergi could see the alien had a long thin tail that whipped back and forth behind him.

The green alien stepped around the forklift, and Sergi's eyes widened when the huge creature suddenly flew backwards. A loud snarl filled the air as the green alien surged to his feet. Two short blades were tightly gripped in each of his hands.

Sergi looked at the alien he had been following. Blood soaked the man's shoulder, and he held a rod in front of himself as he faced off with the green alien. The slender man's stance indicated he knew how to fight, but even still, if Sergi were a betting man, he would have placed a hefty wager on the green alien.

Unfortunately for the green man, Sergi needed information. If he had to choose an ally between Alien One or Alien Two, he'd go for the first one. Decision made, Sergi slipped away from the two and began working his way toward the boulder where the green alien had first appeared.

~

A Few Moments Earlier:

Pain radiated through La'Rue's shoulder, but she ignored it. Silent curses ran through her mind as she simultaneously reached for the stun rod lying in the mud next to her and pulled the pistol from the holster at her side. She had seen the movement a split second too late.

At least you saw him, otherwise you wouldn't be feeling anything, La'Rue, she silently reminded herself as she rolled onto her back and waited for her chance to strike.

She had seen the Turbintan rise up out of the corner of her eye and had already been rolling off the loading skiff, but if she had been more attentive, she wouldn't be injured right now. She tightened her grip on her blaster. She would probably have one chance if this was one of the trained assassins.

Her lips tightened in a line of determination. She wasn't going to give up without a fight. Her finger was poised on the trigger.

Wait for him to come around, she silently cautioned herself. *You need a direct hit between the second and third ribs.*

La'Rue ignored the chill of the mud seeping through her clothing. It was the least of her worries at the moment. Time appeared to slow down as she waited with her eyes closed, listening.

It took every ounce of her courage not to turn and flee when she heard the Turbintan come close to the skiff. She stayed limp, her left arm extended, her fingers open with the stun rod lying in her palm. Her right hand was down by her thigh, half hidden by the coat she was wearing.

The second the assassin rounded the skiff and turned to face her,

La'Rue lifted her blaster and fired on the Turbintan. A huge sense of satisfaction washed through her when the man flew backwards. Rising stiffly to her feet, she held her position. She had seven shots and it would probably take every single one of them to kill the bastard.

As she aimed the gun and tightly gripped the stun rod in her other hand, the deep gash in her left shoulder and she could feel blood dampening her sleeve under the slicker. The Turbintan hissed at her, opening its wide jaws to show off his mouthful of sharp, jagged teeth.

La'Rue ignored him. Her eyes were on the wound in his side. The second he moved his hand, she fired the blaster again. He didn't fly back as far as he had the first time, and he quickly recovered and moved closer. She backed up carefully to keep her balance in the slippery mud. One swipe of his tail and she would be dead.

Her arm shook when she stumbled and fired another blast at the scarred, green man. This one hit him in the shoulder. She pulled her elbow in and tried to keep her arm steady as she aimed for the gaping wound in his side. The blast hit his hip.

"You will die a slow death," the Turbintan growled.

La'Rue shook her head. "You are the one who will be dying," she bravely retorted.

A menacing chuckle echoed through the air. "I will enjoy tearing your guts out and eating them while you scream," he snarled, advancing toward her.

"I hope you know that is completely gross and not normal," La'Rue snapped, jerking backward, aiming for the wound in his side, and pulling the trigger again as he swung one of his sharp blades.

"It is normal for me," he replied with a sharp-toothed grin, not even wincing when the blast hit him.

La'Rue fired again and again at the wound in his side until the charge was depleted on her blaster. Tossing it aside, she held up the stun rod with both hands. Her teeth rattled when the Turbintan's blade struck the rod.

As she stepped backward, her heel caught on a half-buried log, and she fell on her back. The assassin's laughter mixed with the sound of the rain as he nonchalantly tossed one of the blades up in the air and caught it by the handle. He lunged forward, swinging his tail toward her. At the same time, she sat up and shoved the stun rod into the gaping wound in his side. Depressing the button, she discharged a powerful burst from the end of the rod.

Out of her peripheral vision, La'Rue noticed movement behind the Turbintan just before a ghostly figure yanked her attacker's wrist backward. She watched in shock as the man savagely rotated the Turbintan's arm behind him. The sound of the Turbintan's bone snapping sent a chill through her. The man then forcibly bent the man's arm and drove the curved blade up through the Turbintan's back where the tip emerged through his chest cavity.

The assassin's eyes rolled back in his head, and his body fell toward her. La'Rue shoved against the full weight of the collapsing body with all her might. Jerking the stun rod free, she rolled to the side under the trunk of a fallen tree. The assassin slumped face first into the mud – dead.

Her eyes jerked up to the man standing over the assassin. The stun rod had lodged in the trunk of the fallen tree as she'd rolled under it to avoid the Turbintan's falling body. She tried to scramble to her feet, but by this point she was so covered in mud that she kept slipping. The fallen tree was slick with moss on this side and there was nothing else to brace against.

She scooted back when she heard what sounded like a muttered curse in an unfamiliar language. Her heart raced, and she tried once again to move away when the man stepped toward her. Her mouth dropped open when he suddenly stopped, stared down at her, and spoke in a soft, calm voice. He was using the same unknown language that he had uttered a second before, and she didn't recognize a word.

La'Rue put pressure on her bleeding shoulder and warily watched as the man held his hands out in front of himself and slowly sank down into a crouch. Her gaze swept over what she could see of his features – which wasn't much. Like she did, he wore a mask that covered most of his face. The rest of his face was covered with a pale cloth the color of the mud.

He blended in with his surroundings, but the clothing looked different from what she was used to seeing. His hands were covered in a pair of thin gloves that were molded to his fingers. Her eyes swept over the weapon he had over one shoulder before moving down his chest and pausing on the other weapons he wore at his waist.

"I don't speak your language," she said, speaking in Galactic Standard. "What planet are you from?"

The man pulled his arms back to his sides and rested them on his thighs. He didn't answer her at first. After a few seconds, he made a sweeping motion with his hand.

"Take off your helmet and scarf," he ordered with an accent that she couldn't place. Her lips tightened in annoyance, but she decided she didn't have much choice.

If he was another Turbintan assassin, he really needed to go back for more training. Just after that thought ran through her mind, she looked at the dead assassin next to them. The man had silently come up behind her attacker and expertly used the Turbintan's own weapon against him. Those were not things a rookie could do.

Keeping her left arm still, La'Rue used her bloody right hand to angrily pull her scarf down before removing her goggles. She stared back at the man with unblinking eyes. Lifting her chin, she waited for him to decide what he was going to do next.

"You speak English?" the man said more than asked, carefully rising to his feet and taking a step back.

La'Rue shook her head. "I don't know this English, but I know how to speak the universal language just as well as you do," she said, warily reaching for the stun rod.

"Don't," he warned, his head barely turning in the direction she was reaching.

La'Rue glared back at him. "Can I get up? The mud is freezing my ass," she stated.

The man softly chuckled and nodded. "Just don't try anything. I'd hate to have to finish what your friend there started," he replied with a nod toward the assassin.

La'Rue rolled forward onto her feet, her right hand bracing her left arm. She sneered down at the Turbintan. In that moment, she knew for sure that this new man wasn't an assassin, which meant he was here for the same reason that she was – to collect the credits for the pod.

"I'll give you twenty percent," she stated, straightening.

"Twenty percent?" he repeated.

La'Rue's gaze narrowed on his face. It would have been better if she could see his expression. Then she would know what he was thinking. Impatience burned through her. If there was one assassin who had discovered her, there could be more. She needed to get off this planet.

"Alright. I'll give you thirty percent and not a credit more," she countered.

"What will you do with the other seventy percent?" the man asked.

"Disappear someplace away from this war, if I'm lucky. You might want to do that as well. It's going to get worse before it gets better," La'Rue bit out.

She bent over and picked up the stun rod, surprised when he didn't say anything this time. She made sure that she kept it turned away from him. Her gut was cautioning her to be careful. There was something off about this man.

"What war?" the man asked.

La'Rue turned and looked at him with a disbelieving frown. He must have been in some Turbintan prison if he didn't know what was going on. After the devastation done to Jeslean, everyone in the galaxy was terrified.

"Where have you been? Haven't you heard what the Legion did? Director Andronikos ordered the destruction of all major cities on Jeslean. He murdered hundreds of thousands of people," she said, staring back at him with angry tears in her eyes.

"Why would he do that?" the man softly demanded.

La'Rue could feel her lips twist into a sneer. She jerked her head in the direction she had been traveling before she had been attacked. Her eyes flashed with anger.

"Maybe because he can?" she replied in a sarcastic voice. "He wants whoever was in the capsules that fell from the sky. Whoever was in this one is gone, but he has offered a reward for the pods as well. I'll take even Andronikos' credits if it means being free," she said, her eyes flashing in warning. "I claim the pod. I'll give you twenty percent like I promised, but I've claimed it first."

"You said thirty percent a moment ago. There were others...," the man stated, taking a step toward her.

"I know. I followed two signals to this planet. I found this one first. The other... it is in a difficult to reach area. I don't think I'll be able to get to it, especially now," she said, searching for her discarded blaster.

"What of the other three?" the man demanded. "Where are those?"

La'Rue grimaced as she picked up her blaster. She frowned at the man as she slid the useless weapon back into her holster. How did he know there were three more? If he knew there were that many, he should have known about the war – unless....

"How did you know there are three more pods?" she demanded as she slowly lowered the stun rod in her hand.

"We need to find the other one before anyone else does," he said.

She shook her head. "I told you it is too dangerous. The scans show it is out in the open," La'Rue rejected with a wave of her hand. "I'm going to get the capsule in the woods and get off this planet."

"Not until we find the other one," the man stated, reaching out and grabbing her right arm.

La'Rue swung around, aiming the pointed end of the stun rod toward the man's chest. He moved with surprising speed, catching the rod at an angle and deftly removing it from her hands. Her breath caught when she found herself pinned against his taller frame, the business end of her only weapon against her throat.

"Why do you want to risk your life for one pod? I'll give you fifty percent," she offered in a strained voice.

"Where is the other pod located?" he quietly demanded in her ear.

A shiver ran through La'Rue. Her fingers gripped the rod on each side of his hand, straining to hold it away from her throat. Her head tilted back when he pressed a little harder against her pharynx.

"That…that way. Nearly two hundred clicks," she gasped, pointing to the west with her right hand.

"Close your eyes and count to one hundred. If I see your eyes open, I'll slit your throat," he warned.

Anger flashed through La'Rue. In defiance, she lowered her eyelids and began counting out loud and very quickly. He hadn't said how she had to do it; just that she had to do it. His soft chuckle brushed across her cheek. She held the stun rod even after she felt him move away.

The second she reached one hundred, she twisted around to face him. She blinked when she didn't see anything. Muttering curses under her breath, she gripped her injured arm and slowly followed the tracks until they disappeared among the boulders. She took a deep breath and shook her head in disgust.

"Well, his loss! I keep one hundred percent since he's not here," she defiantly muttered.

Turning away, she walked back to the hover lift. Opening a storage compartment, she retrieved a small first aid kit and doctored the wound on her shoulder. Ten minutes later, she was heading toward the pod she had located.

CHAPTER FOUR

The skimmer craft Sergi had scavenged from the dead alien sped across the wide open plains. He leaned forward, protecting his face and body from the icy shards of freezing rain. The wind along the open rocky surface buffeted the bike.

He had figured the man had to have some kind of transportation. The alien had been too clean to have walked in. Sergi had found the hovering bike on the other side of the boulders from where the man had been hiding. It hadn't taken him long to learn how to use it. The principle of operation was similar to that of a motorcycle; twist the handle for power and use the foot pedals for changing gears and stopping.

What had amazed Sergi was that the bike was virtually silent when powered on. It reminded him of the hybrid vehicles that were so popular back home. It must have some type of electric propulsion system.

Leaning to the side, he swept by an outcropping of rocks. His gaze moved to the reading on the woman's tracking device. For a moment, a surprising emotion swept through him – regret.

He focused on the projected path to the signal that the device was displaying even as a part of his mind turned to the unusual woman he had left behind. He had been shocked when she spoke – the husky, feminine tone defiant.

Small strands of dark auburn hair had peeked out from under her hat when she had removed her goggles. She had smooth, tan skin with a faint line of dark spots running from her neck up along one side of her face before fading on her brow. Her eyes were dark brown, almost black. When he'd held her, he had noticed that the wound to her shoulder was superficial.

The top of her head barely reached his chin. He had thought she was taller until he held her close. He briefly glanced down at the device he had taken from her. He hoped she wouldn't need it.

After several kilometers, he slowed the bike. Scanning the area, he made sure he was alone. The wide expanse of rocky plateau was devoid of life. The screen showed his target approximately three hundred meters from his position.

Sergi slowly moved in the direction of the signal until he came to the edge of the plateau. Switching off the power to the bike, he swung his leg over the back and stepped off. He walked around the bike and looked over the edge of the plateau. On the opposite side of the river far below, he saw one of the Gliese's emergency pods resting on a narrow ledge, approximately fifty meters down.

His throat tightened when he saw the number on the side. The pod belonged to Mei. He needed to find a way down over the edge and to the capsule.

He turned back to the bike. There hadn't been time to check if there was anything useful stored in the bike's storage compartments. Now, he hoped there was, otherwise it was going to be a challenging climb down.

Sergi searched the vehicle, opening several compartments. The guy who'd had the bike before him had definitely been a trained assassin. There were enough assorted weapons and equipment for just about any mission requirements. A grin curved his lips when he wrapped his hand around one of the items and pulled it free. The sharp point made him feel relatively positive this was not just for shooting prey. He turned the device over in his hand, studying how it was made. A soft whistle of appreciation slipped from his lips and he nodded as he realized how it worked.

Closing the compartment, Sergi turned back to the cliff. The rain was still falling, but at least not as heavily as it had been a short while ago. He scanned the area once more before pointing the device at the large rock face above Mei's pod. Pulling the trigger, he grunted in satisfaction when he saw the long, thin wire shooting out from the grappling gun.

The sharp point spiraled, piercing the rock. Kneeling, he ejected a small cylinder from the side before holding the butt of the gun against the rock. Flicking off the safety, he depressed the button on the top. A powerful jolt ricocheted up his arm. He tugged on the grappling gun, but it didn't move.

He stood up and turned the small cylinder over. There were two buttons, one on each side. While the top had grooves for fingers, the bottom had a series of rollers. He walked over to the wire and attached the cylinder to it. Pressing one button, then the other, he confirmed that it activated a pulley system function.

"I could definitely have used this on more than one occasion," he murmured.

He walked to the edge and squatted. Testing the wire one more time, he hoped it could handle his weight. Turning over onto his stomach, he slowly slid over the edge. He braced his feet on a narrow ledge – facing the capsule – and reached for the cylinder. Wrapping his hands over each other, he pressed the button on the left-hand side.

His breath caught when he was pulled forward and his feet left the ledge. He glanced down into the deep ravine filled with jagged rocks. Nearly a kilometer below him, a raging river churned.

Sergi refocused his gaze on his target. In less than a minute, he was closing in on the pod. He was almost there when a dark figure stood up on the boulder he had shot the grappling hook into and looked at him. A curse slipped from Sergi's lips when he saw the man aim a weapon at him.

With a flick of his finger, he hit the reverse. His body swung wildly with the sudden change in direction. His strategy worked. The blast swept in front of him. Pressing the switch again, he moved forward once more. Below the ledge the pod had landed on was another wide shelf. Using his forward momentum, Sergi released his grip on the cylinder and fell just as the man fired again. A searing heat cut through the sleeve of his right arm.

He landed hard on the edge of the shelf with a muted grunt, bending his knees, and falling forward. His hands grappled for a hold when the rock began to crumble under his feet and he started to slide. He frantically searched for a stable hold, his feet slipping on the deteriorating rock as it continued to disintegrate. A hissed curse slipped from him as more of the rock fell away beneath his lower body.

Sergi dug his fingers into a crevice. The muscles in his arms bulged as he pulled his lower body up and over the remaining ledge and rolled over. Above him, a rain of small debris warned him that the man who had shot at him was descending from his perch on the boulder.

He waited, remaining frozen until he heard the sound of footsteps above the roar of the water below him. Cautiously rising to his feet, he pressed his back against the rock behind him and looked around as he listened to the man moving overhead.

With grim determination, he turned and worked his way along the edge of the rock. He had to test each grip and foothold as the surface sometimes crumbled under his touch. Moving one foot and hand at a time, he searched for a way to leave his position.

It seemed to take him forever to find a safe route up the side of the rock face. He was finally able to reach a section where he could pull himself over the edge without being seen. Rising swiftly to his feet, he withdrew his pistol, stepped out from behind the rock, and fired.

The man's body stiffened before he fell forward, his body folded over the side of the open capsule with his head and torso inside. Sergi moved cautiously forward. He had counted the number of times the woman shot the other creature. Stepping closer, he could see the pool of blue-green blood slowly sliding from the man's right temple.

He yanked the man away from Mei and froze. The interior of the capsule had a body inside, but it wasn't Mei. The large, partially decomposed body of an alien male lay against the white material.

A frown creased his brow, and he looked around the immediate area. Where in the hell was Mei and how in the hell did she get off this island in the middle of a ravine?

His gaze returned to the capsule. There would be a recording of what had happened to Mei. He reached in and removed the camera.

Sliding the camera into his pocket, he shoved the body of the man he had just killed into the already occupied capsule and closed the lid. A grim smile curved his lips. Let's see what the aliens thought when they found the emergency pod stuffed with their own dead men.

Sergi steadied himself with a hand on the lid of Mei's pod when the ground under him violently shook. A distant rumble grew louder and closer. Jumping up onto the top of the pod, Sergi pulled himself onto the large boulder above him and looked around.

His eyes widened when he saw a wall of water rushing down the ravine toward him. He turned looked toward his bike. A dark mass of churning water was rushing for it across the wide barren plateau. Even if he reached the other side, there was no way he would be able to outrun the flood waters.

Deciding he didn't have another option, he bent his legs and was about to jump back down to the ledge and try to get across the ravine when a blast of air hit him. Looking up, he saw the dark underbelly of a medium-sized ship appear through the driving rain. He steadied himself as it came closer and hovered overhead.

Sergi blinked when the curved doors of a circular hatch slid apart and a platform lowered, revealing the woman he had saved earlier. A sardonic smile twisted her lips before she spoke.

"Get on," she ordered.

"I need to get to the bike," he shouted.

She shook her head. "It is too late," she yelled.

Sergi stumbled and knelt as the boulder under him trembled. He braced a hand on the wet rock as he looked toward where the roar was getting louder. She was right, there wasn't time. He briefly glanced over at the bike, and saw a wall of water hit it. The bike, along with his survival pack and rifle, tumbled like a toy before it rolled over the edge of the cliff and disappeared into the rising waters in the ravine.

He looked up again. The woman had disappeared. Surging upward, he grabbed one of the support bars on the platform as the ship began to rise. He pulled himself up, barely rolling over the side as the initial wave of water hit. As the platform rose, he looked over the edge. The boulder he had been standing on leaned as if resisting the surge before another wall of water hit the large rock. He watched the boulder topple onto Mei's emergency pod. Below him, there was churning dark water as far as he could see. His view was cut off as the platform closed, and he found himself sealed in an alien spaceship.

CHAPTER FIVE

uted red lights lit the interior of the ship. Sergi held onto the bar of the platform when the space craft rocked at a crazy angle, then his body slammed back into the metal grating of the platform when the ship suddenly rose.

A soft curse escaped him when the vessel veered to the left and he felt himself sliding. He held onto the bar as everything tilted. His body twisted when the craft turned the other way. For a moment he wondered if he was on a spaceship or a roller coaster without a seat belt!

His hands slid up the bar as his body floated upward when the ship dropped out from under him. Sergi swore his stomach was in his throat. He couldn't help but think that he would have had a better chance of surviving the rushing flood waters.

The sounds of alarms warned him that his gut feeling might be right. Gritting his teeth, he pulled himself up and braced his feet against the floor. The vessel jolted to a stop. The force of it was enough to rip his hands free from the bar and send him careening across the narrow room. He came to a stop when his back hit the far wall.

Shaking his head, Sergi released a long string of expletives in his native language. He took advantage of the brief stability to rise to his feet and sprint across the long, narrow room to the ladder leading up to the next level. His fingers wrapped around the bars at the same time as the spaceship surged forward. Once again, his feet left the floor. It was only his will to survive that kept his fingers locked around the bars, bearing the full weight of his body plus the momentum of the ship.

After less than a second, his booted feet slammed back to the deck of the ship. He quickly climbed the ladder, emerging into a long, narrow corridor. Alarms continued to ring and the lights flickered. He had an ominous feeling that they were about to lose power – which meant they would crash.

Sprinting down the corridor, Sergi focused on the open doorway at the end. Through the doorway he could see the exterior landscape. Well, he could see the driving sheets of rain and dark gray rock formations that made up this hostile, wet planet.

He held onto the doorframe to keep from falling backwards. "There is a rock," he warned.

"I know there is a rock!" she snapped, twisting the stick to the left.

Sergi grunted when he slid in the opposite direction. The sound of rock scraping on metal echoed through the ship. He really hoped this thing didn't end up like the Titanic.

"Look out!" he hissed, his eyes widening when he saw they were heading for a wall of water that had to be over thirty meters high.

"I see it," she retorted, reaching up to flip several switches.

"Can't you go higher?" Sergi asked, pulling himself forward and sliding into the seat next to her. "You need to go higher. You really, really need to go higher."

Sergi's fingers fumbled for the straps while his eyes remained locked on the wall of water rushing toward them. Once he heard the click of the belt locking, his hands moved to armrests. His fingers clung to the padded sides.

"H, now!" the woman yelled.

Sergi was pressed back against the seat when the ship shot up at a steep angle with tremendous force. The ship passed through the top of the cresting wave and out the other side. Additional alarms sounded for a moment before the woman reached up to shut them off.

Unable to see more than a few kilometers ahead, Sergi could feel the ship descending. He braced for impact when he saw the tall trees rising toward them. He turned to warn her, but bit back his comment.

Her face was stiff with determination and her eyes were grimly focused on the scene in front of them. He couldn't help but admire her calm as she fought for control of the spaceship. His gaze ran over her face. She had removed the hat and he caught himself staring at her thick, auburn hair.

"I have to set us down or we are going to crash. There is a rocky area ahead that will work. At least I hope it will. If it collapses, we are dead," she stated in a tense voice.

"It will hold," Sergi replied with confidence.

She frowned and glanced at him before returning her attention to her chosen destination. "How do you know?" she asked.

Sergi flashed a confident grin that she couldn't see as he was still wearing the cover over the lower half of his face. "It isn't my time to die," he replied.

She gave him a funny look before shrugging her shoulders. "I hope you are right," she muttered under her breath.

He was glad she couldn't see the doubt clouding his eyes as they drew closer to the landing area she had picked out. It looked awfully small from the angle they were approaching. He gripped the armrest as she twisted the spaceship around and set it down with a wobbly thump. Only when she shut off the engines – and the alarms – did he relax his grip.

Turning his head to congratulate her, he found himself staring into the dark barrel of a gun. She had already released the straps to her seat and was standing before he'd realized she had moved. Sergi couldn't keep the dry chuckle from escaping as his eyes rose to meet hers. He slowly lifted up his hands. There wasn't much else he could do while still strapped to the seat.

"You're not an assassin, are you?" she demanded.

Sergi reached up, pulled the cover from his mouth and nose, and removed the military-grade goggles. He heard her swift hiss and saw her eyes open wide when she got her first close-up look of his face. With a wry grin, he answered her questions.

"Sergi Lazaroff at your service, *dorogoy*," Sergi replied, using the Russian word for *darling*.

"Who are you?" she whispered, confusion darkening her eyes.

~

A Few Moments Ago:

La'Rue refused to be distracted by the man sitting next to her. At least, until after they had landed. The moment they did, she released the seat straps and pulled the blaster from her holster. Rising out of her seat, she aimed for his chest.

She was still cursing the fact that she had followed him. If there had been any other way, she wouldn't have, but thanks to the Turbintan assassin and this guy taking her locator, she had been delayed in returning to the pod. She had been within a few kilometers of it when a transport had flown over her and landed.

She'd abandoned her hover lift and crept up to find that two men were not only examining the pod, but they were talking to a Turbintan who La'Rue had no desire to meet, much less cross. Tallei wasn't just a Turbintan assassin; she was a master trainer of the Turbintan assassins. Her reputation put fear in the hearts of the most hardened criminals in the galaxy.

With the loss of the pod and the potential credits, she'd been left with no choice but to go after the other one. She refused to admit that the man now sitting next to her had anything to do with her decision. Unfortunately, the only good thing that had come out of this entire disastrous trip was that she was still alive. She only had a few credits, her ship now needed some major repairs, and she was stuck on a planet where killing was a leisurely pastime. She could really use a drink – after she found out who the man was and what he knew about the other capsules.

Her eyes ran over the man. "You're not an assassin, are you?" she demanded with a frown.

She watched as he slowly lifted his hands. She was about to demand that he remove his protective goggles and face cover when his hands moved toward his face. She released a sharp hiss as his face was revealed.

His hair was short and almost white in color. His eyes were a vivid blue. He had a light coating of darker whiskers along his jaw and chin. His eyes were sharp and glittered with a wry sense of humor. His nose was long and narrow with a slight bump that made her think it had been broken at one time. His voice was deep and smooth with that accent she had never heard before she met him.

"Sergi Lazaroff at your service, *dorogoy*," Sergi replied.

"Who are you?" she demanded, confusion lacing her voice.

The corner of his mouth lifted. "I appear to be lost," he responded in a light tone.

"Lost? How in the hell can you be lost? No one gets lost on Turbinta. No one *wants* to get lost on this miserable planet!" she stated, shaking her head. "If you value breathing, you'd better start talking."

"May I attend to my wound first?" he asked, glancing down at his arm.

La'Rue knew the second her eyes moved away from his face that she had made a tactical error. His hand flashed out, grabbing the barrel of her blaster and redirecting it to the side at the same time as he jerked her forward. He kicked the back of her knee, causing her leg to give out on her. He exerted on her arm, and she lost her balance in the narrow confines of the cockpit, twisting as she fell.

Before she realized what had happened, she was sitting in his lap with his arm around her neck. She clawed at his arm with her free hand. He had trapped her other arm with a steely grip around her wrist.

"I'm really beginning to hate you," she informed him through clenched teeth.

"I can assure you that the feeling is not mutual," he retorted in a voiced filled with amusement.

La'Rue snorted at his comment. His soft, chuckled response to her disbelief heated her blood while his warm breath brushed against her neck. She tilted her head back when he squeezed her wrist. His thumb hit a nerve in her hand that caused her fingers to go numb. The blaster fell to the floor of the cockpit.

"That is much better," he murmured, his lips brushing against the warm skin of her neck.

"Are you kissing me?" she demanded, stiffening in surprise.

"I'm simply making sure you are real," he answered, releasing her.

La'Rue twisted on his lap the moment his arms fell away from her. She stared into his dark blue eyes. He returned her gaze without blinking. She knew her eyes must be filled with confusion. His were filled with heated curiosity.

"I want a drink," she finally said, turning back around and rising to her feet. "Don't mess with anything on my ship."

"Not even you?" he playfully asked.

La'Rue ignored him. Bending over, she picked up her blaster and stepped away before he could stop her. She didn't look back as she exited the cockpit and started down the corridor.

"H! I need a diagnostic report on the ship," she yelled.

She didn't slow her pace until she turned the corner into the galley. Walking over to the cabinet, she twisted the knob and reached up for a bottle of Torrian liquor. She looked over her shoulder when she heard footsteps stop outside the door.

"Is there enough for two?" he asked, nodding at the bottle in her hand.

La'Rue reached up into the cabinet and grabbed a second metal cup. Carrying the items over to a small table bolted to the floor, she slid into the seat with her back to the wall. She placed the cups down in front of her, pulled off the stopper, and poured the light green liquor into each cup. After replacing the stopper and setting the bottle on the table, she leaned forward, and pushed one cup toward the empty seat in front of her.

She kept her eyes on Sergi as he walked into the room. He scanned the room, pausing and frowning at the small kitchen area before he slid into the seat. He casually placed both arms on the table and cradled the cup between his hands. She had a feeling he did it on purpose, to show her that he wasn't a threat. She believed that as much as she believed her ex-lover would cover his own damn debts.

"My name is La'Rue Gant," she stated.

"It is a pleasure to meet you, La'Rue Gant," Sergi said, sitting back in his chair. "This ship, it goes into space, yes?"

La'Rue raised an eyebrow. "What? The *Star Runner*? Of course it goes into space. How else would I have gotten here? Well, it will once H and I repair it. Which better be soon if we want to get off this planet alive," she said, muttering the last part with a grimace.

"Who is H?" Sergi asked, dropping a hand to his lap and casually sitting back. Her eyes narrowed and she mimicked him, sitting back and lowering her hand to the blaster lying next to her on the bench.

"HL-9. He is a modified Harvester Line service bot that I use to help me," she said, lifting her drink to her lips and taking a sip.

A brief frown crossed Sergi's face. "Is there anyone else aboard?" he asked.

La'Rue shook her head and leaned forward. "No. Listen, why don't we cut through the pleasantries and just say what we really want to say? I know you have your weapon trained on me, just as you know I have mine on you. We can either blow the hell out of each other or we can see if we can come to a mutually beneficial business proposition," she suggested, staring him in the eyes.

His lips quirked up and his eyes crinkled, sparkling with mirth. This strange man was driving her crazy! She still couldn't figure out which planet he was from. There were few reasons anyone would want to be on Turbinta and he didn't fit any of the scenarios that she could think of.

"It is obvious you do not care for this planet. Why are you here?" he asked, lifting his hand back to the table again.

"Don't care for this planet?" she repeated in disbelief. "You do know that you are on Turbinta, don't you? The weather isn't the only shitty thing on this planet, so are pretty much all of the inhabitants. The only people on this planet are assassins, would-be assassins, the people the assassins kill in training, and those training the assassins. In case you haven't noticed, I've said the word assassins a few times."

"Yes, I noticed," he dryly replied. "Are there any cities close by? Someplace where they may have taken the person who was in the capsule?" he asked.

La'Rue frowned at Sergi. "The Turbintans are more of a nomadic species, mostly because they are always trying to kill each other to prove who is the deadliest. Personally, I wish they would just kill each other off and be done with it, but they don't really care what I think. There is one major city near us that is considered a 'safe zone' by those delusional enough to believe it. It is where traders from other worlds come to deliver or pick up items. That is why I wanted to get this far. We are on the outskirts of the city and technically are within the zone. It will be dark soon, another reason not to go out. I think all the dreary weather is to blame for the Turbintans being so crazy. If there was anyone in the capsules, they could have been taken anywhere. I've heard there is a tower where they keep the prisoners they plan to use in their training exercises."

"Nice people," Sergi commented, looking down at his drink.

La'Rue looked at Sergi, unsure if he was being serious or sarcastic. She decided it must have been the latter. Sliding out of the seat, she stood up and walked over to the storage. She pulled out a couple of ready-meals and pressed the button on the packaging. Within seconds, steam and the delicious aroma of food filled the room. She opened the pouches and removed the trays.

"I don't know about you, but almost dying – twice – makes me hungry," she said, placing a tray in front of him.

She retrieved some utensils from a drawer and slid back into her seat. Refilling her drink, she held up the bottle for Sergi. He shook his head. She shrugged, trying not to grin when he cautiously stirred the stew she had placed in front of him. She scooped up some of the thick vegetables in broth and blew on it.

"You asked about my home world. I was born on Jeslean, but my family was originally from Tesla Terra. My father left to work at the main headquarters for the Gallant," she said, taking a bite of the hot meal. "So, what about you? Where are you from? You don't look like a Torrian. Are you from one of the outer planets? I've been to a few of them, but not all."

He looked down at his meal for a moment before he looked up at her. That wry smile was back on his lips, but his eyes were deadly serious when he looked back at her. The spoon in her hand froze halfway to her mouth as she waited.

"You could say I'm from one of the outer planets," he slowly responded.

"So, which one?" she pressed, curious to see if she would recognize his accent once he told her.

He placed his spoon down in his stew, and rested his left arm on the table, though his right hand had disappeared under it again, sending a wave of unease through her. La'Rue silently cursed. She had let her guard down.

"Earth. I'm from a galaxy far, far away from this one," he quietly replied.

La'Rue lowered her hand. She could feel her fingers begin to tremble as her mind swirled with sudden insight and the pieces of his odd behavior began to fall into place. The fact that she hadn't seen it right away stunned her.

Flashes of memory shot through her mind. Sergi's sudden appearance when the assassin had attacked her. He hadn't just come upon her and the Turbintan, he had been following her. His strange clothing and his determination to find the other pod had made her think he was after the bounty, but, he had known exactly how many others there were. Finally, his lack of knowledge about the Turbintans and about what happened on Jeslean were too unbelievable to doubt his sincerity.

"Who are you, Sergi?" La'Rue quietly asked.

He gave her a grim smile. "I am the man from the pod. You took my spacesuit. I am not from your world, La'Rue. I'm not even from this galaxy," he answered.

She shook her head. Her gaze swept over his serious expression. This was why she hadn't been able to place where he was from. She groaned and bowed her head, running her hands through her hair as her mind processed the information.

"You don't have to worry just about the Turbintans," she muttered, looking up at him with growing panic.

"Who else would I have to worry about?" Sergi asked.

"Andri Andronikos, the Director of the Legion. He will stop at nothing to find you and the others of your kind," she murmured.

"What does this Director want with us?" Sergi demanded in a soft, calm tone that sent a shiver through her.

"Your support or your death," she replied.

CHAPTER SIX

Jeslean: City of the New Legion

*A*ndri Andronikos stood near the window and looked out at the dozens of transports lifting off with supplies for his warships. The war had officially started. He turned when he heard the incoming communication signal.

"Connect," he ordered.

General Coleridge Landais appeared in a hologram on the center of the table. Andri could see the frustration in his half-brother's eyes. In the background, he saw the gray clouds of Turbinta. Andri would have ordered the destruction of that planet as well if he hadn't needed the skills of some of the inhabitants on occasion.

"What do you have to report?" Andri demanded.

"We discovered where a pod landed, but the pod itself was missing. The signals from both pods have faded. There is a considerable amount of interference due to the climate here. I have men looking for them both," Coleridge replied.

Andri's mouth tightened in annoyance. "Have you discovered any information about Roan?" he queried.

Coleridge's eyes narrowed and his frustration turned to a

simmering anger. General Roan Landais, one of the Legion's best Generals, Coleridge's son and Andri's nephew, had disappeared a few days ago. While Coleridge had insisted that Roan would not betray them, Andri was not as confident. Roan had always been independent.

"Nothing yet," Coleridge acknowledged.

"Do not disappoint me, Coleridge," Andri warned in a calm voice.

"I haven't yet, Andri. I will deal with my son if it becomes necessary. I have Commander Taug searching for the missing pod and its contents. I will notify you the moment it is located," Coleridge promised.

"See that you do," Andri reiterated before ending the communications.

He turned back to the window. A dark haze covered much of the planet due to the number of buildings that were still burning and smoldering. He ignored the devastation. The flattening of the cities on Jeslean had been necessary to erase any hope that a rebellion would be successful. He had needed to set an example and he had done so by striking at the heart of their heritage.

Jeslean had been the home of the Ancient rulers, the Knights of the Gallant Order, an elite group of men and women devoted to the protection of the galaxy. Hutu Gomerant had been the only remaining active Knight of the Gallant Order – until the mysterious ship and the pods appeared.

The initial strike against his iron-fisted rule had been on Tesla Terra. One of his commanders had tracked the first pod to a forest not far from Jemar de Rola's vineyards. Jemar had also been a Knight of the Gallant Order, but the old Knight had retired years ago after Andri had ordered the assassination of his wife.

At Andri's behest, the Legion commander in charge of investigating the pod had killed Jemar and his young son during a confrontation. Instead of discouraging further rebellion, however, de Rola's daughter and a stranger to the known galaxy had defeated a squadron of highly trained Legion forces – and then escaped.

Andri knew that Cassa de Rola had then met up with General Hutu Gomerant, the legendary Gallant Knight and close friend of her family, and the stranger had met with another who had arrived in a pod.

Andri had hoped that leveling the ancient city of the Order of the Gallant would strike fear into the hearts of his enemies. Instead – fueled by the false hope that at least two of the 'Ancient Knights' themselves had returned from a distant galaxy – the rebellion was gaining power and followers. Now, there was the possibility of two more knights surviving their arrival in those damn pods. He needed to find at least one of the aliens from the pods and demonstrate that they could die, just like anyone else.

"Where did you come from, and what brought you here now?" Andri murmured, staring out the window as he thought of the strange capsules.

～

General Coleridge Landais sat back in the chair of his office aboard the Legion warship. He stared at the blank screen in front of him, his mind on the issues at hand. Rising from his seat, he walked over to the bar and poured himself a drink. The chime at the door drew his attention.

"Enter," he ordered. The doors slid opened to reveal his first officer. "What is it?" he asked.

"You asked to be informed when we were within deployment range of Turbinta, General Landais," the First Officer replied.

"Prepare an away team. I want fighters on standby. Any ship trying to leave is to be redirected back to the planet and thoroughly searched," Coleridge ordered.

"I'll instruct the fighters to be prepared. Will you want me to lead the search, General?" the First Officer asked.

Coleridge was silent for a moment before he shook his head. "No, I will personally oversee this mission," he instructed with a dismissive tone.

"Yes, sir," the First Officer replied with a bow of his head before he backed out of the room.

Coleridge walked back over to his desk. He reached out and tapped a series of commands. After several seconds, he slammed his hand down on the desk. Liquid from his glass sloshed over the side onto his other hand.

His lips tightened in irritation when he saw that the tracking signal he'd had embedded in his son's arm was offline. Coleridge had suspected that Roan was aware of Andri's suspicions. Coleridge hadn't felt the same reservations about Roan – until now.

"Do not betray me, Roan," Coleridge murmured.

He lifted the glass in his hand and drank the clear liquor in one gulp. Placing the glass down next to the computer, he stepped around the desk, and strode toward the door. Once he located the pods, he would locate his missing son.

∿

Turbinta: Aboard the *Star Runner*

"We have to get off this planet," La'Rue stated. "H, I need you."

Sergi followed La'Rue down the long corridor to a ladder that led to the lower section of the ship. A small robot with eight legs scurried by him, and he muttered an oath as he jumped to the side. He shook his head.

After La'Rue had dropped her nuclear bomb of a statement, they had eaten the rest of their meal in silence. He hadn't minded since it gave him time to appreciate the complexity of the situation he was in – and the woman across from him. Not to mention, the silence gave him time to absorb the fact that he was still alive and in an alien world unlike anything Earth's scientists could have imagined.

He'd been to his fair share of movies during his life. If he ever made it back to Earth, he would have to tell a few scientists that they needed to hire some writers because the men and women making up that shit were doing a pretty realistic job.

Sergi watched as La'Rue bent down and descended the ladder, the eight-legged freak machine right behind her. He shook his head and wondered if perhaps he had fallen through the universe's version of a rabbit hole into an alternate reality. It wasn't such a far-off concept.

"Will more of your people come to help you once they realize you are in danger?" she asked, glancing over her shoulder at him as he jumped to the deck.

"No," he replied, looking around the rectangular room.

"H, work on the engine circuitry. What do you mean 'no'? Do they not value your life?" she questioned with a frown.

"My people.... Let's just say that it would be very difficult for anyone to come to my aid," he dryly replied. "I need to find the other pods. Mei was not inside the one in the gorge. That means she must have escaped."

"Or she could have died by falling into the ravine or drowning," La'Rue countered. "Might I remind you that you almost died? You're welcome by the way."

Sergi felt a flash of amusement even as he shook his head in denial. Yes, she had saved his life, but he refused to believe Mei was dead. That tiny, formidable Chinese woman was much too resourceful to have plunged to her death.

"Chert voz'mi!" Sergi cursed.

"What does that mean?" La'Rue asked, looking up at him from where she was pulling a series of circuit boards.

"I will be back to help you," he replied as he turned around and gripped the ladder.

He paused when he felt a hand on his arm, and he turned to look at La'Rue. Her dark eyes were filled with confusion and a hint of suspicion.

"What did you just say? The 'chert voz'mi'," she said, slowly repeating what he had said.

Sergi chuckled and cupped her chin. "A word unfit for a lady's ears," he said, bending and brushing a kiss across her lips. "I need to check something."

He turned away from her bemused expression. Climbing the ladder, Sergi pulled the video recorder from his pocket. Its battery was dead. He needed to rig a power source so he could see what had happened to Mei.

Returning to the galley, he opened and closed the cabinets. In a side drawer, he found what he'd been looking for – a conglomeration of tools and discards. Some things appeared to be universal – even in an alien galaxy.

In minutes he had rigged a power source for the video recorder. The recording started as soon as the lid was opened. In the background behind Mei, he could see the Gliese 581 ship shaking violently, lit by blinking lights. The alarms sounded tinny through the recorder's speaker. Behind her, he could see his pod and then Julia's.

"What about Ash and Josh?" Mei worriedly asked as she climbed into the pod.

"We have to trust that they will be able to guide us through this," Julia stated above the alarms.

"Sergi...."

He could see Mei's eyes move to his pod, her expression filled with worry and regret. Julia's reflected the same emotions – along with resignation and grief. He watched as Julia climbed into her own emergency pod. Neither woman wore a spacesuit.

"We've done all that we can, Mei. He is stable. In the end, he may be the luckiest one of us all if he never realizes what is going on," Julia replied.

"Catastrophic hull breach imminent. Prepare for emergency pod evacuation," the computer warned.

"It has been a great honor and privilege to be a part of this mission, Julia," Mei quietly replied before she laid back and closed the lid of her capsule.

Sergi's throat tightened when he saw the tear escape from the corner of her eye and slide down the side of her face. The interior of the pod grew dark for a few seconds before the interior lights kicked on as it slid into the ejection tube.

Mei bit her lip to keep from crying out when the capsule shook violently. Nearly ten minutes passed from the time Mei entered the capsule until it was ejected. He watched as her breathing sped up before it finally slowed, and a look of wonder filled her eyes. The video became less shaky, and he wished he could see what Mei was seeing. A moment later his wish came true when she turned the camera so that it angled outward. His breath caught when he saw the Gliese 581 breaking apart. Minor explosions lit the darkness, but it was the pieces spinning in slow motion that held him captivated. It was as if someone were spilling the pieces of a puzzle out on a black velvet cloth.

There was no way to know if all of the emergency pods made it safely away from the ship. He knew his own and Mei's had, but what of Julia, Josh, and Ash? Without being able to enlarge the image and analyze, it was impossible to tell if any of the moving pieces of wreckage were the ship or a pod. He listened as Mei began to speak in a soft voice filled with awe and grief.

"I do not know if anyone will ever see this video, but I do not want us to be forgotten. The Gliese 581g project was Earth's first mission into deep space. We learned that we are not alone in this beautiful universe. There were five of us aboard the Gliese 581: Commander Joshua Manson, Commander Ashton Haze, Sergi Lazaroff, Julia Marksdale, and myself, Mei Li Hú," she said before her voice faded and she turned the video back toward her face. *"The pod is going into conservation mode. I will sleep now. I do not know if I will ever wake up again. If my father should ever see this, please know that I have died with honor."*

Sergi watched Mei's eyelashes flutter before her face relaxed, and he knew the low dose of sedative to slow body function had been released. The camera remained locked on her sleeping face for several more minutes before it went black. Then there was a flicker.

He frowned when he saw the camera screen flicker. It was only meant to come on if it detected motion. He fast forwarded until the video began to play again, and he saw Mei pushing open the lid of her emergency pod. She moved the camera to show what she was seeing. The view showed the interior of a spaceship. There was a large collection of debris. All of the junk reminded Sergi of a garbage dump.

He grinned when he saw the way Mei slipped over the side of the pod and turn in slow, measured movements. The intense scrutiny, plus the way she analyzed her surroundings, validated her military training. This was the part of her that she kept hidden from the rest of the crew. His grin grew when she turned and began removing a wide variety of weapons and supplies from the pod. A few of the items and weapons that she held up made him whistle under his breath and wish that he had checked out her capsule when he had a chance.

"*Milaya*, Mei. You have very good taste in weapons," he chuckled.

After she had secured all of her weapons, she turned back to the camera. There was a look of fierce determination in her gaze. Once again, he could see the calm that came with being focused on a mission.

"*I'm alive. I don't know where I am. It looks like some kind of alien spaceship. If we ever had doubt that life existed elsewhere, we have found undeniable proof now. I will do everything I can to stay alive as long as possible. Sergi, I know you are a member of the FSB. I wish you were here now. I would feel better with a few more weapons. I hope you and the others made it. If it is possible, I will search for any survivors. If not... Fight well, my friend,*" Mei added the last in Mandarin.

His features hardened when he noticed a movement behind Mei. A large man appeared out of the shadows behind her. The useless warning on his lips died when Mei suddenly turned, sensing she wasn't alone. The combination of darkness and the limitations of the camera view made it difficult for him to see exactly what was happening. He could hear the sounds of masculine grunts mixed with Mei's more feminine ones.

Sergi jerked back when a male's unfamiliar face suddenly appeared in front of the camera. The man's expression was frozen in shock even as his eyes glazed over in death. The handle of a knife was the only thing visible against the skin of the man's throat. The blade was completely buried in his neck.

Sergi had wondered how the body ended up in the pod. He now had his answer as he watched Mei – with a lot of grunting and a few surprising, but impressive curses in Mandarin – push the man into the pod and close the lid.

Sergi pause the video when he noticed the writing on a door behind Mei. He stared at the characters, committing them to memory.

If the symbols were unique to the ship that Mei was on, then it would be possible to find her. La'Rue might know who the ship belonged to. If nothing else, she could tell him what it said.

He pocketed the video camera and slid it into the leg pocket of his cargo pants. Rising from his seat, he made his way back down to where La'Rue was working. His lips twitched when he heard her yelling for H.

"What do you need?" he asked, sliding down the ladder.

She scowled at him. "A billion credits would be nice," she retorted. "The auto-navigation is shot, the engine needs six new fuel rods, and we are on a planet where shit doesn't come cheap and stranded customers end up dead, so they can sell your ship to the next unsuspecting victim."

"You need the parts, we get the parts," Sergi replied with a shrug. "The question I have is where do we find what you need."

La'Rue grimaced. "Tribute. It's Turbinta's only large city – well it's large compared to the villages dotting the rest of the planet. Tribute is that so-called sanctuary I mentioned, where killing is discouraged and if there is a bounty on your head, you can't be touched. It's a lie, Sergi. If we go in, we won't come back out."

Sergi raised an eyebrow. "So we'll just stay here, then. That is the plan? Live off the supplies you have until we live no more?"

La'Rue scowled. "The Turbintans can look like anyone, you know. They can sound like anyone too. They usually have tattoos to represent their tribe and mark how many kills they've made. Slate met a Turbintan once. He was lucky he wasn't the target. The pirate he was with wasn't as fortunate. The Legion is not exactly at the top of the list of people you want to run into either. Actually, with the price on your head, you might have to stay away from *everyone* no matter where you are." She wiped her hands on a rag that had been hanging on a hook, her expression thoughtful.

Sergi folded his arms. "That might be a little difficult. How much has this Legion offered to pay?" he curiously enquired.

La'Rue pursed her lips and looked down at her dirty hands, hiding her expressive eyes as she rubbed at a spot. Dropping his arms to his sides, he stepped forward and cupped her chin. She tilted her head back and looked up at him.

"How much, La'Rue?" he quietly repeated.

"One hundred thousand credits," she replied.

Sergi could see a faintly wistful expression in her eyes, though he could tell she was trying to keep her expression neutral, and he wondered, *Are you desperate enough to trade me for the reward?*

CHAPTER SEVEN

$\mathscr{L}$a'Rue started to pull her chin away from Sergi's hand, and was surprised when his arm slid around her waist. He gazed down into her eyes with a searching expression. She tried to look away but found it impossible.

"You could use those credits to fix your spaceship," Sergi reflected, watching her carefully.

She raised an eyebrow at him. "Yes, I could, couldn't I?" she replied before she glowered up at him. "I may be lots of things, but I still have some standards. You saved my life. I don't turn in people who do that, even if I could use the credits."

She shivered when he lightly stroked her jaw and tangled his fingers in her short hair. She took a deep breath when he lowered his head closer to hers.

"You saved my life as well," he reminded her.

She swallowed. "I... guess that means... you can't turn me in either," she murmured, her gaze dropping to his lips.

La'Rue leaned forward and pressed her lips to his. She wanted to deepen the kiss, but the sound of an alarm made her quickly pull away. He released her and looked at her with a concerned expression.

"I... have to go help H before he blows up the ship. I'll be back," she said in a breathless voice.

"I think that is an excellent idea. I would rather not be blown up. Almost dying in space and drowning were enough for me," he murmured.

Sergi stepped to the side when she reached for the ladder. She was halfway up when she heard his chuckle and soft comment. A smile curved her lips. She liked that he had a sense of humor.

~

Four hours later, La'Rue tiredly walked down the corridor to the repair room. She was wet, tired, muddy, and hungry again. Outside, the constant rain had turned into a savage lightning storm. The thick hull of the ship insulated them from the sounds of the raging storm.

She stored her tools in the cabinet and secured the door so it wouldn't open. Her mouth opened in a huge yawn and she ran a hand through her wet hair. Turning, she released a startled squeak when she saw Sergi leaning against the doorway, watching her. She lowered her gaze to the large circuit board in his hands.

"What are you doing with that?" she suspiciously asked.

He looked down at the board before he held it up. "It is the one you were working on before you disappeared to prevent H from blowing up the ship. I did a little trouble-shooting on the issue and repaired it," he commented before he looked her up and down. "What did you do? Fight in a mud ring?" he asked.

"I should have let you drown," she grumbled, reaching for the circuit board.

She raised an eyebrow at him when he pulled the board away and out of reach. A retort hovered on her lips, but the caustic remark changed to a soft hiss when he raised his hand and twisted a damp swathe of her hair around his finger.

"You should have come in when it started raining harder. If I had known you were still outside, I would have insisted you get out of the weather. Your skin is like ice," he murmured.

"It's cold outside," she remarked.

He stepped to one side. "You should get cleaned up and into dry clothing," he said.

"The circuit board…," she started to argue.

"You can see if it works after you are dry. I do not want you ruining my work," he replied. "I will prepare us something to eat while you get cleaned up."

La'Rue was shocked when she nodded in agreement. She watched Sergi turn and stride down the corridor. Since when was she obedient?

Since I know he is right. Water and circuits don't mix, she reminded herself before she grudgingly headed for her cabin.

Twenty minutes later, she was stepping into the cramped galley. The circuit board Sergi had been holding earlier was on the table. She walked over, sank down into the chair, and picked it up. She was surprised when she saw the burnt-out modules were now gone and new components were soldered in their place.

"Where did you get the parts to fix this?" she asked in an incredulous tone.

Sergi looked over his shoulder and smiled. "If I told you, you would probably kill me," he said with a crooked grin.

La'Rue looked over at him and frowned. Her eyes scanned the counter. Something was missing. It took a moment for her to realize what it was.

"Where is my cooker?" she demanded.

Sergi turned with a plate in each hand. "Is that what it was? I thought it looked similar to a microwave," he replied, placing the plate of hot food on the table in front of her.

She looked down at her plate then over at the antiquated cooktop. "You actually cooked this on that thing? I didn't know it still worked," she muttered with a glum look. "I really liked my cooker."

Sergi reached over and grabbed her hand. She looked up at him and saw the crooked smile on his lips and serious look in his eyes. The same strange warmth filled her when he touched her.

"I'll find you a better one," he promised.

She snorted. "You better or I might have to turn you in. I don't know anything about cooking and would probably starve otherwise," she teased. "H and I were able to fix most of the stuff, and with you repairing the panel, the only thing left to do is to get the new fuel rods. If I can find some that have been recharged for a decent price, I might have enough credits to cover it. I've got a few things I can trade as well," she said. "We can go to the city tomorrow. It is too late tonight. Between the storm and the dangers of reaching the city on a good day, we'd be stupid to go tonight."

He nodded in agreement. She looked down at her plate, suddenly starving. Picking up her utensil, she began eating. A soft moan of pleasure escaped her as the hot food hit her stomach. She could feel Sergi looking at her, and when she glanced up, she was drawn into his heated gaze. She was finally warm, and not just from the residual heat of her earlier cleansing and the food. Sergi's company heated parts of her that hadn't been touched in a very long time.

She studied him from under her eyelashes, and her fingers itched to brush the messy strands of his white-blond hair away from his wide forehead. His blue eyes were locked on her face, and she blinked when she realized that he was returning her scrutiny.

"What happened to you?" she suddenly asked.

Sergi shrugged his shoulders. "I don't remember much. There was an accident," he lightly replied.

La'Rue placed her utensil next to her empty plate and cupped her hands under her chin as she leaned forward. She didn't miss the reservation that came into his eyes. He didn't want to tell her.

"What kind of accident?" she pressed.

Sergi held her gaze. "I believe I died," he answered, rising to his feet.

She sat back in her seat, stunned. She reached out and grabbed his arm when he reached for her plate. Her eyes locked with his in confusion.

"What do you mean you died? How...?" she murmured, her eyes scanning his face.

"I hit a live power cable. Do you have any clothing onboard that might fit me? I lost my pack when the bike went over the cliff," he said.

La'Rue nodded, accepting the change of subject, for now. She released his arm. "Yes. I have some stuff that might fit you. We can pick up some more tomorrow as well," she said, rising to her feet.

Sergi caressed her cheek. His fingers paused on her chin and he stroked along her lower lip with his thumb. She could see a hint of confusion in his eyes before it disappeared and he dropped his hand.

"I would like to get cleaned up," he admitted, turning away.

La'Rue nodded. "I'll show you where everything is. While you are getting cleaned up, I can see if the circuit board will work now. If it does, it will be easy enough to get a new cooker on another planet – one where I don't have to watch my back and I know I'll pay a reasonable price for it," she stated.

"There was a symbol that I saw. If I drew it out for you, do you think you could tell me what it means?" Sergi asked.

"If I can," she replied with a puzzled frown. "Where did you see it?"

"On a ship," he responded vaguely, turning to carry the dishes to the cleaning unit.

She hesitated at his deliberate lack of specificity, biting her lip. Secrets could be good or bad. In her personal experience, almost all of the secrets she had ever discovered had turned out to be bad – for her. Her ex was a perfect example of that. She just hoped she didn't get screwed by helping Sergi.

Who am I kidding? she thought in self-disgust. *If the Legion ever finds out I knew – much less helped – someone they were hunting, I'll be dead!*

For a brief second, she considered again what it would be like if she were to turn in Sergi. She didn't know him. Heck, she'd only met him this morning. With a hundred thousand credits, she could fix her ship and start over without having to worry about Slate or anyone else.

No sooner had the thought crossed her mind than she pushed it away. Yes, she had only just met Sergi, but he had more honor in his little pinky than Slate had in his whole body. There were always ways to make a few credits. She had the *Star Runner*. As long as she had her freighter and kept it functioning, she could make a living. She looked at him when he turned away from the dish-cleansing unit.

"There are two cabins on the freighter. I sometimes carry passengers looking to relocate undetected. You can use the other cabin. There are some clothes in the cabinet in there. Slate is a little bigger than you, but I don't think you'll have any issues finding something. H can modify the clothes," she explained.

"Who is Slate?" Sergi asked, following her down the corridor to the cabin.

La'Rue looked over her shoulder. "My ex. If you ever meet him, you're welcome to kill him," she replied with a sweet smile.

CHAPTER EIGHT

*S*ergi lay on the bed in the room that La'Rue had shown him earlier. He stared up at the ceiling; his mind was processing everything that had happened since he woke in the emergency pod. The memories of what had happened before were fragmented. He remembered everything up to the point when he hit the cable.

Frustration ate at him. He knew a little of what had happened after he'd passed out, thanks to Mei's video. There would be no going home. The Gliese 581 was gone, and he suspected the gateway they had traveled through was, too.

There was only one option left – adapting and learning to survive in a possibly hostile alien world. Well, not completely hostile. He had found La'Rue.

Unable to sleep, Sergi sat up and swung his legs over the side of the bed. He had never felt as unprepared for a mission as he did now. Rising to his feet, he pulled on a pair of dark brown trousers, and reached for the tan shirt he had picked out. He pulled it on and buttoned it. He finished off his new outfit with two pairs of socks and a pair of scuffed, brown boots. He'd been surprised to discover the boots were a close enough fit if he wore two pairs of socks instead of one and tightened the buckles on the sides.

He grabbed the dark brown leather jacket and pulled it on as well. His weapons were limited to what he had been carrying when he went across the ravine. He cursed the fact that it had been too dangerous to wear the backpack. He'd searched the freighter while La'Rue was outside and discovered that as far as weapons went, she was in worse shape than he was.

His thoughts moved to the woman he had saved this morning. When she had removed her head cover and goggles, he had been struck with an instant attraction that had startled him.

He had met his share of beautiful women. La'Rue wasn't beautiful in the classical sense, but there was an inner exquisiteness that he had reacted to on a physical and visceral level – and her sarcastic retorts had really struck a chord in him.

A stunning woman with a dry sense of humor and an air of innocence was a potent and dangerous combination. He had never had such a powerful reaction to a woman before, and it was... disconcerting. His relationships had always been very carefully formed with a focus on superficial enjoyment without commitment or true intimacy. That was the way it'd had to be due to his line of work on Earth.

I am no longer on Earth, though, he thought.

He shook his head. The first woman he meets – hell, the first alien he meets – and he is thinking of a long-term relationship.

"I must have hit my head," he muttered to himself under his breath.

He tightened the belt around his waist and adjusted the sheath holding his knife. Last, he bent over and picked up his gun and the extra magazines for it. He slid the magazines into the inside pocket of his jacket and tucked his gun into the waistband of his pants at the back. On impulse, he also picked up the video recorder that he had taken from Mei's pod and the Project Gliese 581g patch he had cut from his shirt and slipped them into his pocket.

He ran his hand over his smooth jaw. He had shaved off the extra growth and trimmed his hair before he showered. His tongue ran over the smooth enamel of his teeth. La'Rue had given him a liquid that had turned out to be a cross between mouthwash and toothpaste. All he had to do was take a swig, swish it around in his mouth, and spit it out.

A quick glance around the room showed that he had everything he needed. He wasn't sure how late it was, but he knew that La'Rue had retired shortly after he had. Since he couldn't sleep, he would do a little exploring to become more familiar with the ship and with the alien technology.

Sergi silently stepped out of his room. He looked both ways before deciding the best place to start was the cockpit of the freighter. He briefly paused outside of La'Rue's room. The door was open, and he could see her peacefully sleeping.

A sudden ache formed low in his belly. He was surprised once again at his reaction to her. If things had been different, he'd have joined her.

His gaze swept over her face. She lay on her side, facing the open door. Her eyelids moved as if she was dreaming and her plump lips were slightly parted. A powerful urge to capture her lips pierced him.

His gaze moved over her shoulders and along her arms. She had one hand tucked under her pillow. Sergi had no doubt that she was holding her blaster. Her other hand was under her cheek.

The blanket covering her was bunched around her waist. She was fully clothed. He knew it was because she wanted to be ready in case something happened. Her fear of being here had been very evident in her constant reiteration of the dangers.

Sergi forced his attention away from La'Rue and continued down the corridor. He climbed the short ladder to the bridge and he reached for his pistol when he caught a movement out of the corner of his eye. He relaxed when he saw that it was HL-9.

"So, is there any way you could help me, little robot?" he murmured.

H crawled across the ceiling and down along the wall before pausing in front of him. Sergi slid into the seat and looked at the controls. His eyes narrowed on the strange symbols written in different places.

"What does this mean in Galactic Standard?" he asked, not really expecting an answer.

Booster....

Sergi blinked in surprise when the symbol and the word popped up next to each other in a holographic image. Curious, he pointed to another symbol.

Oxygen....

Excited, he pointed to every symbol he could find and repeated them several times before he was satisfied he had memorized what the symbols meant. At least this was a beginning. The sooner he learned the language, the better prepared he'd be in this new world.

"Show me the alphabet in both languages," he ordered.

H projected each symbol and letter. Sergi created several short phrases and had the bot translate them. Over the course of the next two hours, he slowly began to recognize the patterns. Satisfied with his progress, another idea came to him.

He pulled out the video recorder. Turning it over in his hand, he wondered if there was a way he could have H translate what the alien said to Mei.

"H, is there any way you can upload the video on this and play it with subtitles?" Sergi asked, holding up the camera.

Two of the long silver legs reached out and plucked the camera from Sergi's hand. The spider-like bot turned the camera over between its legs several times before it removed the battery and touched the two connectors with different legs.

Sergi watched the small bot's eyes flicker and glow. He sat back in his seat as the bot projected the video in front of him. This had been a hell of a lot easier than his rigging it for power earlier!

"You are indeed an amazing little robot," Sergi murmured in approval.

He chuckled when the little bot's back two legs danced a jig of delight. He turned his focus to the video, watching it with the same intensity he had earlier. The little bot added a scrolling caption to the bottom so the words spoken were in both English and whatever language the man was speaking.

"Pause," he ordered, leaning closer to the projection. "Can you enlarge on the words on the wall?"

H enlarged the scene. There was another set of words that he hadn't seen earlier on the small camera screen. His fingers lifted instinctively to touch them, forgetting for a moment that it was a projection and not a tablet. He growled when his fingers passed through the visual, distorting it.

"What do the words on the back wall say?" he said, pulling his hand back.

Cryon II 5469220

"Is that the name of the ship? Is there a way to locate it?" Sergi demanded.

The screen flickered again before changing. Sergi frowned when he saw the word Torrian. La'Rue had mentioned Torrian. He was about to ask H what it meant when the image of a planet appeared. H zoomed in until Sergi could see an alien spaceport.

"Torrian is another planet," he murmured.

Sergi stared at the image, his mind swirling. If the spaceship that Mei had been on was now there, then that was where he was going. Pushing out of his chair, he started to turn away before he remembered the video camera. Holding out his hand, he motioned for the little bot to release it.

The small black camera dropped into the palm of his hand. He quickly pocketed it before turning to exit the bridge. Regardless of the dangers, they still needed to get the fuel cells.

He strode down the corridor toward La'Rue's cabin. The sound of her voice raised in anger had him slowing his steps and walking more quietly. He paused outside of her room, listening as a man spoke.

"*Jabeti lo gaya*," the man said.

"I don't care if you owe credits, it isn't my problem. I told you when I left that I wouldn't be responsible for any of your debts, Slate," La'Rue angrily responded.

"Why are you speaking in the old tongue?" Slate demanded.

In the reflection of the mirror hanging on the wall Sergi saw

La'Rue toss her head and run her hands through her hair, making the short lengths stand up.

"Because I want to, Slate," she said irritably. "I can't help you. I have enough problems of my own. The *Star Runner* is currently out of commission and unless I can find a good deal on fuel cells, I won't be getting out of this place alive without a miracle. I cut all ties with you, and you still used me. I had to transfer a good portion of my savings to the bounty hunter who came after my freighter because he was looking for you!" she said.

"Half the *Star Runner* should be mine," Slate stated.

Sergi watched as La'Rue's expression turned from shock to fury. She leaned closer to the device she was holding. Sergi could understand why La'Rue had said he could kill this man if they ever met, though he had a feeling she didn't know he would actually do it without a second thought, especially now.

"My father gave me the *Star Runner*, and I refurbished it by myself. I own her – every nut and bolt. You never spent one credit on her even though I ran trades for you. If you try to use her for credits again, I'll kill you, Slate," she threatened.

"Too late, Rue. I owe another ten thousand credits to pay for a cargo delivery the Legion confiscated from me – illegally, I might add. It was honest, recorded merchandise," Slate replied.

"Another ten thousand credits! On top of the thirty thousand?! Are you insane? Who did you owe that kind of cargo to?" she hissed, sitting back.

"Aires, this time," Slate responded with a sigh. "I didn't have anything else to promise him, La'Rue. He is worse than Bog. I needed to buy some more time, especially after he found out I was already beholden to Bog. He was afraid I wouldn't be able to repay him."

La'Rue shook her head in disbelief. "You're a dead man, Slate. If Aires doesn't kill you, I will. You've got to make another deal with him. I don't have those kinds of credits," she said.

"Is there any way you can get it, Rue?" Slate said in a desperate voice.

La'Rue hesitated, a momentary flash of indecision sweeping across her face before she hid her expression. Slate had noticed it as well.

"What is it? Do you have a job?" Slate eagerly asked.

La'Rue started to shake her head. "No... not really," she muttered, looking away from the screen.

"Rue, you know what Aires does when he doesn't get his cargo. I might be able to renegotiate with Bogs, but Aires won't budge. I need your help," Slate pleaded.

"La'Rue. My name is La'Rue. You can't call me Rue anymore. I don't have much left thanks to your last screw up, Slate, but I do have a lead on something that could pay off. If – and it is a big *IF* – I'm successful, you've got to swear you will never contact me again," she stated.

"I swear, La'Rue. If you help me this time, I'll pay you back and never contact you again," he swore. "I love you, Rue. I always will. Contact me when you have the credits. I have to go now."

Sergi watched the light from the tablet in La'Rue's hand grow dark. She tossed it to the side and fell back against the pillow. He watched as she lifted her arm and covered her eyes and groaned.

"If only I didn't need the credits," she whispered, her voice filled with regret.

Her soft words hit him harder than he would have expected. He silently stepped away from her door and pressed his back against the wall. Closing his eyes, he let her betrayal wash through him.

He opened his eyes when he heard the bathroom door in her cabin open and close. Stepping away from the wall, he shot a quick look into her cabin to make sure she wasn't in it before he passed by the door and continued down the corridor.

At the end of the long passage, he descended the ladder to the lower section of the freighter. Within seconds, he was on the circular platform as it descended from the ship's belly to the ground. Luckily, the rain had slowed to a light mist.

Drawing from his memory of the map that La'Rue had shown him earlier, he oriented himself to his surroundings. Once he was confident he knew which direction to travel in, he pressed the button to close the lift.

"Good luck, my beautiful but deceitful alien," Sergi murmured. "Perhaps one day we will meet again."

He pulled up the collar of his jacket and silently left the shelter of the freighter, disappearing into the night.

CHAPTER NINE

"*I* can't believe he left!" La'Rue growled, storming down the corridor to the platform. "H! Where are you?"

La'Rue grabbed the stun rod from its charger. She scowled at HL-9 when the robot suddenly appeared. There was no telling how long Sergi had been gone.

"Make sure nothing happens to my freighter," she ordered, stepping onto the platform.

The robot's eyes flickered in acknowledgement. She pressed the button and held on as the platform lowered to the ground. She had already scanned the area to make sure it was clear, but it never hurt to be extra cautious.

Clutching the stun rod in her hand, she set out in the direction of the city. If she was lucky, she'd find the fuel rods that she needed and Sergi. She hoped the first wouldn't cost her an arm and a leg – or her life. The second – well, she wasn't making any promises that she wouldn't take a life.

"I can't believe he would just disappear like that," she muttered, refusing to think of his kiss. "So much for his promises; they are just as worthless as the ones Slate made."

It would take her nearly an hour to reach the city if she didn't encounter any delays. She kept a wary eye out for any movement. Breaking into a fast jog, she let the fury building inside her fester until she almost relished the thought of someone getting in her way.

Sergi better hope our paths don't cross again, she savagely thought.

~

Tribute: Sanctuary City on Turbinta:

The two men struggled to get the mud-covered capsule through the doorway and into the bar. Tallei, the owner of the bar and a master assassin, stood to the side, scanning the capsule with her one good eye.

"Where did you find it?" Tallei said, walking over and running her long staff along the top.

"In the forest southeast of here," one of the men replied.

"There was nothing in it when we found it. The interior was ripped up pretty bad," a second man said, nervously swallowing when Tallei turned her gaze to him.

"And the Legion?" Tallei inquired, walking around the capsule before pausing once again in front of it.

"We took it out from beneath their noses," the first man promised.

Tallei fixed her clear eye on the man. "Make sure that all tracks are covered and tell no one about this," she instructed.

"Yes, Tallei," the man replied.

"And find the missing contents. It will be a man who is unlike any others you have seen. Bring him to me – alive," she ordered.

"Yes, Tallei," the man said again.

Tallei waved a dismissive hand at the two men. She had closed the bar early, unwilling to chance anyone discovering the capsule was here and trying to take it from her.

She waited until they left before she opened the capsule. Using the staff in her hand, she moved the ripped pieces of cloth to the side to reveal the underside. Her dark green lips were pinched in irritation.

There was nothing of use or value in the pod – but, she thought, her eyes glimmering with malice, the pod itself could be useful. Tallei reached up and closed the lid. Her pupil, Kella Ta'Qui, had betrayed her. The reports that Tallei had received stated that Kella was in the company of an unusual man. Kella had what she wanted – and she had not brought him to her.

Tallei pulled a small portable communications device from the pocket of her pants. With a sweeping gaze, she scanned the empty bar. The establishment in the city gave her extra credits, but mostly it gave her opportunities to gather information and it was a source of potential new recruits, though she no longer took in full pupils, not after Kella.

Kella was her niece by blood. Tallei had stolen her away after killing Kella's parents. As one of Turbinta's most powerful master instructors, it was only fitting that she had one of the most powerful students. She had seen the possibilities inside Kella the moment she met the young girl. Unfortunately, there was also a weakness. Kella liked to collect treasures, things that she cared about. Tallei had tried beating that weakness out of her young charge, and she'd thought she had succeeded, but clearly, she had failed.

Opening a private communication line, she sent a signal to Kella's spaceship. It did not take long for her niece to answer. She studied the defiant young face reflected on the screen.

"Tallei," Kella greeted, her head lifting.

Tallei was silent for several seconds. She studied Kella's expression. There was something different about her niece. It took a moment for Tallei to recognize what it was – fear. Tallei could use that to her advantage against her young protégée.

"Your time is up," she stated in a cold, calm voice.

Kella vigorously shook her head. "I have two days left," her niece argued.

"Not any longer," Tallei sharply countered.

Kella's voice became hard. "The contract specified the time period. I have two days left," she insisted.

Tallei's irritation flared into an icy fury. It seemed Kella would not give up her treasure without another of their lessons. Or it was time to kill her. Tallei suspected she would do the latter. It was dangerous for the master to have a pupil as skilled as Kella no longer in their control.

Tallei's lips pursed in irritation. "Bring the alien to me, Kella, and I will not kill you," she ordered.

"No," Kella stubbornly replied.

"The Legion forces are here. Bring the alien to me. I order you to obey," Tallei impatiently commanded again.

"No, Tallei. I will not bring him to you. I no longer answer to you," Kella quietly replied.

Tallei could feel her lip curl in disgust. "Do you think you love him, Kella? Do you wish to collect him and place him in a box with your other treasures?" she asked.

Satisfaction coursed through her when the alien male reacted to her goading and stepped into view. She ran her eye over him, assessing how dangerous an opponent he would be. There was no doubt in her mind that Kella would have told the man who she was and of what she was capable. The contemptuous expression on the man's face and the mocking look in his eyes provoked an unusual emotion in Tallei – doubt.

The man returned her scrutiny with his own. "Damn! I say daam-mmn, but how do you spell bitch? You know, they have places for psychopaths like you," he commented in a scornful tone.

Tallei's eye narrowed and she could feel the vein at her temple beginning to throb. "You are arrogant," she stated in a cold voice.

"Yep, to the bone," he agreed.

Tallei's grip tightened on her staff. A fierce desire to wipe the insulting smirk from his face swept through her. Kella and the man would die a slow and very painful death. From the man's protective stance over her niece, she suspected it would be especially painful for him to watch Kella die such a death. Tallei's only regret was that she could not keep her niece alive to watch her kill the foolish man, too.

"You are reckless," she sneered.

The man's grin grew until she could see his even, white teeth. "And handsome, witty, charming, and a host of other lovely adjectives. I'll send you a dictionary if you need help with the definitions," he retorted.

"You will come to regret your disdain of a Master Turbintan, alien," she promised.

"Not likely, bitch. Kella is no longer under your thumb. If you come near her again, you'll have to deal with us both," he stated.

Tallei felt a chill of unease course through her. She had faced adversaries before who thought they could defeat her, but never had she met an opponent who had dared to look her in the eye and mock her like this man was doing. It would be interesting to see if he was still as arrogant when they faced each other without the protection of distance.

"Oh, I will deal with her – and with you when you come to me. You'll come quickly if you wish to rescue the other one of your kind," Tallei said with a triumphant smile.

She stepped to the side and held the communications device out so that both her niece and the man could see the pod sitting in the center of the room. The sound of their reactions empowered her. They would come, and she would be ready for them. She turned the communications device back to her face.

"You know where to come, Kella. You have one hour, or I will use the alien I found inside to show you what happens to those who displease me," she ordered before she cut the transmission.

An ominous screech rent the air as she dragged her metal staff across the top of the metal pod. Her mind was no longer on her niece and the man, but on the Director of the Legion. Andronikos had promised a substantial number of credits for finding a pod and even more for the contents. Her good eye glittered with avarice. She would have both.

"But... there is still a third," she murmured. She opened the communications device once again and pressed in a code.

"Yes, Master Tallei," a soft voice replied.

"I have a job for you," Tallei said.

~

Sergi grinned as he pulled the skirt over his trousers and fastened it at the waist. The long folds of dark gray material fell to his ankles. He had appropriated it from the clothing hanging from a line under an eave. Until he knew exactly what he was dealing with, he would scout the area in disguise.

He pulled the long, heavy gray shawl over his head and adjusted it, then picked up the thick piece of wood he'd found to use as a cane, and made sure the clothes and shawl covered everything but his fingertips. He couldn't help but wonder what La'Rue's expression would be if she could see him now.

"Ah, my little alien, if only we had met under different circumstances," he muttered under his breath, unable to stop thinking of the vixen with the red hair, sharp tongue, and enticing lips.

Stepping out of the dim alley, he shuffled along the narrow walkway. There weren't very many people out this early in the morning. He suspected that most transactions were done later in the day. He moved slowly, pausing as if needing to take a rest, but actually focusing on the names written on the buildings, trying to decipher what they meant.

Continuing down the walkway, he was about to turn the corner when a man swept around it. Sergi fell back against the wall, hiding in the folds of his skirt the knife he had automatically pulled. The small, orange-striped male glared at him. Sergi's hand tightened around the gray shawl covering his head and he bowed his head enough to keep his face hidden.

"Move, old woman, or I'll slit your throat," the man snarled.

Sergi didn't argue. La'Rue had mentioned that Turbintan assassins wore a tattoo signifying their clan, and given that he was on Turbinta and this guy had a prominent tattoo on his neck, Sergi thought it was a good bet that this was an assassin. He wondered if the kill marks La'Rue had told him about were somehow incorporated into the clan tattoo or if they were some elsewhere on his body. He would love to take the guy down a peg or two, but revealing his identify was not worth satisfying his desire to teach the man a lesson in etiquette. Instead, he shuffled back several steps and kept the walking stick and the knife ready in case the man followed through on this threat. Sergi warily watched the man stride down the sidewalk. The sudden, humorous thought that the man really did have Little Man Syndrome flashed through his mind.

Big knife, little dick, he silently mused.

Three hours later, he was making his second circuit through the compact area where it appeared most of the businesses were situated. He stepped into a covered area in front of one business when he saw a familiar figure weaving a determined path through the growing crowd of merchants and pedestrians. La'Rue was wearing her goggles and face cover, but he recognized her lean body, long stride, and the stunner she liked to carry everywhere.

Curious, he kept his head down until she passed by his position. His lips twitched when he heard her muttering to herself. He wondered if she had been cursing him since she left the freighter.

Sergi stepped out of the shadows and began following La'Rue. A silent groan whispered through his mind as he did. The gentle sway of her hips made his body think of things other than the fact that he was on an alien world and dressed in drag.

You have been without a woman for far too long, Sergi. Keep your focus, he cautioned himself.

Of course, his body didn't want to listen to what his mind was telling him. La'Rue had somehow wiggled her way under his skin during their brief encounter. He turned left at the corner and followed her down a covered alley with shops on each side. He knew there was a shop at the end selling parts.

He frowned when she passed the shop and kept going. What concerned him even more were the two men who stepped out of the shadows in front of him, their eyes fixed on her. The one on his left fingered the weapon at his hip. Sergi picked up his pace a little when he saw La'Rue glance over her shoulder. She turned another corner up ahead.

A silent curse filtered through his mind when the men sped up. He reached behind his back and wrapped his fingers around the grip of his gun. Pulling it free, he kept it close to his side as he turned the corner. He could see the two men standing in front of La'Rue at the far end.

"You picked the wrong person to rob. Now, get lost," she said, aiming her weapon at the two men.

One of the men turned and spit on the ground. "Give us your credits," he replied.

"Wrong decision, Marastin scum," she jibed, lowering her blaster and shooting the man in the leg.

The second man surged forward, wrapped his beefy hand around her wrist, and twisted her arm. Her blaster hit the ground. She swung the stun rod at the man, but he grabbed her other wrist.

The man on the ground released a series of loud curses as he reached for the weapon at his side. Sergi lifted his gun and fired a single bullet into the man on the ground. The silent thud made little sound in the narrow alley. The man fell back to the filthy ground, his weapon falling from his limp hand.

La'Rue took advantage of the other man's distraction at his comrade's sudden collapse to kick the man in the groin. Sergi swore he could hear the man's balls crunch. The moment the man released her, she kicked him backwards onto the ground and pressed the end of the stun rod into his chest.

"Mess with me again and I'll rip your balls off," she swore.

Sergi pointed his weapon at the man and fired a shot. La'Rue jerked backwards in surprise and raised the stun rod toward Sergi. He strode forward and toed the man's arm out to reveal the knife he had been about to throw.

"Never give them a chance to strike again, *dusha moya*," Sergi instructed, pulling the shawl back to reveal his face.

"Sergi...," La'Rue breathed, her eyes widening in shock before they darkened in fury. "You... you... you...."

Sergi pushed the stun rod to the side and stepped forward. His other arm swept around her, and he pulled her close against his body. The fury in her eyes changed to uncertainty as he bent his head close to hers. He captured her lips in a desperate kiss that made him wary of how easy it would be to lose control with La'Rue.

Her lips parted under his onslaught. He wished he could tousle her hair between his fingers. If they weren't out in the open, he would seriously consider burying himself inside her. The overpowering urge to take her for his own was completely out of character for him.

His tongue tangled with hers for several long seconds before he reluctantly released her lips. They gazed at each other, their breathing heavy and their bodies taut with desire. He winced when she suddenly punched him.

"What was that for?" he demanded, releasing her and stepping back.

"You left," she stated, pushing him farther back so she could step to the side and pick up her blaster.

He turned and watched her walk over to the two men. A shudder shook her lithe frame, and a look of disgust swept across her face as she bent over and gingerly searched both men. He frowned as he watched her.

"I can do that, if you prefer. Are you looking for something specific?" he asked, curious when she carefully pulled a bag out of the pocket of the first man he had killed.

She looked over her shoulder at him. "I need credits for fuel cells. They are dead, so they don't need them anymore," she stated, turning back around and picking up the dead man's weapon. She slid it into an inside pocket of her coat.

"*You* are robbing the dead?" he asked in a dubious tone.

La'Rue looked at him and scowled. "We are on Turbinta. These men would have stripped the clothes from my dead body. I'll at least leave them that. They can't use the credits and I need them to get off this dark cesspool of a planet. I also need more weapons. They are expensive. I guarantee you that in less than ten minutes, even the bodies will be gone. Someone will sell those as well," she rationalized.

Sergi shook his head. "I am not judging you," he muttered, rubbing his side.

His hand paused when he saw her watching the movement with

concern. A slight smile twisted his lips. She was such a contradiction of toughness and compassion. Her attention shifted to searching the second man. She released a soft whistle and grinned as she stood up.

"I was hoping they would have a fair amount of credits on them and they did! I bet I have enough for the fuel cells without touching my own funds," she said, tossing one of the black bags up in the air.

Confusion darkened Sergi's brow. "What do you mean you were 'hoping they would have a fair amount of credits on them'? You knew they were following you?" he demanded.

"Of course I knew! It was only a matter of time," she said, sliding the two bags of credits into her pocket before removing two round disks from her utility belt.

Sergi bit back a retort and frowned unhappily as he watched her slap a disk to each man's chest. He was glad she could use a dangerous situation to her advantage, but the fact that she was in danger at all felt absolutely intolerable. "You could have been killed or worse," he couldn't help grumbling, flashing back to Mei's incredulous glares whenever his new and bizarre protective instincts had flared up around her.

"But I wasn't," she said, stepping past him. "You might want to step away."

Sergi turned and followed La'Rue as she walked back down the alley. He stopped when she paused near the end, turned, and depressed the button on a thin, silver cylinder. His gaze moved to where she was looking. The bodies of the two men glowed for a few seconds before they became two piles of ash in the alley.

He turned to look at her with a wary expression. "I think I may have underestimated you," he ruefully admitted.

She gave him a wry smile as she slid the cylinder back into her utility belt. "Most people do. It is how I stay alive," she retorted before she grew serious. "Why did you leave without telling me?"

Sergi studied her face as he mentally debated what he should say. After her reaction to his kiss, he wondered if he may have drawn the wrong conclusion earlier.

"I overheard you telling Slate that you knew how to get the credits he needed. If I remember correctly, you told me that the Legion is offering a large bounty for me," he confessed.

La'Rue's eyes widened briefly in understanding, and she ran her fingers along the coarse, gray material of the shawl that rested near his temple. Her eyes followed the movement as her knuckles brushed along his smoothly shaven cheek. She paused and looked into his eyes.

"I might be a lot of things, Sergi, but I don't betray a trust or turn my back on a friend, even if that friend is an ass. There are some runs I can make that pay a lot. I can do a couple of them and make the credits Slate needs," she said, her eyes turning away from his.

Sergi lifted his hand and cupped her cheek, forcing her to look up at him. "These runs – they are dangerous to you, *da?*" he demanded.

"Yes, they are dangerous, but I'm good at what I do and the *Star Runner,* when she is in good running order, is one of the fastest freighters out there," La'Rue stated.

"Why would you risk your life for a man who has betrayed you?" Sergi probed, feeling another emotion he had never felt before – jealousy.

La'Rue's expression filled with regret. "Because life doesn't always let you pick and choose who will be there to watch your back," she murmured, tweaking the shawl before she released it. "This is a good disguise. I never looked twice at you."

Sergi grinned. "I would have preferred a nice red or royal blue," he teasingly reflected, replacing his gun in the waistband of his trousers.

"You're crazy," she chuckled with a shake of her head.

"Only for you, *dusha moya,*" he replied, catching her hand and lifting it to his lips.

"What does *dusha moya* mean?" La'Rue faintly asked, gazing up at him with dark, curious eyes that made him want to kiss her again.

Once again, he was shocked to realize that he had only met this incredible woman the day before. So much had happened in the past twenty-four plus hours that he was still trying to process everything.

"My soul," he answered in a deeper voice.

CHAPTER TEN

"Stay here. It will look strange if you come in at the same time," La'Rue said, pausing outside of the parts shop that they had passed a short while ago.

Sergi nodded. "I will be here when you come out," he promised.

He watched as she disappeared into the parts shop. Bowing his head, he gripped the sturdy walking stick and stepped across the narrow alley until he was standing under the protective overhang of the building facing it. From this position he could see La'Rue inside through the large open doorway.

Sergi silently watched as merchants and customers went about their daily activities. He noticed that they moved in pairs or small groups. Every once in a while he would see a lone figure that made him wonder if it were one of the assassins who lived here. One thing that stood out was that there wasn't a lot of talking between people, instead people looked suspiciously at each other as they passed. After what had already happened to La'Rue, he could understand their distrust.

He narrowed his eyes when he noticed two men come out of the parts shop and walk across to where he was standing. He hunched his shoulders and pulled the shawl down a little more over his face before he casually leaned against the walking stick. He was surprised when the two men turned and leaned against the wall beside him, acting as if he wasn't even there. One of them pulled out a long, narrow flute from the inside of his coat and lifted it to his lips.

"We need to leave here before the Legion has a chance to close off the planet," one of the men muttered, his eyes following the movements of a merchant carrying supplies down the alley.

"You heard what Andronikos did to Jeslean, didn't you?" the other man asked.

The first man nodded. "He'll destroy anyone who gets in his way," the man grimly replied, lifting the flute to his mouth once more.

The other man drew in a deep breath before he released it. Both men grew silent while several people passed by them. He waited to see if the men would continue their discussion.

"They say that two of the Ancient Knights of the Gallant have returned. I heard from another source that one of them defeated a Legion squadron single-handedly on Tesla Terra," the second man said.

The first man nodded. "I heard the same thing. I also heard that the Director sent a squadron of warships to flatten the cities on Tesla Terra only to have his fleet intercepted and destroyed by the rebels in a surprise attack. They say the Ancient Knights have returned to lead the rebels," he added.

"Do they think any of the Ancient Knights are here on Turbinta?" the second man asked.

The first man shrugged his shoulders. "I don't know why they would come here. The Turbintans won't join in the fight unless they are paid to do so. The rebels wouldn't stand a chance if the Legion were to hire these bloody assassins," he growled with distaste.

"I heard from another freighter captain who was in a market on Torrian that there was a Turbintan seen with an Ancient Knight. She was fighting with him against the Legion forces there, not against him," the second man shared.

Sergi could sense the first man's surprise. His own desire to ask for more information about who these Ancient Knights were made him want to shake both men and demand answers. Instead, he gritted his teeth and hoped that they would continue to talk.

The men looked up when a third man appeared in the doorway across from him. They straightened when the man walked over to them. Sergi could sense the man's gaze sweep over him before the man dismissed him. An old, infirm woman was no threat, after all.

"The parts will be delivered to our bay," the man said. "I could use a drink. That damn merchant demanded almost twice what the part was worth." The man paused and looked around with a frown. "Has anyone seen Germ and Amaric?"

"No, and I'm not waiting on them. You should never have hired those two. They are trouble," the first man replied, sliding the thin flute back into his coat.

"The merchant told me the Legion is here searching for those two missing pods. Word has it that Turbintan natives are evacuating the city. He said General Landais himself is here – the older one, not the younger bastard. We need to get the ship repaired and then get off this damn planet," the man continued.

"We were just talking about that. I heard that they are searching for pods of some sort. They are offering a large bounty for one and even more for a pod's contents," the second man replied.

The man who had stepped out of the shop nodded. "I heard the same thing – and that one of the pods was already found and taken to Tallei's bar. There is no way I'm messing with that deranged assassin or the Legion. We repair the ship and get the hell out of here," the man ordered.

"I'm with you, Captain," the first man agreed. "I've got a family."

Sergi watched the three men walk away. His mind swirled with this new information. He looked up when he saw La'Rue appear in the doorway. She was carrying a box by its handle. She looked up and down the alley before she crossed over to him.

"Did you get everything you needed?" he asked, watching as she placed the box down on the ground and began removing the long, silver tubes.

"Yes. Cost me twice what they should have, but they are in good shape. I made the merchant test each one in front of me," she answered, sliding the tubes into a bag she had pulled from the pocket of her coat. "With the repairs we did yesterday and these, we should be able to get off the planet."

"There is something I need to do before I leave here," he murmured.

La'Rue straightened and looked at him with a frown. She lifted the straps of the bag over her shoulders and pulled the tabs to tighten the bag securely against her back. Her gaze searched his face as she waited for him to continue.

"I overheard two men talking about someone named Tallei. She has one of the pods. I need to see which one it is," he said.

"No!" La'Rue loudly hissed before she lowered her voice. "No, Sergi. Tallei isn't just an assassin, she is a *master* assassin. You *know* there were two pods on Turbinta. One was yours; the other was washed away by the flash flood. The merchant said the Legion forces are here as well. Not *just* the Legion, but General Coleridge Landais. He is as bad as Tallei. If either one of them sees you.... Sergi, they *would* kill you and it wouldn't be a pleasant way to die because they will get whatever information they want out of you first," she warned.

Sergi almost smiled at the worried expression on La'Rue's face. He started to lift his hand to caress her face before he caught himself. He clenched his fist and looked toward the end of the alley to the main road. Returning his gaze to La'Rue, he nodded.

"We'll go back and repair your freighter," he agreed.

Her shoulders relaxed, and she gave him a brief smile before she pulled her goggles down over her eyes and used the material around her neck to cover her lower face. He sighed regretfully, already missing the sight of her face.

I have it bad. Mei and the others would never let me live it down if they knew, he ruefully thought.

He drew in a deep breath. He knew that Mei had survived and there was a strong possibility that at least one or more of the others had as well. He also had two other planets as possible landing sites – Torrian and Tesla Terra.

"We need to hurry. I've got a bad feeling that things are about to go from bad to worse rather quickly. Have you noticed that even the merchants are closing up shop?" La'Rue commented.

"Yes," Sergi murmured.

Merchants were moving to seal their doors while the few customers who had been out and about seemed to have vanished into thin air. They reached the end of the alley and turned the corner. Sergi scanned the area ahead, sweeping over the few people still out on the main road. He was about to turn back to La'Rue when a lone, cloaked figure caught his attention.

There was something very familiar about the way the man was walking toward them. Sergi couldn't see the man's face, but he had a nagging feeling that there was something important here. He had learned a long time ago never to ignore such strong feelings.

He drew La'Rue behind him when the man was almost to the corner where they were standing. As he got closer, disbelief washed through Sergi when he heard a familiar soft chuckle followed by a voice he recognized.

"Damn, I feel like I'm back in Vegas," the man said, though he wasn't slowing down and didn't appear to have noticed Sergi in his disguise.

Sergi remained frozen as his mind processed who he was seeing. He didn't know how, but Ashton 'Ash' Haze was on Turbinta. His mind raced as he wondered if Ash had somehow been able to trace the signal to Sergi's pod. If he had, he was walking into a trap.

"What is it?" La'Rue said, after the man had walked past them.

"Get to the freighter and repair it," Sergi instructed, trying to keep his eye on where Ash was going.

"Sergi...," La'Rue started to protest.

Sergi turned to La'Rue and reached up to cup her cloth-covered cheek. He wished things could have been different – that they had met in a different time and place – a different life.

"I can't go with you. Repair your freighter and get out of here," he ordered, wishing he could see her eyes.

"What is it? I'm not going to leave you, Sergi," she protested.

"You have to. That man – he is from my world. I have to go, and so do you. Something far too dangerous is about to happen, and I don't want you anywhere near it. You are a very special woman, La'Rue. Perhaps...," he started to say before he shook his head, pulled down the cloth that had covered her mouth, and pressed a hard kiss to her lips. "Stay safe, *dusha moya,*" he instructed before he released her.

"Wait— I... You be safe as well, Sergi," she said, brushing a kiss to his lips before she withdrew and pulled up the cloth over her mouth and nose again.

Sergi watched her look back and forth before she hurried down the walkway in the opposite direction. She didn't look back at him. For a split second, he almost followed her instead of Ash. It was only the knowledge that this might be his only chance to connect with another member of the Project Gliese 581g mission and the possibility that Ash was walking into a trap that stopped him.

CHAPTER ELEVEN

Legion transport outside the city of Tribute:

oleridge Landais stood looking out of the window of the military transport. The craft moved above the trees toward the main trading city of Tribute. His piercing gaze swept over the dull, gray landscape, constantly searching. The craft passed low over an isolated stand of trees. A frown furrowed his brow when he thought he saw a ship on the ground below them, but when he looked again he decided it must have been the combination of light, weather, and shadows that had made him think so. He returned his focus to the structure coming into sight ahead of them.

The city of Tribute was as depressing as the rest of the planet. From the transport's current position, he could see the entire city. Gray stone buildings lined the main road and divided the city into two sections with numerous side alleys branching off. The spaceport was located in the northwest section of the city. He could see the Legion shuttles scattered among the other spaceships.

"Are all transports being thoroughly searched before they are released?" Coleridge asked, turning to look at the Sergeant standing at his side.

"Yes, sir, just as you ordered," the man stated.

"Do not allow any more ships to depart," he ordered.

"Yes, sir," the Sergeant replied, turning to relay the General's orders into the communications link attached to his ear.

Coleridge's grip on the metal support tightened as the transport swung around the outskirts of the city. The moment it touched down, the doors opened. A cold blast of air swept through the vessel along with the heavy mist.

"Move out," the Sergeant yelled above the sound of the engines.

Coleridge jumped out of the transport and strode toward the main street. Behind him, the Sergeant, along with half a dozen men, followed him while another half dozen spread out in formation and moved ahead of them.

Tallei's bar was at the end of the street and to the left. Coleridge reached down and withdrew his weapon from the holster at his side. On each side of the street, the doors to the businesses were closed, and the sidewalks were deserted. A sense of satisfaction swept through him. He would have to convey to his brother that even the Turbintans were not immune to the overwhelming power of the Legion.

~

The small, orange-striped Turbintan wiped his blade on the front of the dead Legion Commander's shirt. Blood smeared across Commander Taug's name tag. Zoak had saved the Commander for last. All he had learned was that his master was in danger. His lips curled into a snarl.

He stepped over the body of the Commander, but not before ripping the man's name tag off his shirt and adding it to his collection. He liked to collect one memento from each of his kills. He bent his knees and jumped. While small in stature, he made up for it in speed and strength. He could jump twenty feet in a single leap and was an excellent climber.

It didn't take him long to return to where he had left the hover glide. Releasing the handle, he slid his feet into the foot grips and grasped the controls. In seconds, he was weaving through the forest and heading back to town.

~

Sergi followed behind Ash, searching for anyone else doing the same. He wasn't sure what was going on, but it was obvious that Ash was on a clearly defined mission. Sergi paused along the walkway when Ash slowed, adjusted his cloak, and opened the door to an establishment a short distance away. Sergi stayed by the building across the street from where Ash had entered as three other men walked up to the door Ash had just gone through. They were speaking intensely to each other in a language he didn't understand.

When one of the men glanced in his direction, Sergi looked down and scooped up a basket that had been left outside the closed business he was standing in front of. Covertly sliding his knife inside the basket, he casually carried it on his arm as he followed the men into the building.

He silently slipped around the small group of men, using their bodies to help conceal his own as he made his way toward a dark corner. Sergi's glance skimmed over his emergency pod in the middle of the room. The two men who had entered before him were now sitting at a table while Ash sat at a table near the window.

Sergi watched from his dark corner as a tall woman appeared from the back of the bar. The woman had a series of intricate tattoos on her neck. Another Turbintan assassin – the master La'Rue was afraid of, if the hair on his nape standing up was any indication.

"*Nebi mau keti mi*," the woman ordered, waving a dismissive hand at the men. Sergi's eyebrow rose at her low, menacing tone.

Sergi was impressed that one lone woman, especially one who was blind in one eye, could scare three large men. He curiously watched as she sneered and shut the door. She pulled a large key out of her pocket and twisted it in the lock. A wry grin curved his lips when she turned the full force of her irritation on Ash.

"*Nebi mau keti mi!*" she snarled again in a language that Sergi didn't understand but was pretty sure meant 'Get the hell out of here' as she unlocked the door again.

Sergi watched as Ash leaned forward, pulled the hood off of his head, and gave the woman one of his best shit-eating-grins.

"Sorry, bitch, I don't understand what you're saying, but I have to say, if your tone is anything to go by, you need some serious counseling on how to run a business," Ash commented, looking at the woman with just the right amount of derision to feel like nails on a chalkboard.

The woman's expression changed from irritation to pure malice. "You!" the woman snarled.

Sergi sat back in his seat and listened as Ash formally introduced himself. He frowned when he heard Ash state that the two of them were going to be related, realizing in that instant that this was about more than just the pod in the center of the room – this was personal for Ash. Sergi's gaze moved back to the woman and he winced. He wouldn't want to be related to that woman for all the natural resources in Siberia.

The woman's lip curled into a sneer. "I could not care less what you are called. Where is Kella?" she demanded.

Sergi turned his head when another woman appeared from a back room of the bar. His gaze swept over her, noting her confident walk, the number of visible weapons strapped to her body, and the tattoo on her neck. His eyes moved from the young woman to the expression on Ash's face and back again. His mind tried to connect the woman with the smooth, forest green complexion and clear, dark brown eyes with Ash – the playboy pilot of the Gliese 581.

He had to hand it to the younger woman – she looked like she was ready for battle. His fascination with the unfolding events increased when she stopped and aimed a blaster at the woman, her chin lifted in determination and defiance. There were going to be fireworks.

"I am here, Tallei," Kella declared.

Ash stepped around the table, his expression taut and focused. "I wouldn't, lady. I promised myself I'd never kill a woman if I could help it. Please don't make me break that promise," he warned.

Tallei turned to look at Ash. "The legend is true? The Ancient Knights of the Gallant Order have returned?" she sneered.

Sergi frowned, adding this conversation to the intel he'd previously gathered: Ancient Knights returning to lead the rebels, two of them. One was helped by a Turbintan on Torrian – the same planet Mei's spaceship had been tracked to – and the other knight had single-handedly defeated Legion squadrons on Tesla Terra. *Is this why the Legion Director wants us? These people think the members of the Gliese 581 are some kind of prophecy come to life?* he thought in disbelief.

Sergi listened with growing concern as Tallei, the evil bitch of the west, as he was beginning to think of her, tried to bribe Ash into turning over the woman in exchange for 'the one who was in the container'. Then he saw a flicker of red light as Tallei dropped what could only be an explosive device. Rolling out of his chair, he took the heavy table with him. In the background, he heard Ash yell out a warning.

The loud explosion shook the room. The sound was deafening, but a discharging blaster could still be heard. Sergi rolled to his side. From his position, he could see Kella lying on the floor with a knife embedded in her shoulder. Unsure if she was still alive, he struggled to his feet. A quick look around showed him that Ash was locked in a fierce battle with Tallei.

Pushing the table to the side, he crawled over the debris to the woman. She was perfectly still, her face paler than before. The blade was embedded in her right shoulder. Sergi hissed out a warning when she lifted a hand and gripped the knife, but she swiftly pulled the knife out anyway. He released a long string of curses in Russian even as he pulled the shawl off of his head and wadded it up to apply pressure to the wound.

"Ash needs you alive, *dorogoy*," he muttered.

Kella's eyes widened when she looked up at him. Her lips parted in surprise. Sergi gave her a gentle, reassuring smile.

"So, you know Ash, yes?" he inquired as if there wasn't a major fight going on behind him.

"You are...." she started to say before she turned her head to look toward the woman. "Help me up."

Sergi started to protest but the fierce, determined expression in Kella's eyes warned him that she wasn't going to stop until she was standing. He wrapped his arm around her and helped her to her feet. She swayed and her face turned an alarming shade of pale green. Sergi couldn't help but wonder if the blade had been tainted with poison.

She pushed his hand away from her shoulder. Sergi decided that Ash had either discovered a true Amazon from the legends or a woman with a spine of steel.

"What did you do to my parents?" Kella demanded in a trembling voice.

Ash and Tallei looked towards him and Kella. Sergi grinned when he saw Ash's disgruntled expression and Tallei whipping her head back and forth as she tried to absorb his sudden appearance. It was either that or they were trying to figure out why he was dressed like a woman.

"Hi, Ash," Sergi replied with a grin.

Ash's lips pursed together for a moment. "How long were you planning on just watching?" he demanded.

"I don't know. When you greet a woman by calling her a bitch, I figure it is probably a personal disagreement, and I should stay out of it," he replied with a shrug.

"What did you do to my parents?" Kella asked again in a quiet voice.

Sergi decided right then and there that if Ash didn't kill the bitch, he would. He felt the shudder of pain and grief that shook Kella's slender form. Her softly spoken words tore through him, bringing back memories of his own painful loss.

"I remember...," Kella whispered.

"Sergi, catch her," Ash ordered at the same time as Tallei attacked again.

Sergi jerked when Kella suddenly moved with surprising speed, aiming a smaller but no less deadly pistol at Tallei, and firing. The older woman briefly stiffened before she collapsed.

No one spoke for a moment. Sergi looked over at Ash, and his lips twitched when he saw Ash's stunned expression turn to a dark scowl. Sergi pointed at Kella.

"She did it," he said with a grin.

Sergi scooped Kella into his arms when her legs suddenly gave out from under her. "She is in shock," he cautioned.

Ash nodded and took Kella out of his arms. He saw Ash looking for a place to lay Kella so he could attend to her wound, but there wasn't time. A look through the front window showed that they were about to have company – a lot of company.

"We need to leave," Sergi said, nodding to the window. "Immediately!"

"The cellar – there is a tunnel that leads to the spaceport. It comes up under my freighter," Kella murmured.

"Go. I will be there in a moment," Sergi replied, his eyes glittering with a touch of vicious anticipation.

Sergi watched Ash and Kella disappear through a door leading to the back. He would catch up with them in a moment, but first he needed to do a few things. With a flick of his wrist, he discarded the skirt.

He kept a wary eye on the approaching soldiers as he opened the lid to the pod. Grabbing the cloak that Ash had worn, he wrapped Tallei's body in it and deposited the bundle in the emergency pod before he closed the lid.

Next, he turned and kicked the skirt out of his way as he retrieved his knife. It had fallen to the floor when he flipped the table. An idea began to form in his mind as he slid the knife into the sheath at his waist. He reached into his front trouser pocket and pulled out the patch he had cut from his shirt. He toed the basket upright and dropped the patch into it.

If the Legion wanted a prophecy, he'd give them one. With a last glance, he grabbed two bottles of wine off the shelf as he passed the bar. In seconds, he was closing the door to the cellar behind himself and descending the stairs to the tunnel.

He grinned when he heard Ash's impatient voice up ahead demanding to know where he was. The grin faded when he saw Kella's pale face and pain-filled eyes. He crossed the room and held up the two bottles of wine.

"No worries. I thought we might need some refreshments to celebrate finding each other," he said with a wink at Kella.

Ash nodded for him to follow Kella. "You are crazier than I am!" he muttered.

Sergi chuckled, his sharp eyes taking in the long tunnel. "You are just now figuring that out?" he joked before his expression became serious. "Do you know if anyone else made it?"

"Josh did," Ash replied.

"What of Mei and Julia?" Sergi asked, pausing to look at Ash.

"We don't know. I'll tell you once we are out of this place," Ash said, cutting in front of him so he was behind Kella.

"I hope there are better planets than this one. It reminds me too much of Mother Russia," he responded.

Sergi drew back, allowing Ash and Kella a little space to talk. Seeing them together, he couldn't help but think of La'Rue. Perhaps Ash or Josh would know a way to contact her and make sure that she was safely off this planet. They had found each other. It should be a hell of a lot easier to find La'Rue since he knew her name and the name of her freighter.

I'll find you, dusha moya, he thought as they came to the end of the tunnel.

CHAPTER TWELVE

*C*oleridge stood in the center of the bar. It was obvious there had been a fight here. His gaze swept over the bloodstained floor, overturned tables, and shattered chairs to the alien pod sitting in the center of the room.

The bottom of the pod was covered in leaves and mud from the forest floor. He motioned to two soldiers standing beside the large rectangular box.

"Open it," he ordered.

Coleridge impatiently waited as the two men struggled to open the lid. When the top finally released, he stepped forward. A frown creased his brow as he studied the cloak-covered body inside. The material was dark gray, with dried mud along the lower edges of it.

Snapping his fingers at the soldier standing near the top of the pod, he motioned for the man to remove the covering. A heated wave of fury swept through him when he saw the frozen features of Tallei staring blankly up at the ceiling. Coleridge turned to the soldier who had been next to him on the transport.

"What is your name?" he demanded.

"Sergeant Ri Manta, sir," Manta replied.

Coleridge glanced down at the dead Turbintan Master. "Commander Manta discard the body, and have this pod delivered to the Battle Cruiser, then order the destruction of the city, including any ships leaving the spaceport," Coleridge ordered.

"Yes, sir," the newly promoted Commander replied.

Coleridge listened as the soldier barked out orders to dispose of Tallei's body. He walked over to the window, lost in thought. Behind him, he could hear the men working to clear the debris out of the way so that the pod could be removed.

His thoughts ran through what he knew of the strangers who had appeared. He was now in possession of two empty capsules, and there had been another pod's signal transmitting from Turbinta that had disappeared before it could be tracked. That meant three Ancient Knights of the Gallant. There were confirmed sightings of at least two survivors.

The Knights were spread throughout this star system, with one sighted on Tesla Terra, one on Torrian, and the possibility of two more here on Turbinta. While he had ordered the leveling of Tribute, whoever had been in the pod might no longer be in the city. There was still a chance that Roan had discovered the location of the second pod on Turbinta – and hopefully the Knight inside it. From the corner of his eye he saw Manta quietly approach.

"Sir, the transport is ready for pick up," Commander Manta informed him.

He lifted his hand to indicate he had heard the man. Still lost in thought, Coleridge turned and looked around the relatively bare room now that the pod was no longer in the center of it. His gaze swept over the righted tables that had been pushed out of the way by his men. In the corner, someone had picked up a basket and placed it on a table.

The basket looked out of place in the bar. Walking over, he peered down into the woven basket. Lying in the bottom was a piece of heavy cloth with a colorful symbol and strange markings on it. He reached in the basket, picked up the piece of cloth, and turned patch over in his hand. The pattern was the same as the ones found on Torrian and Tesla Terra.

His fingers curled around the scrap. The message was clear – 'we are here'. For the first time, Coleridge wondered if perhaps the legend of the Ancient Knights' return might not hold some validity. Fury swept through him.

"Let's go," he snapped to the man silently standing and waiting for him.

He turned and strode out of the bar. The sooner the city was flattened, the sooner the message would spread throughout the star systems that even the most deadly of the Turbintans was no match for the powers of the Legion. His half-brother was right. The only way to control the masses was through fear. They would strike terror in the hearts of the inhabitants and annihilate anyone who dared to resist.

He needed to know what the emblem and the strange configuration of stars meant. The archives on Jeslean had been destroyed when Andri laid waste to them. The scholars who knew of the legend would also have been eliminated. A grim smile curved his lips. While all the resources about the legend had been destroyed on Jeslean, there was still one source who knew the legend better than anyone else – the Secretum on Plateau.

"The destruction will begin as soon as the last Legion vessel has evacuated, General Landais," Manta informed him.

Coleridge climbed into the transport. "Very good," he replied. "Order all ships to return to the Battle Cruisers and prepare to leave once the city is leveled."

"Yes, General," Manta replied with a bow of his head.

～

La'Rue stumbled when the ground shook beneath the freighter. She made sure the lift locked into place before she turned and stored the stunning rod in its spot next to the lift. She quickly reached out to steady herself when the ground violently trembled again. She gripped the metal railing of the ladder and began to climb. Once on the upper level, she slid the straps of the bag free from her shoulders. Her fingers were tightly wrapped around the straps as she took off down the corridor.

"H, what is the status outside?" she yelled.

The service bot met her in the corridor. She glanced at the screen it flashed in front of her. From the brief glimpse, she could see that the city was under attack.

La'Rue strode into the engine room. She crossed to the sealed compartment that housed the fuel rods. Placing her bag on the floor, she straightened and punched in the code to unlock the compartment. She bent over and opened the top of the bag to reveal the replacement fuel cells.

She withdrew a silver cylinder. She bent her knees to regain her balance when another explosion sent a shockwave through the ship. Biting her lip, she slid the cylinder into one of the empty sleeves. With a firm twist, she watched the light turn from red to green.

"I can't believe the Legion would attack the Turbintans. Even Slate is smart enough to know better than to piss off a nest of assassins," she muttered under her breath as she carefully installed the remaining fuel cells.

"H, check the tracking device I activated," she ordered, trying to focus on what she was doing while the world exploded around her. "No, not that signal. I don't need that one anymore. You can deactivate the first device."

She had forgotten that the tracking device she had placed in Slate's favorite jacket was still active. That was how she had found out the bastard was not only lying to her, but cheating on her as well. At the moment, Slate was the least of her worries, she thought as the ship continued to rock from the Legion's attacks.

She snapped in the last cylinder and twisted it, then looked up at the map that HL-9 was displaying. A relieved laugh shook her body when she saw the signal moving rapidly away from the planet. Sergi had escaped the devastation. The laugh faded when a new, even more disconcerting thought occurred to her – what if he was in the hands of the Legion? It was possible he hadn't escaped after all, but was a prisoner.

The thought sent a chill through her. She needed to find out. If he was in the hands of the Legion, she didn't know what she could do.

"It wouldn't be the first time in your life you got into something that was over your head, La'Rue. You'll just have to figure it out. You've got brains – use them. Let's just hope he was able to find his friend, and his friend had a nice spaceship. I like that scenario much better, don't you, H?" La'Rue said, looking at her eight-legged companion with a hopeful expression.

HL-9 blinked his eyes to show he'd registered her question. La'Rue sealed the compartment, and glanced down at the silvery fuel cells with satisfaction when she saw that all of them displayed a green light. She picked up her bag and turned, almost falling again when a prolonged series of explosions rattled the ship.

"We've got to get out of here, H. Set a course to follow the tracking device DL980," she instructed, exiting the engine room and heading for the bridge.

It was growing dark outside by the time the last of the explosions faded. Short-range scans showed a limited number of spaceships leaving the planet, but none arriving. Sliding into the pilot's seat, she strapped in and engaged the engines. All systems came online.

"Well, I might starve to death if I can't figure out how to use the old cooktop, but at least my ship works again," she muttered, lifting off.

She swallowed and brushed a hand across her eyes as she cleared the atmosphere of Turbinta. Bright flashes of light lit up the map on the console in front of her where fires still raged in the city below. While she had no love for the Turbintans, the level of destruction hit her hard, and all the lives lost here were minimal compared to the lives lost on Jeslean – all because of Andronikos' greed for power.

She guided the *Star Runner* through the debris of ships that had been trying to escape. The Legion forces had shown no mercy to anyone. La'Rue hardened herself against the fear that the *Star Runner* would be seen and felt only resolution.

She might be a lowly freighter captain looking for a way to make a few credits, but she knew how to fight when she had to. The reflective paint and signal distorter that she had designed had never truly been field tested until now, but her ship hadn't been discovered yet, which meant they had proven successful against the Legion's technology. Maybe they would be of help to the rebellion.

When she had first heard that the Knights of the Gallant were rising up again, she had thought it a joke. Everyone knew that the old Knights had died out. Talk along the trade lines had been that the rebellion was a puny attempt by a group of disgruntled citizens trying to fight against the Legion's iron-fisted control on trade and taxes.

The attack on Jeslean had sent a shockwave of disbelief throughout the star system. Some still couldn't believe that such widespread destruction was possible. Heck, even she hadn't believed some of the tales that had come from those who had managed to escape. She knew once word spread about the attack on Turbinta, total terror would sweep through the various worlds.

"Oh shit, H. How could I be so stupid?" she suddenly murmured.

She had been after the pods because Andronikos was offering a bounty that was impossible to ignore. She had heard rumors before she left that the pods contained one of the Ancient Knights of the Gallant. She swallowed as all the pieces came together.

"The pods contained the Ancient Knights – Sergi...."

She shook her head in disbelief. The legend was true. The Ancient Knights of the Gallant would return when the star systems needed them most. That was why Sergi had been so insistent about finding the others of his kind.

"Have you locked on his location?" she asked, looking over at the small robot plugged into the navigation system.

A new map displayed beside the map of Turbinta. She studied the star chart. There were several planets in that region, including Tesla Terra. She would follow the signal and see where it took her.

"Whether we like it or not, H, I think we are now part of the rebellion," she said, locking the freighter's navigation onto the signal.

CHAPTER THIRTEEN

*S*ergi walked down the passage. Up ahead of him, he could see Ash checking on several panels outside of the bridge. When he got closer, he leaned against the wall, silently watching for several minutes until Ash was finished. Ash closed the panels and turned to look at him with a wry grin.

"One of the modules was burnt out," he replied.

"It is always something," Sergi commented. "I've patched up Kella. She said she heals quickly."

"Yeah, she does. It's part of her genetics and another reason Tallei wanted her," Ash quietly replied.

Sergi nodded in understanding. He had heard enough in the bar to piece together what Kella's life must have been like. She had shared a little more while he was administrating first aid to her injury.

There hadn't been much time for talking before. They had transferred from the Legion shuttle that they had used to escape Turbinta to Kella's more agile – and vastly more weaponized – spaceship near one of Turbinta's more distant moons. Sergi had been extremely impressed with what he saw and couldn't wait until he had a chance to explore what Kella had added to the spaceship.

Overall, he was still trying to process that Ash had fallen for the Turbintan assassin. "She's real quiet," Sergi said with concern.

Ash glanced down the passage to where Kella was resting before he turned to look back at Sergi. Ash gave him a brief nod of agreement.

"She's been through a lot. Thanks for staying with her and doctoring her up," Ash replied.

"Thank you for getting us off the planet without getting us blown up," Sergi murmured, his mind turning to La'Rue.

Ash leaned forward and looked intently at him. Sergi grimaced, knowing that he had let his guard down and his thoughts must have been reflected on his face. He folded his arms across his chest and waited.

"What is it? You've been distracted since we took off," Ash commented.

"I met a woman. She saved my life," he admitted with a shrug of his shoulders.

Ash raised an eyebrow. "And you left her behind?" he asked in an incredulous tone.

Sergi frowned. "She returned to her spaceship. The vessel was several kilometers from the city. La'Rue's freighter needed repairs. We were in the city so she could get the parts she needed when I saw you," he said.

"Damn, Sergi. The Legion…. There isn't much left of Tribute," Ash said with a shake of his head.

"I know," he quietly replied.

"I'm sorry, man. If I had known, maybe we could have done something," Ash murmured.

Sergi didn't reply. Instead, he reached into his pocket and pulled out the video camera that he had taken from Mei's pod. He held it out to Ash.

"What's this?" Ash inquired, reaching for the camera.

"It is the camera from Mei's emergency pod. She is alive – or she was at the time of the recording," he said.

"Mei! What about Julia?" Ash questioned.

Sergi shook his head. "I don't know. I was hoping either you or Josh might," he admitted with a tired sigh.

Ash turned the camera over in his hand. "We heard about your capsule and another one, which I now know must have been Mei's, that landed on Turbinta. Shit was hitting the fan. Turbinta isn't a planet that I wanted to get lost on, and Kella came up with the plan that she and I would go after you since she knows the planet and – well, I know you and Mei," Ash explained.

"I am thankful you came, my friend," Sergi responded.

"Have you watched this?" Ash inquired, leaning against the wall.

"Yes. She is – was – on a spaceship. The name of the ship was the *Cryon II*. The last known location of the ship was a place called Torrian," Sergi said.

Ash's eyes widened and he grinned. "Well, on a positive note, I know where that planet is. On a negative note, so does the Legion. They are crawling all over it like fleas on a hairy dog," he replied.

"We have to search for her," Sergi insisted, his jaw tightening.

Ash held up his hand. "I never said we wouldn't. There are a few things you don't know, Sergi. Things are bad. How much do you know about the Legion?" he asked.

Sergi was quiet for a moment before he shook his head. "Not much. La'Rue said the Legion had placed a large bounty on our heads," he answered.

Ash nodded. "There's a reason the Legion's Director wants us. I don't understand the whole thing, but the Director of the Legion, a guy named Andri Andronikos, has been slowly taking over the Gallant Order. It was once ruled and protected by an elite group of men and women known as the Knights of the Gallant Order. Andronikos was elected Director of the Gallant Order more than ten years ago. Anyway, over time, the other Knights and members of their families began to die in mysterious accidents. They were replaced, mostly by supporters of Andronikos and his half-brother. Now, I'll fast forward to today. While the Knights were all but extinct, there were still a few members of the council who opposed Andronikos and the growing influence he had over the Legion. They felt it was not in

keeping with the ancient laws passed to protect the different worlds –
laws that promised freedom and protection in return for a commitment to democracy and a united agreement to follow the rules set
forth by the Gallant Order. Andronikos has been aggressively
violating the laws instituted to prevent invasion or a military rule.
Things shifted several weeks ago."

"What happened?" Sergi asked with a frown.

Ash looked back at Sergi. "We happened. Word is getting around
and people think we are the Ancient Knights of the Gallant, the myth-
ical Knights who left long ago vowing to return when the people
needed them the most," he dryly replied.

"Have you or Josh thought about explaining that we are just lost
astronauts from another galaxy?" Sergi suggested with a bemused
expression.

"Oh, we tried…. Then, we kicked some Legion ass, and after that,
no one believed us," Ash chuckled.

Sergi shook his head. "And Mei thought I would be the trouble-
maker of the group," he groaned and ran a hand through his hair.
"Where are we going and what are we going to do about Mei?"

Ash's expression turned serious. "We are headed to a secret rebel
base on a cold ass moon near Tesla Terra. Once we are there, I know
someone on Torrian who can help us search for Mei," he explained
before he released a sigh. "I need to check on Kella."

Sergi grinned. "You teach me how to fly one of these and I'll be
happy to take over. I'll go sit up front. If I see any bad guys, I'll play
with some of the weapons your girlfriend loaded on this thing," he
joked, gleefully rubbing his hands together as he turned and headed
for the bridge.

"Just don't blow anything up!" Ash called in a distracted voice
behind him.

Sergi chuckled and paused in the doorway to the bridge. He
turned and strode back down the passage. He decided it would probably be best to find out exactly which buttons controlled the ship's
weapons system before he touched anything. He stopped at the
doorway to the cabin when he heard Ash and Kella quietly talking. He

glanced into the room. His expression softened when he saw them embracing.

Turning, he retraced his steps back to the cockpit, stopping briefly to pick up one of the bottles of wine he had taken from Tallei's bar. He decided there would be plenty of time to ask questions about the weapons systems later. Stepping into the cockpit, he sank into the pilot's seat and opened the bottle of wine.

He murmured a soft toast to Mei and Julia before he lifted the bottle to his lips and took a long swig. Lowering it, he leaned back. He stared out into the blackness of space as the modified freighter sped to a distant moon at a speed the engineers back on Earth could only dream about.

He leaned his head back and thought of La'Rue. He wondered where she was and if she had made it safely off of Turbinta. Most of all, he wondered whether they would ever meet again.

"Ah, *dusha moya,* if only you knew how much I hope our paths do cross again," he murmured.

With a sigh, he shoved one hand into the pocket of his jacket as he raised the bottle of wine to his lips again. A frown creased his brow when his fingers touched a small, round disk. He slowly lowered the bottle of wine to rest on his thigh as he pulled the disk free.

Turning it over in his hand, he noticed a small flashing red light and a set of symbols on the disk – DL980. His mind flashed back to the alley where La'Rue had pressed a hard kiss to his lips. Her hands had slipped under the shawl to his jacket.

"You are a very sneaky woman, La'Rue Gant," Sergi murmured with a grin. "But… I am an Ancient Knight of the Gallant, my greedy little freighter captain, who happens to know a thing or two about spy devices."

Thirty minutes later, Sergi was watching the dot on the map in front of him that was shadowing their course. A soft chuckle escaped him and he took another drink from the nearly empty bottle of wine. His woman was as smart as she was beautiful.

"And you are mine, La'Rue. I will not be letting you go again," he vowed, sitting back in his seat.

CHAPTER FOURTEEN

Turbinta: Ruins of Tribute

Zoak pushed aside the drunkenly hanging door to the bar. The interior of the bar lay in ruins like the rest of the city. His eyes quickly adjusted to the dim lighting. He climbed over a thick ceiling beam, and looked around the devastation.

Rain fell through large gaping holes in the ceiling. Shattered tables and chairs mixed with those that had miraculously survived undamaged. He wormed his way through the maze of debris, searching for Tallei.

He found her body near one corner. Pushing aside the table that had partially collapsed on her, he saw the evidence he'd been seeking – she had not died in the destruction of the city, but by a shot from a blaster. The death of his master did not free him from his assignment; he simply had an additional objective: hunt down and kill whoever had killed his master. Whichever student accomplished that, would then become the Master to Tallei's protégés and have the right to collect and train more students.

Zoak knew the Legion had been searching for the alien pod. It was possible that Tallei had been killed by the Legion General, but Zoak doubted that was the case. His gaze turned back to Tallei. She was tangled in an unfamiliar cloak. He knelt, and touched the material. It was thick, but soft. The material was made from a Torrian plant fiber.

His eyes narrowed when he noticed a basket under a chair. He stood and stepped over Tallei's body. Grasping the leg of the chair, he tossed the broken piece of furniture over his right shoulder.

He lifted the basket, which pulled another long section of material with it that was caught on some of the straw. He was about to discard the material when he noticed the splotches of blood staining it. With a strong tug, he pulled the rest of the material free from where it had been stuck under some fallen debris.

Lifting the fabric to the two slits that comprised his nose, he drew in a deep breath. The remembered scent of Kella's blood filled his nostrils. His eyes glittered with outrage. If Kella had killed Tallei, that meant Kella would be his new Master, which was unacceptable to him.

He growled as he sniffed the material again.

There was a second fainter scent clinging to the fabric. He shook the fabric out, noticing that it was a woman's skirt. He lifted a section of the waistline to his nose this time. This part of the skirt would have made the most direct contact with the person wearing it. Memorizing the new scent, he lowered the skirt and carefully studied it.

There was something familiar about it. He looked at the basket – and beyond it to a chair that sat undisturbed in the corner. Dropping the skirt, he reached between the debris and pulled a gray shawl from the chair. This one had a large amount of blood staining it. He held it to his nose. The scent of Kella's blood was strong on the coarse material.

The mental image of the old woman he had bumped into on the sidewalk suddenly hit him. The old woman had worn this shawl draped over her bowed head. In her hand she had carried a long branch, still covered with mud. Her hand....

"Fingers... Pale fingers... Young, thick fingers with light hair on *his* knuckles," Zoak murmured, his own fingers tightening around the shawl.

Turning, he looked back down at the cloak covering Tallei. He bent over and pulled up a section to his nose. A third scent washed through his senses. Three – there had been three assassins here. To find the unknown two, he would first need to locate Kella.

He released the material and straightened. His mind began to plot how he would complete his mission of locating the missing person from the pod. Before Zoak had killed the Legion Commander, the man had told him that Tallei had the pod they had been searching for but not the contents. The destruction of the city had begun before he had returned, preventing him from reaching Tallei in time – though he suspected she had died before the city's destruction now that he knew Kella was involved.

A cruel smile curved Zoak's thin lips. "I will find you, assassin, and I will find the ones you protect," he said, bending to pick up one last memento – Tallei's laser whip.

Zoak turned and retraced his steps out of the building. He mounted his hover glide and pushed it to its limits. He would need a plan to track Kella before he returned to the secluded area several hundred clicks from the city where his spaceship was docked. Fortunately, with the right persuasion, people talked in his experience.

~

Rebel Base - Ice Moon of Tesla Terra:

"Let me go," La'Rue growled, jerking her arm away from her guard's grasp. "I know how to walk."

La'Rue's scowl turned to an expression of awe when she saw the huge man walking toward them. His dark red skin and piercing eyes swept over her. Fortunately, the expression glinting in his eyes was more curious than hostile.

La'Rue drew to a stop, once again shrugging off the guard's hand. She pushed back a strand of hair that had been tickling her cheek. She didn't miss the raised eyebrow the huge man directed at the thick metal cuffs that restrained her wrists.

"General Gomerant, there was only the woman and a small service bot onboard the freighter. Teams continue to search for any hidden compartments and tracking devices," the guard said.

A shiver ran through La'Rue when the General turned his dark brown eyes on her. There was a sense of power exuding from him that made La'Rue now second guess her decision just to fly into the hidden military base. Of course, she hadn't realized there was a base here. Her first thought had been that the ship Sergi was on had crashed on the frozen moon, and he needed help.

Honestly, if it hadn't been for HL-9, La'Rue wouldn't have made it either. She needed to remember to give the little service bot an extra oil dip for his amazing navigation through the ice cliffs. *If I get a chance,* she thought. She had been shocked when from out of the blinding storm, two fighters had suddenly appeared and flanked her.

"Do you have any?" General Hutu Gomerant asked.

La'Rue blinked, she had forgotten what the question was. "Any what?"

"Hidden compartments or tracking devices," General Gomerant inquired.

La'Rue nodded. "There are two false walls where I store valuables when I'm making a run. One is in the engine room and the other in the galley," she replied.

"And the tracking device?" General Gomerant asked, his tone deeper and filled with a thread of warning.

"Only the one she put on me," a familiar voice announced while walking toward them across the hangar.

La'Rue's eyes widened and her lips parted in relief. "Sergi!" she breathed, ignoring the other three men and starting forward. She turned to growl at the guard when he grabbed her arm again.

"I will see to her. Check the compartments she mentioned and run another scan over her ship," General Gomerant ordered, stepping to one side.

"Yes, General Gomerant," the guard said with a nod to his comrade.

"Wait, bracelets?" La'Rue asked, twisting just enough to lift her wrists up without breaking contact with Sergi's eyes.

The guard waited for the huge Torrian's nod before he pressed a series of buttons and pulled the cuffs from her wrists. La'Rue dropped her hands and pushed past the General. She looked up when Sergi stopped in front of her, her lips parted on a teasing retort. The words never formed as they were smothered by his powerful kiss.

Any concern that he would be upset that she had tracked him down melted along with her body against his when he drew her into his arms. Her hands slid over his shoulders and up around his neck.

The sound of a throat clearing finally reminded them of the fact that they were standing in the middle of a hidden hangar and that they were not alone. La'Rue looked up at Sergi with a bemused smile. He smiled back at her before turning his attention back to General Gomerant.

"This is La'Rue Gant," Sergi introduced. "La'Rue, General Hutu Gomerant."

"Welcome to the rebellion, Captain Gant," Hutu greeted with a warm smile.

"General," La'Rue politely replied, turning in Sergi's arms to look around her in amazement. "What is this place?" she asked, staring around her.

"Hope," Hutu responded.

～

Sergi walked next to La'Rue through the tunnels of the moon base. He had notified Josh and Hutu several days before of La'Rue's imminent arrival and warned them that she was not to be harmed. Hutu had not been happy when he'd been informed that she had placed a tracking device on Sergi. Nor was the Torrian General pleased that Sergi had not destroyed the device after he first discovered it.

In the end, Hutu had acquiesced, mostly due to Josh and Ash

vouching that Sergi would never do anything that would endanger the base or the rebellion, though Hutu had insisted that La'Rue's approach was to be carefully monitored to ensure that no one else was following her. Sergi had remained in the control center as she approached the moon. He knew the base's defense system would automatically activate and fighters would be deployed. What he wanted to ensure was that they did not open fire on the *Star Runner.*

As soon as the freighter had landed, Sergi had made his way down to the landing bay. He had wondered as he crossed the large open hangar filled with rebel fighters if his physical reaction to La'Rue a week before would be any different now. He'd had a lot of time to think about his attraction to her over the last few days. What really shook him was the fact that he couldn't stop thinking about her.

"You found your friend?" she asked as they walked down the excavated corridor.

"Yes. I found Ash, as well as Josh," he replied, wrapping an arm around her waist as they stood to the side to allow several motorized carts filled with supplies pass them.

"They were both there on Turbinta?" she asked with surprise.

Sergi shook his head. "No, Ash and Kella, a Turbintan, had traveled to the planet searching for the pods," he explained.

La'Rue turned to look at him in horror. "A Turbintan? As in a merchant or as in an assassin?" she quietly exclaimed, looking around them.

Sergi chuckled. "I think Kella would definitely qualify as an assassin. She killed the woman you warned me about," he said, turning her around and guiding her down the corridor again once it was clear.

"Tallei? She killed a Master Turbintan?" La'Rue breathed in disbelief. "Sergi, this woman is very dangerous. I've heard stories about the Turbintans. When a student kills their master, they then assume the master's title and position. The other students can either accept or assassinate the new master in order to assume the position of master themselves. Just the thought of always having to look over my shoulder would drive me insane."

Sergi turned the corner and paused outside of a set of lifts. They entered one when the doors opened. He didn't say anything until he knew they were alone. Ash and Kella had been dealing with that same Turbintan reality and subsequent unease since their arrival.

He ran his hands up La'Rue's arms and looked down at her. "Ash and Kella love each other, La'Rue. Tallei murdered Kella's family, stealing her away and forcing her to be trained as a Turbintan assassin. She has already risked her life for the rebellion and fought beside Ash. I'm asking that you keep an open mind when you meet her. She has been through enough without people judging her without knowing who she really is," he shared.

He could see the conflict in her fade. A rueful smile curved her lips and she nodded. Her next words took him by surprise.

"Just like you, Sergi," she said, leaning up to brush a kiss on his lips. "We all have a story."

The lift stopped and opened before Sergi had a chance to ask La'Rue what she meant. He held her hand as they stepped onto the level reserved for living quarters. His jaw tightened and he paused. La'Rue's assigned dorm was to the right and his quarters to the left.

"What is it?" she asked when he didn't proceed in either direction.

"You've been assigned shared quarters," he said, looking down at her.

"Oh." She bit her lip and looked down the passage before she turned to look back at him. "What about you? Are you sharing quarters with anyone?"

A soft, inviting smile curved his lips. "One of the benefits of being considered an Ancient Knight of the Gallant Order is having my own living quarters," he admitted.

She tilted her head to the side and ran her tongue along her lips. "Would you be opposed to some company?" she murmured, stepping closer to him.

Sergi could feel his groin tighten. Oh, yes…. He had been alone far too long. He knew his eyes must have conveyed his desire because La'Rue released a soft hiss.

"I only have one bed," he commented with a slight challenge in his voice.

"That's all we'll need," La'Rue replied, boldly running her hand down his stomach.

"Remind me to thank Hutu for leaving us alone," Sergi stated, turning and grabbing her hand. "My quarters are this way. I'll inform Josh and Ash we will be fashionably late.

CHAPTER FIFTEEN

Plateau: World of Floating Islands

*G*eneral Roan Landais carefully guided his spaceship through the treacherous outer rings of Plateau. It was an isolated planet in the outermost regions of the known galaxy. This very isolation and distance had protected the planet and its inhabitants from the notice and reaches of the Legion – for the most part. If his father and uncle were to know what he suspected, nothing would save this world from the same devastation that Jeslean had suffered.

His ship broke through the upper atmosphere and glided down through a pristine blue sky. His breath caught at the magnificent sight of the floating islands which hung above the vast blue-green ocean below. Plateau was known to the very few who had visited it as The Floating World. The residents lived on the floating rock structures that were inter-connected by thousands of hanging bridges. The islands were made of a porous lava rock that absorbed the lighter than air gases released from the ocean below.

He carefully navigated the sleek long-range fighter to an island floating a greater distance away from the others. Only a single bridge connected it to the nearest island. Carved into the massive center peak was a large cathedral.

He flew over, carefully searching the island before he circled around and then landed on the nearest island tethered to it. Shutting down the craft's systems, he unstrapped and stood. Within minutes, he was stepping off the narrow landing platform and onto the fine gravel surface.

He could sense the eyes of the residents following him as he strode toward the wide hanging bridge leading to the island of the cathedral. The difference between the eyes watching him here and the eyes that watched him elsewhere was that they would not be filled with fear, hatred, or suspicion – these people accepted his presence and were merely curious.

Roan crossed the bridge and walked up the path to the steps leading into the elaborately carved structure. Workers paused and bowed their heads to him in greeting. Roan stiffly returned the greetings. He paused at the bottom of the steps and looked up. There were new statues on display since the last time he had been here. His eyes rested on one statue in particular – the likeness of Jemar de Rola stood tall and proud with his hand resting on his young son's shoulder. The message was clear. This was a tribute to the fallen Knight of the Gallant as well as the future knight lost too soon.

His mouth tightened and he pushed away his regret. There was nothing he could do to bring back the old knight and his son. He could only focus on the future.

He climbed the steps and entered the surprisingly bright interior. Anyone looking at the cathedral from the outside would think it would be dark and dreary on the inside. Instead, strategically placed mirrors reflected the abundant sunshine coming through the narrow windows and shining off of the polished black walls.

He walked along the wide nave centered between the towering arched columns. At the far end was a beautifully carved spiral staircase that led to the upper levels and terraces. He would find the person he needed to speak with at the top.

Twenty minutes later, he emerged at the top of the stairs. Through

a set of large carved double doors, depicting the history of the formation of the stars, he spied the tall elegant woman he was seeking. He
entered the room, bowing his head in respect to the women standing
guard on each side of the open doors. His footsteps slowed to a stop
when he was within a few feet of the woman silently looking out at
the vast ocean below.

"Grandmother," he politely greeted.

"Roan," Roanna murmured, turning to smile at him. "It has been
too long since you last visited."

"Yes," Roan replied, not elaborating on his reasons. "How is
Grandfather?"

"Calstar is tending his plants and talking to the wind. He would
enjoy it if you would ask him yourself," Roanna replied with a tender
smile.

"I don't have much time," he confessed.

Roanna's smile faded and grew sad. She turned away from him to
stare back out at the ocean. Guilt ate at him. He walked over to stand
next to her.

"I'm looking for something that came from a distant world," he
quietly murmured.

"Why do you seek it, Roan?" Roanna quietly asked.

"The capsule is here, isn't it? Who was inside it?" he asked in a
voice harsher than he meant for it to be.

Roanna lifted her chin. "Yes, it is here. We will not give you what
you seek, though," she stated.

"Grandmother, it is dangerous to have the pod and the person it
contained here. If my father or Lord Andronikos learn that you have
had either one here, they will destroy this world," Roan warned.

"You would have us give you the life of another to save our own?
This is not our way, Roan. It was not the way of your mother, either,"
Roanna quietly replied.

A muscle ticked in Roan's jaw. He was well aware that it was not
the way of his mother. Her refusal to accept the overweening ambitions of his father and uncle had been a contributing factor to her
death. In the end, it had been her refusal to allow Coleridge Landais

and Andri Andronikos to corrupt her son with their own ambitions that had forfeited her life.

"One life for many thousands, Grandmother. Where is the pod and the contents?" Roan demanded.

Roanna tilted her head and considered him a moment. "Find your grandfather and you'll find what you seek," she finally instructed.

"Thank you," he said in a gentler tone, pausing and bowing his head before he turned on his heel and left.

Roan had a pretty good idea of where his grandfather would be. He descended the steps and retraced his path back to his ship. Soon, he was flying away from the larger islands and out toward the open ocean where several smaller untethered islands dotted the horizon.

He searched over almost a dozen of the islands before he discovered what he was seeking – an island with a small hut and a large garden. The smaller islands tended to float further above the ocean, drifting along on an invisible current of air. He landed once more on a narrow, flattened section of ground. In minutes, he was walking up a different path.

Roan saw the old man kneeling in the garden at the foot of a woman's statue. His eyes moved from his grandfather to the young woman kneeling beside him. The woman rose first, looking at him with curious eyes before she turned and bent to help his grandfather stand up.

He had found it. What his father and uncle were willing to kill thousands of innocent lives for– one of the Ancient Knights of the Gallant – and she looked nothing like he'd expected. He slowly walked forward, then paused a few feet away, his gaze locked onto the woman's delicate features. His eyes followed the movement of her hand when she lifted it to brush away a strand of hair that blew across her cheek in the gentle wind.

"Roan, you have come. I knew you would," his grandfather said in a trembling voice.

Sergi rolled to his side when the comlink buzzed for the second time. His fingers fumbled for the device on the table next to the bed. He looked at the image that flashed across the screen and groaned.

"Who is it?" La'Rue asked, rolling to face him.

"Josh this time," he replied, stroking his hand down her bare back. "I have to go."

"I'll go part-way with you. I need to check on my freighter and H. That little bot can get rather wacky if he is left to his own devices too long," she said with a sigh. "Or, I can just stay here and keep the bed warm."

Sergi chuckled. "I like that idea better," he admitted.

He released a soft curse when the comlink he had been given chimed again. Picking it up, he pressed the connection link.

"I received the first message," he growled.

"Hey, don't blame the messenger, but I thought I should warn you that Hutu is about ready to send a security team to your living quarters to make sure that La'Rue didn't kill you in your sleep," Ash informed him in an amused voice.

"Tell the large red bastard that if anyone comes in my rooms uninvited, I will be the one doing the killing," Sergi shot back.

"Ouch! Didn't you get any... well, you know... any?" Ash asked.

"I have a lot of time to make up for," Sergi retorted.

"Really? I thought that you and Mei...," Ash started to say before Sergi's snort cut him off.

"Mei and I did not have that type of relationship, Ash. I will be there in ten minutes," he replied, severing the link.

"Mei? Isn't she the one you almost died trying to find?" La'Rue asked, sitting up and pulling the blanket with her.

"Yes. You have no need to worry. I thought of her more as a younger sister," Sergi replied, sliding his legs over the side of the bed and standing up.

He looked over his shoulder when he felt La'Rue run her hand over his bare buttock. She had that damn pleased expression on her face that made him crazy with desire. His reached out and traced the pattern of spots that ran down from her forehead to just above her waist.

"You are beautiful, *dusha moya*," he murmured.

La'Rue twisted until she was kneeling on the bed. She placed her hands on his bare shoulders and stood up. He raised an eyebrow at her when the covers pooled around her ankles.

"You aren't so bad yourself – for an Ancient Knight," she teased, brushing a kiss across his lips. "We'd better get dressed before Hutu's security team gets here. I don't relish being back in wrist cuffs while being paraded nude through a military base."

Sergi wrapped his hands around her waist and drew her against his hard body, the evidence that he was still aroused pressing against her stomach. He gave her a devilish smile.

"I can think of some very interesting things to do with you naked and bound," he murmured, bending to run his lips along her neck.

"I'll have to ask Hutu if I can borrow a set," La'Rue quipped, slipping around him and heading to the bathroom. "Oh, can you see if they have a cooker here for me to use? I still can't figure out how to use that old cooktop, and eating cold rations sucks."

Sergi chuckled. His gaze affectionately ran over La'Rue as she disappeared into the bathroom. Only when the door had closed behind her did he finally focus on getting dressed.

He pulled his mind away from the woman humming in the other room to the matter at hand – finding Julia and Mei. During the past week, he had learned a lot about what was going on. Everything Ash had touched on during their journey here had been expanded upon until the full story – or at least as much as was known – had been shared.

In a nutshell, they had activated a gateway left behind by an advanced species of alien travelers. Their resulting appearance had been serendipitous for the rebellion in an escalating civil war between the Legion and the Order of the Gallant. The Order had originally consisted of men and women trained by this advanced species to protect those who needed protection. The Legion, fearing that their arrival would spur hope and advance the cause of the rebels, had placed a huge bounty on their heads, anticipating that their deaths or capture would debilitate the rebels' ability to win the war. When the rebels had been inspired to fight to protect the Gliese 581 crew members instead of turning them over, the Legion had destroyed the home world of the Order of the Gallant on Jeslean. Lord Andronikos and his half-brother, General Coleridge Landais – aka Count Landais, said in Ash's best Bela Lugosi imitation – wanted to get their hands on at least one of the members of the Gliese 581 crew. They could then use the crew member's execution to demonstrate that they really weren't these superhero aliens. And the Legion then assumed it could more easily cow the disillusioned people and crush the rebellion.

All-in-all, the entire thing reminded him of the struggles he had faced back on Earth. He hadn't had much choice of who he worked for there, but he sure as hell had a choice here. This time, he fought because he wanted to; not because he had been ordered to do so.

Sergi finished dressing just as the door to the bathroom opened and a fully dressed La'Rue stepped out. Her face was still flushed from their lovemaking and she was sporting a few marks on her neck that weren't there naturally. This was something else he had chosen – falling in love.

He drew in a deep breath at the thought. He wasn't sure if their relationship was the beginnings of love, but he wanted to find out. Wrapping an arm around her when she started to walk by him, he pulled her back against his body and pressed a heated kiss to her neck.

"Keep your comlink on you. If you need anything, let me know. I'll find you a new cooker and have it delivered to the freighter," he said in a slightly gruff voice.

La'Rue turned her head and pressed a kiss to his lips. "You'd better or I'll haunt you after I starve to death," she replied, stepping away from him when he released her. She turned to look at him with a serious expression. "Sergi...."

Sergi lifted his hand and touched his fingers to her lips. "One day at a time. I want to see where this takes us," he said.

"I do too," she admitted.

He squeezed her hand before moving around her. The door

opened and they stepped out. They walked together down to the lift. He would escort her as far as the landing bay before he headed for the conference room.

"I'm glad you found your friends," she said, lifting a hand to tuck a wayward strand of hair behind her ear.

"It was good to know they made it. Josh saved my life," he said.

"I'm glad he did. I thought I saw him with a woman from Tesla Terra," she said, running her hand down along the marks on her throat. "It was nice to see there are quite a few rebels from my home world willing to fight."

Sergi nodded. "Cassa, and her brother Packu, have paid a heavy price. The Legion is responsible for the deaths of their parents and younger brother, as well as the destruction of their vineyard and home on Tesla Terra. It was the price of protecting Josh," he explained.

"I never realized the extent of the war against the Legion," La'Rue said, walking quietly beside him.

Sergi threaded his fingers through hers and squeezed her hand. "The Legion Director has a lot to answer for. He has killed a lot of innocent people. That does not sit well with Josh, Ash, or me. Josh was correct when he said the Legion brought the fight to us, not the other way around. Humans tend to take things personally – especially when some asshole thinks he can rule the world... or galaxy," he said

"My parents were originally from Tesla Terra. My mother was a member of the Knights of the Gallant. Both of my parents were killed in a shuttle accident shortly after Lord Andronikos came to power. Slate's parents were killed as well. After that, it was just the two of us trying to survive on Jeslean," she shared in a quiet voice.

CHAPTER SIXTEEN

*S*ergi stepped into the conference room and glanced around. He noted that he wasn't the only one running late. Ash and Kella came into the room a minute after he did, followed closely by Josh and Cassa. He was surprised when he didn't see Hutu.

"Where's Hutu?" Ash inquired, sliding into the chair next to him.

"There were reports of attacks by the Legion on three additional planets. He is assigning more resources," Josh said, pulling out a seat for Cassa before he sat down in his own chair.

"What about Tesla Terra? Have you heard if Andronikos is going to send more troops there?" Kella asked.

"My friend, Bantu, is monitoring the Legion's transmissions. His knowledge of the Legion's communications and programming has been extremely helpful in anticipating Legion movements. So far, we've been able to warn our bases, and they have taken the appropriate measures to minimize damage," Cassa explained.

"What have you found out about Mei and Julia?" Sergi asked.

"General Kubo, Hutu's father, is on Torrian," Josh said. "He has his men searching for information about the freighter that was on the video. There are records indicating that several shuttles of materials were off loaded to the spaceport, but there was nothing out of the ordinary registered, and so far, all the merchants say they never saw an unusual woman. That doesn't mean that Mei couldn't have snuck down on a shuttle and disguised herself as Ash did."

"What if she didn't transfer down to the planet, but stayed hidden on the ship?" Sergi said, trying to think like Mei.

"That is why we are searching for additional records. We have the ship's ID. We just need to identify where it may have stopped en route. With dozens of planets and thousands of spaceports, that may take us a while," Cassa replied with a sigh.

"What about Julia's pod? Have we heard anything about it?" Sergi asked.

Hutu and Bantu stepped into the room just as Sergi asked his question. Sergi could tell from the tense lines around the men's mouths that the news they had received hadn't been good. The room grew quiet as everyone waited for Hutu to speak.

"Nobo Sands on Torrian has been destroyed. Thanks to Bantu, we were able to evacuate most of the civilians, but we lost four squadrons of fighters during the battle. The civilians have been moved underground into the Nobo Caverns and amongst the Canyon Dwellers. General Kubo has also sealed the gates to the ancient city," Hutu explained. "This attack was in retaliation for the earlier deaths of several Legion soldiers. A video was left on the body of one of those Legion soldiers for us to find."

"Is there anything we can do, Hutu?" Cassa asked in concern.

"General Jubotu, with whom you have met, has begun a counter-offensive. I've also requested additional fighter support be sent to Torrian. The Torrians will not fall. There are thousands of miles of underground tunnels, and the sand covering most of the planet absorbs the powerful bombs being deployed. It is primarily the structures above ground that have been destroyed, including the landing sites. I've asked Bantu to give an update on the last known signal we were tracking," Hutu reassured them, nodding to Bantu.

"Good afternoon," Bantu began. "I've written a program based on the information Josh and Ash gave me regarding their pods and the debris field that the Legion had been collecting, and we are now able to track Josh, Ash, and Sergi's pods. The other two pods posed a problem, however. From what you've shared and what the limited available footage shows, it seems Mei's pod was picked up by a Cryon salvage ship. The Cryon have a large fleet of ships which travel throughout the star system, primarily picking up and recycling space debris. It is no surprise that the *Cryon II* is part of Dorane LeGaugh's fleet. He is one of the wealthiest and most elusive men in the star system. He has powerful friends and doesn't always play nice, but the biggest advantage we have is that he doesn't like the Legion and they don't want to mess with his private army – which is made up of mostly Turbintan assassins and other cutthroats. He has his own private moon, by the way, with a strictly enforced invitation-only policy for visitors. As for the last pod, belonging to...." Bantu paused to look at the screen he was holding.

"Julia Marksdale," Sergi supplied.

Bantu nodded his thanks. "I was able to collect enough data and piece it together to estimate a rough projection of her pod's path, which at least gave us the most likely trajectory of her pod. However, it is proving more difficult to pinpoint the landing site. The transponder stopped emitting a signal nearly two weeks ago, and even then, there is no way to verify that the last intercepted signal came from her pod – or if it even was her signal. If the pod did locate the nearest habitable planet as it was programmed to do, then there is only one probable planet it could have gone to – Plateau. There isn't a lot of information about the planet except that no one ever goes there. The planet is purported to be covered in water with large numbers of islands floating in the air above their oceans. If Julia's capsule did make it that far, the likelihood of her surviving is, unfortunately, very slim. First, the question is if she would have had enough oxygen. The distance from the wreckage to the planet is almost three times as far as any of the other emergency capsules traveled. Second, if she did make it that far and she was still alive, then the pod would have had to land on a floating island. If it missed, it would fall into the ocean and sink hundreds, if not thousands of feet below the surface. This might account for the loss of signal," Bantu explained, bringing up a map to display the details he was outlining.

"I think she might have made it," La'Rue said from the doorway. Her eyes sought out Sergi's. "I was scanning some of the different channels and overheard a member of a freighter crew, who I know, talking about seeing an unmarked Legion long-range fighter heading for the Void. That's our name for the area of empty space between Plateau and us. I just thought you might want to know. Oh, and another friend said they overheard that General Landais is planning on going there – the old one, not the young one. No one knows where Roan Landais is at the moment. He supposedly disappeared after meeting with Andronikos and the older General Landais."

She paused and gave everyone a wry grin. "Freighter captains and crews gossip a lot. There really isn't much else to do on the long hauls."

～

An hour before:

La'Rue warmed up some soup, inhaling the delicious aroma. She'd been shocked when a technician had met her at the platform for her freighter with a brand-new cooker. In minutes, the technician had it installed in her galley for her. Starving and unable to resist trying it out, she had pulled out one of her favorite soups and placed the package in the unit. Now, her stomach and her heart were filled with warmth, thanks to Sergi.

Carrying the soup to the bridge, she slid into the captain's chair and propped her feet up on the chair across from her. She spooned a mouthful and swallowed before she looked up at where H was hanging down from the ceiling. She grinned when the little service bot flipped and landed next to her feet.

"How about we check out what some of the other captains are up to?" she mumbled around a noodle.

No sooner had the words come out of her mouth than her communications screen lit up. A groan escaped her when she saw it was Slate. He'd probably gotten himself into more trouble and was trying to drag her down into it with him.

"Hit the scrambler. I do NOT want him knowing where I am," she informed the little robot.

A moment later, Slate's face was displayed on the screen in front of her. She frowned at him. He looked gaunt and tired.

"What have you done now?" she demanded, sliding her feet off the chair and twisting around to face him.

"I... nothing, Rue. I was just wondering how you were doing," he replied.

La'Rue shook her head. "For some reason I'm not buying that. You look like crap and the last two times you've contacted me, it was because you borrowed credits against *my* freighter," she heatedly reminded him.

"Yeah, well, about the credits. You don't have to worry about helping me with those anymore," Slate said.

La'Rue placed her barely touched soup to the side and sat forward. Something was definitely wrong. She'd known Slate her entire life and he had never been this nonchalant – nor told her she didn't have to worry anymore about anything.

"What's really going on, Slate? What did you do now? You can tell me," she insisted.

Slate gave her a sad smile. "Nothing's wrong, Rue. I was able to make some great runs and the missing cargo turned up. You were right. It was wrong for me to use you that way or ask you to do things I know you don't like doing," he admitted.

La'Rue could feel her head shaking. "You are scaring me, Slate. Where is the jerk I know? You know, the one who will hustle anyone and who loves the good life?" she demanded.

"He's still here," Slate reassured her. "Have you heard the news? The Legion flattened Tribute. I bet that is going to upset a few of those assassins. It isn't often that they get a little taste of their own medicine."

La'Rue grimaced. "Yeah, I heard about that," she replied. "Anything else?"

"Not really. People are still saying the Ancient Knights of the Gallant have returned, but no one has really seen them. Nobo Sands got hit as well and it is making the other captains nervous. That was one of the biggest markets for us," Slate shared.

"It sounds like things are going to get much worse before they get better," La'Rue agreed, sitting back in her seat and picking up her soup again. "So, what kind of runs have you been doing that paid so well?"

Slate shrugged and looked away, not meeting her eyes. "I was able to get some high paying jobs due to all the unrest. Listen, I've got to go. I... I just wanted you to know I've always loved you, Rue, and that I'm sorry for being a bastard at times," he said with a strained smile.

"Are you sure you are okay, Slate? I hate to say this, but you really don't look so good. Maybe you should see a healer," she said, her eyes dark with concern.

"I'm good, Rue. I've been working a lot to get out of the hole. Be safe. Life... It can sometimes throw you a black hole when you weren't expecting it," he warned.

"I'll be safe," she said, frowning when the transmission ended. Sitting back in her seat, she propped up her feet again and shook her head. "I swear that man is getting stranger the older he gets," she muttered. "How about doing a channel search and we'll see what everyone else is up to?"

Twenty minutes later, she was hurrying to find Sergi. If there was one thing she knew, it was that freighter captains were very observant of what was going on around them. If they saw Legion ships heading for the black void, then there was something there worth looking at.

∾

Legion Battle Cruiser:

"Coleridge, what have you found?" Andri demanded.

Coleridge studied his half-brother's stiff expression. He had been following what his brother had been doing – and trying to keep his own temper under control. Andri was good with the politics of controlling vast groups of people and their worlds. He was not good at the required military aspect of it. Coleridge had taken the blame more than once during the early years for Andri's less than effectual impulsiveness.

"I have one of the pods," he stated.

"And the contents?" Andri asked.

Coleridge could suddenly feel the vein in his temple pulse with tension. "The pod was empty. I have a lead that I am following," he stated, not bothering to mention the fact that Tallei had been found inside the pod.

"I was not yet ready to order the attack on the Turbintans. Their services might still be needed," Andri stated with irritation.

"One Turbintan has already joined the rebellion. Would you risk having them all join?" Coleridge snapped.

"Tallei...," Andri began.

Coleridge waved his hand, cutting off his half-brother mid-sentence. "Tallei is dead, killed by her Turbintan student and two of the Ancient Knights. Once word escaped, more would have followed her lead. I did what was necessary, Andri. Your attacks on Jeslean, Tesla Terra, and Nobo Sands did little to strike true fear into the heart of the rebellion. When you kill those who are feared more than any others, that is when you put fear in their hearts. If the Turbintans can fall to the Legion, then there can be no hope for anyone else to triumph against us," he stated in a blunt tone.

Andri's mouth turned down and his eyes flashed. Coleridge released a sigh. Angering his half-brother would only increase the chances of his drink being the next one to be poisoned. Another factor Andri appeared to have forgotten is that the more resources they destroyed the fewer they would have access to for own their military needs.

"I have a promising lead on the location of another pod and one of the Ancient Knights. Once we have one in our hands and can prove that the legend is a myth, then we will have won, brother," Coleridge shared.

"You'd better be right, Coleridge," Andri snapped. "I have worked too long to fail now."

"You will not fail, Andri. The Ancient Knights are a myth. Once that is exposed, the rebellion and the last of the Knights of the Gallant will become just another myth as well," Coleridge assured his half-brother before he ended the communications.

Sitting back in his seat aboard the Battle Cruiser, he thought about his destination. He'd had one brief marriage to a young and very beautiful woman who he met during a diplomatic visit to the Jeslean capitol. Their courtship had been swift. It was not until after their marriage and the imminent birth of Roan that Nia decided that she would like to return to her home world to give birth and visit her family.

At the time, Andri was just beginning his rise to power within the Order of the Gallant Council. Coleridge would be the first to admit that he had been jealous and possessive of Nia. He had not questioned her visits home at first, but her stays grew longer as Andri and he began to put their ambitious plans into action.

After the birth of Roan and the first of the mysterious deaths of the Knights of the Gallant Order and their families began, Nia went home with Roan and informed Coleridge that she would not be returning. In a fit of rage, he had followed her to Plateau. He had taken Roan from her and returned to Jeslean. Nia in turn had followed him, refusing to allow their son to be raised in what she called a cruel and heartless environment devoted to nothing but power and greed.

She had picked up Roan and attempted to leave with the small boy. He had forcibly removed Roan from his mother's arms. During the struggle, he had violently pushed Nia and she had fallen down a flight of stairs, breaking her neck. He had sent her body home to Plateau, but not their son. Now, he would not be surprised to discover that Roan was much more like his mother than himself after all. If that turned out to be the case, then his son, too, would join his mother in a violent death.

CHAPTER SEVENTEEN

*B*antu brought up a star chart of the two places they suspected Mei and Julia could be located, and La'Rue listened as they discussed different options to reach the two locations without being discovered, frowning as she mentally worked through the best possible ways to reach each destination without getting caught by the Legion.

"We both have freighters, Kella and I. Why don't we use them both?" La'Rue asked.

"Tell us what you are thinking, La'Rue," Sergi encouraged.

La'Rue pushed her chair back and stood up. Walking around the table, she quietly said, "Dorane LeGaugh has some of the tightest security in the galaxy and the deadliest private army, save for that of Andronikos, but freighter captains and their crews are a relatively close-knit group, and I know someone who can get you clearance to deliver to him, though I have to tell you, that is going to be the easiest part. We need someone who wouldn't be suspicious to LeGaugh's security, someone who knows how to get into places most of us couldn't, and looks like the kind of person LeGaugh would hire," she said, looking at Kella with a crooked grin.

Kella's lips twitched. "Someone like a trained Turbintan assassin," she agreed.

"Oh, hell no! There is no way I'm going to let Kella go alone if it is as dangerous as you say," Ash protested.

La'Rue's grin grew. "Of course not. You are her amusing co-pilot who has offered her your undying loyalty if she promises not to slit your throat," she said.

"Kella's comedic sidekick…. It's perfect. I like it," Josh said, looking at Ash with an amused smile.

Ash lifted his fist and acted like he was winding up his middle finger as he had once seen it done in a movie. Kella and La'Rue looked at the three men in confusion when Sergi snorted with laughter and the other two men chuckled.

Kella shrugged her shoulders. "Men… I find their sense of humor very strange at times," she replied with a glimmer of humor in her own eyes.

"So, you suggest that Ash and Kella search for Mei. What about Julia?" Sergi asked.

"I've been making runs out through the Void for a couple of years now. I took over for another captain who grew tired of making the run because it was too far out. The planet has a few natural defenses that help protect it besides the fact that there is nothing else out there. Unless you know how to get through the rings, and then where to find the floating islands, you'll either get crushed or sucked into the ocean. The inhabitants are very polite, but don't talk much to strangers. They already know me, though, so it won't be a problem," she said with a grin.

Sergi looked at Josh. "It makes sense. One of us needs to be on each mission, and the women have the skill sets and civilian transports needed to complete it," he acknowledged.

Josh looked at Hutu who had been quietly monitoring their discussion. "I agree with La'Rue's assessment, Hutu. What do you think?" he asked.

"I, also, agree. In addition, I think a little diversion might help," Hutu said, rubbing his chin.

"What kind of diversion?" Cassa asked.

Hutu looked around the room. "I think it is time to make a public introduction of one of the Ancient Knights of the Gallant Order," he replied.

"Draw the attention to me while the others go on their covert missions after Mei and Julia," Josh agreed with an emphatic nod of his head.

"And give hope to the peoples of our worlds," Hutu added.

"I'd love to be a fly on the wall in Andronikos' office when Josh gives him the middle finger salute," Ash chuckled.

"When do we leave?" Sergi asked.

"The sooner, the better," Josh said before he looked at La'Rue. "What do you need for your freighter?"

"Weapons," Sergi immediately replied.

La'Rue nodded and looked back at Josh. "Weapons," she agreed.

~

Zoak sat in the back of the bar in the underground city of Nobo Caverns and twirled the knife in his hand. The establishment was filled to capacity thanks to the Legion forces leveling most of Nobo Sands above ground. He had been searching for any information he could find on Kella and the dark-skinned knight who accompanied her.

He didn't touch the drink in front of him, instead he watched and listened to the patrons. Information flowed through establishments such as this. Most of the conversation was about the destruction of Tribute. There was much speculation that the Turbintans would attack the Legion, but Zoak knew that they wouldn't – not without there being a monetary reward to do so. That was the misconception that many other species held about the Turbintans. Others cared for their own world, their own people, and the items they collected. The Turbintans did not. They were defined by who and what they were, not by where they lived and owned.

There was one conversation that attracted his attention. A group of freighter pilots sitting at the large round table next to him mentioned a sleek fighter heading for the Void.

"It had to be a Legion ship. The only other person I know who has a ship like that is Dorane LeGaugh. It was heading for the Void as I was coming out," one of the freighter captains shared.

"I wonder if it has anything to do with those pods they are looking for. Word has it that the Legion has found two, but not the others," another man commented.

A third placed his empty glass on the table with a low bang and wiped a hand across his mouth. "The Legion may have found the pods, but they didn't find what they were transporting. One of the Ancient Knights is on Torrian. I saw him and a Turbintan, along with a bunch of Torrian Sand Warriors, wipe out a squadron of Legion soldiers. I've never seen fighting like that before," the man stated.

"How do you know he was one of the Ancients from the pods?" the first captain demanded.

"He carried the Staff of a Gallant Knight and he definitely knew how to use it," the third man replied, lifting his glass and waving to the waitress.

Zoak listened until the men began discussing issues they were having with some of their runs because of the Legion's activities. His mind focused back on what the first freighter captain had said – that a Legion ship had been seen traveling to the Void. Only a Legion officer with a lot of power would have access to the type of long-distance fighter the men were talking about. It was a viable lead. If these men suspected the Legion may have located another pod and the Knight inside, then Zoak had no doubt that the rebellion leaders would also know. They would need to send someone to retrieve the Knight – preferably someone who already knew them.

Like another Ancient with a Turbintan assassin to guide him, Zoak thought.

He was about to leave when the first hologram message appeared on a device across from him. Pulling out his communicator, he tuned it to the same frequency as the broadcast. In seconds, he was receiving the same message.

"...Commander Joshua Manson. I came to your star system from a planet far, far away. Many have come to consider me an Ancient Knight of the Gallant Order. I am a trained soldier. When Jemar de Rola opened his home to me, the Legion attacked – killing him, his young son, Jesup, and many of the workers at his vineyard on Tesla Terra. Andronikos attacked innocent men, women, and children, murdering them in cold blood when he ordered the destruction of Jeslean. He tried to do the same to Tesla Terra and in return the rebellion gave him a taste of what is to come – his defeat and that of the Legion. He ordered the destruction on Turbinta to demonstrate that he fears no one, but he does. He fears the Ancient Knights who have come to help stop the spread of his evil – he fears me. My message is to those who are willing to fight against tyranny. I did not ask for this war, it was brought to me. I came in peace, but I stand at the helm of the rebellion. I will not give in. I will not give up. I will not disappear. If the Legion wants a fight, I stand with the Knights of the Gallant and the New Order. I stand with the peoples of this star system."

Zoak calmly watched as the man lifted the staff belonging to the Knights of the Gallant, extending the staff, before twirling it in his hands and giving the ancient ceremonial salute. The video then replayed, and Zoak pressed record on his device as the video began again with "My name is Lieutenant Commander Joshua Manson..." When the speech finished, and the video replayed again, Zoak transmitted the saved file to his ship, then answered the call coming in to his device.

"Speak," he murmured.

"This is Lord Andronikos. You are an apprentice of Tallei's," Andri said.

"I was," Zoak replied.

"I have a job for you," Andri stated.

Zoak leaned back against the wall. "How much?" he demanded, lovingly caressing the handle of his knife.

Andri paused. "One million credits," he answered.

"I want the full amount up front. I will notify you of the information I need. If I do not receive it within one moon cycle, the contract is void," Zoak instructed.

"You will have the credits and the required information. I will send the job description through this link. You have one week to complete the assignment. Failure to do so will result in your execution," Andri replied.

"I do not fail," Zoak countered.

He scanned the information that appeared on his communication device with a sense of satisfaction. A smile curved his thin lips, revealing the tips of his sharp, pointed teeth. He would be able to complete the assignment that Tallei had given him before her death, kill Kella, secure his right to the line of the Master Turbintan, and become very wealthy at the same time.

The questions he'd planned on asking became unnecessary. He looked up at the larger image projected above the bar and studied the alien male speaking on the video screen. The man's broadcast was being replayed over and over.

Rising to his feet, Zoak tossed a credit coated with poison into his drink. He might not drink the liquor, but he also didn't give anything away for free. If an unsuspecting patron thought they might get a free drink off of him, they would pay a heavy price for their assumption.

He exited the bar and made his way along the upper caverns to where his ship was located. He would need additional supplies for the long journey. Residents everywhere were talking about the broadcast as he passed them.

The Knight had accomplished his objective – he had given hope to the people. He had also energized them. Zoak knew that was what had drawn Andronikos's attention. The Director of the Legion needed one or more of the Ancient Knights to use against the others and to crush the growing rebellion.

The communication device vibrated in his hand and he glanced down at it. His stride grew longer as he hurried through the crowded cavern passages. The money had been deposited with the final instructions.

Kill any who get in your way. Return with one Ancient Knight still alive, the message read.

Zoak abruptly closed his communication device and slid it into his pocket. He turned and made his way to one of the less populated sections where small groups guarded 'less accessible' items. His fingers rested on the blasters on each of his hips.

Several men warily watched him as he approached. A short creature with dark, beady eyes narrowed on him from within the dark pelt that covered his entire body waved his guards away. Zoak came to a halt in front of the merchant.

"I need supplies," he stated.

"Come in, come in. I am sure I have what you need," the merchant replied with a wave of his hand, guiding Zoak into the makeshift store.

CHAPTER EIGHTEEN

The soft sound of an alarm woke La'Rue from a fitful sleep. She opened her eyes and blinked in the dim light. Behind her, she could feel Sergi's warm body pressed against her back, buttocks, and legs as he molded his body to hers.

"Cease alarm," she murmured.

The annoying chime immediately stopped. She sighed in contentment when a pair of warm lips pressed against her shoulder. The past couple of weeks had made La'Rue aware of several things – mostly good things – like her feelings for Sergi, but also some bad – like the overwhelming feeling that she could lose him.

"You were restless. What is wrong?" Sergi murmured against her skin.

La'Rue wrapped her hand around his and brought it up between her bare breasts. She threaded her fingers through his and held his hand tightly. A soft groan escaped her when she felt him move. Rolling onto her back, she gazed up at him.

"What is wrong?" he requested again in a slightly more insistent soft voice.

Her eyes searched his face, memorizing every line, every feature.

She released his hand so that she could run her fingers along his chest and over his shoulders. She would never get tired of touching him.

"I'm afraid that something will happen to you," she confessed, looking up at him again with worried eyes. "If the Legion...."

Unable to go on, she closed her eyes. Sergi silenced her fears with a hard kiss to her pursed lips. Her arms wound around him and they held each other for several minutes before the sound of metal tapping on metal drew their attention. Opening her eyes, she turned her head and smiled.

"Hello, H. How is everything going?" she asked when a set of glowing red eyes moved up to peer over the side of the bed.

Sergi rolled to the side and sat up. "I don't think I'll ever get used to waking up to those beady eyes," he muttered, running his hands through his hair.

"You know you'd miss him if he didn't come in every day to make sure we were awake," La'Rue chuckled, feeling the overwhelming panic she had woken up with beginning to recede.

"Alarm clocks with moving legs are not normal," Sergi insisted.

She laughed again and sat up. Sliding her feet over the side of the bed, she released a soft gasp when Sergi wrapped his arm around her waist and leaned her back in his arms. Her gaze softened when she saw the concern in his eyes.

"Everything will be alright, *dusha moya,*" Sergi promised.

"Our world must seem so different from yours with the ongoing war," she murmured, her eyes darkening with regret.

Sergi bent and pressed another hard kiss to her lips before releasing her and sliding off the bed. She gripped his hand when he held it out. His eyes were serious as he gazed down at her.

"Not as different as you would think," he quipped in a light tone. "Come, let us get ready."

La'Rue nodded. Her mind was already on the dangers ahead of them. If the Legion was here, then that meant extreme danger for Sergi. She had wanted to land and approach the Guardian first to get a feel for the situation.

The people of Plateau were a peaceful society. They would never turn away someone in need. If one of Sergi's friends had landed here and was still alive, the Guardian would have offered them sanctuary.

Sergi had insisted that he go with her. La'Rue had rejected the idea. She knew it was due to an irrational fear caused by the nightmare she had right before she woke. The details of the nightmare had faded until she couldn't remember them, but the remnants of what she had felt in the dream remained and left her with a presentiment of grave danger.

Please, don't let the Legion be there, she fervently wished.

Outer rings of Plateau:
  Two hours later

In the large closet that he had set up as a workroom, Sergi packed the last of the weapons he would take with him. He'd spent his time over the past few weeks becoming more familiar with the vast array of alien weaponry that had been given to them before they left the frozen moon base in orbit around Tesla Terra.

His fingers ran over the unusual staff that he had found at the bottom of a box when he was looking for some parts to repair an electrical short. The staff reminded him of the ones that Josh, Ash, and Hutu carried. He'd meant to ask La'Rue about it. He started to set it down when he heard La'Rue's voice.

"Sergi, we are approaching the outer rings. You won't want to miss this," La'Rue said over the communication speaker.

He looked up and slid the staff into the deep pocket of the coat he was wearing. He paused in mid-turn. Turning back, he picked up a small, round disk from the bench. He thoughtfully twiddled the device between his fingers before he added it to his pocket as well.

Turning toward the door again, he exited the closet into the larger area of the storage bay. Striding down the corridor, he thought about their mission. If it was true that a Legion officer had journeyed to

Plateau, then there was a real possibility that Julia, if she was here and had survived, was a prisoner of the Legion. If that was the case, then the mission would change from search and recovery to search and extraction. Fortunately, he was well trained in both procedures.

He entered the cockpit of the *Star Runner* and slid into the seat beside La'Rue. Grasping the straps, he fastened his safety harness. A soft whistle of appreciation slipped from him when he caught his first sight of the planet.

"It looks as if the rings are rotating at different velocities," he observed.

"The rings are tidal-locked to each other and with the planet," La'Rue explained as the *Star Runner* neared the brilliant blue and white world that reminded Sergi a little of Earth.

"I never imagined anything like this before," Sergi admitted, gazing at the varied patterns of the rings.

"Plateau is a very unusual planet," La'Rue agreed.

Sergi nodded, fascinated as they moved through the dense clusters of rings. Each of the rings was composed of different materials and was multi-layered. The rings were varied in depth, width and distance between each other, much like the rings of Saturn were back home. He noticed that La'Rue merged into the different layers through the intermittent dark spaces that formed in between them.

He warily noticed a boulder the size of their freighter heading toward them. He sat back and gripped the armrest on the co-pilot's seat. Unable to stop himself, he lifted a hand toward the front screen as if to fend off the approaching boulder.

"La'Rue, ...*dusha moya,* there is a boulder coming at us. Perhaps a little evasive maneuvering would be conducive to our continued existence," he suggested through gritted teeth.

"Not yet," she replied with a grin.

Sergi's head was shaking in disagreement. "No, love, I think now would be a very, very good time," he muttered.

"I can't until the next space becomes available," she said.

"We do not have time," Sergi retorted in a choked voice.

He released Russian curses that grew louder and more elaborate the closer the boulder came toward them. His eyes widened when the impact alarm echoed in the cockpit of the freighter. He knew his knuckles had to be white as his fingers gripped the armrest. He fought the urge to close his eyes when the massive rotating boulder got closer and closer until everything else was blocked out of the view-screen.

"La'Rue!" Sergi hissed in alarm when the freighter reached the asteroid. "What the…?"

Sergi's voice faded as they continued on … and passed through it. The whole asteroid was composed of space dust whose particles were loosely attracted to each other to form a seemingly solid mass. The dust collected together again after they passed. He shot La'Rue a heated glare when she snorted with laughter.

"I wish you could have seen your face," she commented with an amused grin, still chortling a bit.

Sergi shook his head at her. "Remind me to whip your ass later," he said.

"Promises, promises," she laughingly teased even as her body heated at the idea. She flashed him an amused look. "You aren't going to have a meltdown like you did yesterday, are you?"

The 'meltdown' that La'Rue was referring to was caused by his numerous defeats on an alien first-person game called Battle Sands. The game pitted players against each other as they chose different teams of alien warriors and fought their way through a variety of scenarios on different worlds. Each character was based on a real species and had their traits and capabilities. If he'd had any doubt that the Turbintans and the Torrians were fierce opponents in battle, he only needed to watch them in action in the game.

La'Rue had suggested the game. She said it would give him a better understanding of the different planets, the species who inhabited the worlds, the strengths and weaknesses of each species and their capa-bilities and probable tactics during a fight. Plus, she added, it helped to break up the monotony of the long flight. He learned very quickly what moves to look out for, but the game proved he still had a lot to learn.

"I did not have a meltdown. The virtual Turbintan was dead and should not have been able to attack again, and the poison hurt like hell. Virtual games should not come with pain. I still think that the game cheated," he retorted with an exaggerated outraged expression reminiscent of a young child.

"The game doesn't cheat. The pain is to keep you motivated not to lose – at least that was what Slate and Crock always told me. You just need to learn all the aliens' battle strategies. The Gailock have the ability to regenerate damaged tissue," she explained, referring to the orange-and-black-striped lizard-like species in the game. "The only ways to kill a Gailock are to cut through the main artery in their upper left thigh, remove their head, or burn them to ash. The problem is their blood is poisonous, so the first two methods are dangerous for the attacker. If they splatter blood on you, it'll eat through your skin and enter your bloodstream. If you are lucky, you'll only absorb a little and feel sick. If you get enough blood on you – well, you're dead," she informed him with another flash of amusement.

"I still think the game was rigged. I didn't get as much blood on me as the first time and I still died," he retorted. His expression changed when he looked through the side window of the freighter and watched another of the boulders they had passed through reform. "This is just incredible." He shook his head.

She nodded. "In this layer you can pass through the boulders. In the second ring, the one closest to the planet, you can't. If you try to do so, you'll end up with a real boulder inside your freighter with you," she warned.

He nodded, focusing on the planet below. Wispy white clouds dotted an otherwise vivid blue world. There was no evidence of land yet. Darker swirls of blue mixed with lighter shades and highlighted the ocean's variations of depths.

"Where do all the people live?" Sergi asked. Then, as they emerged through the clouds, he got his first look at the islands floating above the ocean with their cloud halos. He said in a soft, stunned voice, "This is... magical. How is this possible?"

La'Rue shrugged. "Crock told me the rocks are lighter than air, they capture the rising gas pockets underneath them, and use the updrafts of oxygen from the water. I didn't understand most of it. Of course, I was like you, more awed by just seeing all of this," she admitted.

Sergi couldn't help but wish the other members of the Gliese 581 crew were here. He knew all of them would be as fascinated as he was by the magnificent alien world in front of him. He leaned forward, to get a better look at them as La'Rue expertly guided the freighter between the floating islands, steering clear of the bridges that connected them.

"Plateau, this is the Tesla Terran freighter *Star Runner* requesting permission to land," La'Rue said into her comlink.

"Welcome, *Star Runner*. Please follow the landing path. May your visit be bountiful," the soft, feminine voice on the other end responded.

Sergi raised an eyebrow when a series of white lights flashed from one island to the next. In the distance he could see a flashing red light. He turned his head and watched from the side window as they passed huge rocks draped in abundant dark green foliage. Children paused as they crossed the connecting bridges to wave at them overhead.

Along the lower elevations of the floating islands, he could see buildings and structures carved into the black and gray cliffs. Staircases snaked back and forth as they wound around the islands' contours to the upper levels. From what he could tell as they flew by, the residents lived primarily along the lower portions of the islands. Their buildings for businesses, government activities, meeting places, and parks were located higher above the residences. The elaborate terraces for agriculture and manicured areas of forest were at even higher elevations.

Long, thick tubular green vegetation spiraled down over the islands' shores to the oceans below. From above, numerous waterfalls fell from fresh water rivers fed by the green tubes which siphoned and filtered the sea water to them. Lush, green fields were interspersed between thick forests and rising mountains.

"I should warn you that Plateau is primarily ruled by women," she said while she guided the freighter in for a landing.

Sergi turned to look at her in surprise. "It is a matriarchal society? Do the women look down on their men?" he asked, looking back at the floating cities with a wary expression.

La'Rue chuckled and shook her head. "No, they don't. There are more women than men on this world, but obviously the majority doesn't always rule. Personally, I think it is because they are a nurturing people, and the women tend to pick up the characteristics to which Plateauans aspire more readily than men do," she replied. La'Rue expertly rotated the freighter and gently set the spaceship down on the landing pad. She reached up and shut down the engines. "I really think it would be best if you stayed here. The people here know me and will be more willing to talk with me," she finally said, turning to look at him with a pleading expression. "A stranger will cause more gossip, Sergi. If we want to locate your friend quickly, I think it would be best if we didn't cause a scene."

"La'Rue...," Sergi started to argue before he unwillingly bit off the protest and nodded. "I will wait here. If you discover any information...."

"I'll let you know immediately – I promise," she reassured him, releasing her seat harness and turning to look at him with a relieved smile. "It shouldn't take me long to find out if there is a stranger here."

Sergi reluctantly nodded. "I'll wait for you," he said, releasing the harness to his seat and rising when she did. He reached out and gripped her arm to stop her. "Be careful, La'Rue."

"Always," she said with a crooked smile.

Sergi brushed his hand down along her cheek before releasing her. He followed her down the passage. He noted that she had replaced her antiquated blaster with two sleek Torrian laser pistols, one holstered on each hip.

She walked with a confident stride. He followed her down to the end of the corridor where it opened near the ladder which led to the lower level hatch. She turned and grabbed the handrail on each side and stepped onto the top rung. He stood next to the ladder.

"I should be gone a couple of hours. I've programmed HL-9 to scan for any ship arrivals or departures. He'll let you know if anything is coming or going," she said, looking up at him.

Sergi leaned forward and brushed a kiss along her lips. His hand slid along the collar of her jacket, his fingers skimming the soft exposed skin of her nape. He felt his body tighten at her immediate response.

"I'll monitor the video feed as well," he said.

He released her and stepped back as she descended the ladder. He watched the platform under the ship as it lowered. A moment later, she was gone. Turning, he retraced his steps back to the cockpit.

"H, show me the video feed," Sergi ordered as he stepped back into the cockpit.

From the cockpit, he could see across the landing area. With the windows shielded, he could see out but others could not see inside. He slid into the captain's seat and watched La'Rue's progress via the small camera she had attached to the front of her jacket.

"H, activate the tracking device as well," Sergi added.

That little device had not been a planned addition. He had suspicioned that La'Rue would insist on going alone despite his objections. He understood her reasoning and couldn't deny her logic, but that didn't mean he liked the idea or wanted to accept it. In the end, he had remained behind because he didn't want to draw dangerous attention to La'Rue.

He could admit to himself now that he was in love with her. He'd never felt it before, but the signs were clear to him. The past few weeks alone with her had only increased his attraction and commitment to her. He reacted to her on an almost primitive level. There was an overwhelming need to protect her. His body responded to her nearness with a mind of its own, often leaving him hard and aching. He wanted to see her, touch her, hear her voice, and he craved her touch in return.

He enjoyed her sense of humor, intelligence, and sarcastic wit, but at times he felt an irrational fear, as if he might wake and she would be gone. He enjoyed the sound of her voice. The smooth, accented tones sent a wave of calmness through him, just as her laughter sent a wave of heat. He felt calm, balanced, in control when she was near.

"Now that I realize what I am feeling, H, how should I tell her of my sentiments?" Sergi mused, looking over at HL-9. "This is not something I have ever told a woman before."

The little robot didn't respond to his question. Sergi chuckled and shook his head. It would appear he was on his own in this matter. Refocusing his attention on the video screen, he watched the woman, who had broken through the walls encasing his heart, walk across an alien bridge straight out of a fantasy artist's painting.

He sat forward, his eyes suddenly glued to the unfinished carving in the side of the massive black cathedral that came into view. Sculptors were still working on the statue of a woman standing next to the rectangular box. The upper portion of the female figure was standing tall and looking upward toward the stars, one hand raised as if pointing to where she had come from while her other hand rested on the faithfully carved statue of the Gliese 581 emergency pod.

"Julia," Sergi murmured, his eyes transfixed on Julia's serene carved face.

CHAPTER NINETEEN

*L*a'Rue drew in a deep breath as she watched the historians carve the new representations into the exterior of the Cathedral of History. She had been enthralled by the beauty of the structure the first time she had seen it. How the people of Plateau knew so much about what was going on elsewhere while they lived so remotely was beyond her. She imagined that much of their knowledge came from visitors like herself, but still, some of the carvings reflected events that she was pretty sure that *she* hadn't even heard of yet.

She paused to ensure that Sergi could see what she was seeing. Her first impulse was to contact him, but she decided she needed more information first. Swallowing, she started down the path that led up to the front entrance. She climbed the stairs, and crossed the polished landing to the Cathedral's massive doors that always stood open.

La'Rue stepped inside. She swore she could feel a surreal energy flowing through the building. It wasn't an unpleasant feeling, just one that spoke of things in the galaxy that she didn't understand.

This was the first time she had ever actually stepped into the sacred site. She slowly walked down the center aisle of the nave. Everything inside was made of the same black stone that had formed the islands. The walls, pillars and floors were highly polished and contained swirls of gold, diamonds, emeralds, and other precious gems. She looked up as she passed under one of the massive arches that supported the upper levels.

She turned in a circle and carefully studied the ceiling. A colorful mural was painted in panels along it. It had scenes so life-like, she wished she could touch the panels to make sure they were really paintings. She studied the paintings for several seconds before she realized that Sergi wouldn't be able to see what she was looking at. Sliding her hand up she unbuttoned her jacket and she tilted the camera so he could observe along with her as well.

"Sergi, are you getting this?" she murmured, her mind trying to process what she was seeing. "It's the history of the Ancient Knights."

"I see it," he replied.

She walked backwards, studying the stars painted above. She recognized them and the planet in the first panel – Jeslean. On the right side one panel appeared to be a star map while on the left side many panels showed scenes depicting the histories of the Ancient Knights. They looked different than she'd expected. They were tall, slender, and ethereal in stature. There were dozens of them in the paintings.

"You wish to know of the Ancient Knights?" a calm voice asked behind her.

La'Rue turned so fast that she became dizzy. Releasing her jacket, she lifted her hand to her head. It took a moment for her to realize who the woman standing in front of her actually was – Roanna, the matriarchal leader of Plateau. Unsure of what she should do, she bowed her head in greeting.

"The images are breathtaking. Greetings, Lady Roanna," La'Rue added with an inner wince, realizing she should probably have said that first.

"You returned sooner than we expected, La'Rue. I cannot help but wonder what cargo you have – or hope to take back with you," Roanna said.

La'Rue looked up at Lady Roanna when she heard the slight sound of amusement in the other woman's voice. A rueful smile curved her lips. "Can you read minds?" La'Rue asked impulsively.

Roanna smiled and motioned with her hand for La'Rue to walk with her. The lack of a response made La'Rue a little uneasy. She wondered if it were possible to make her mind go completely blank or if she should start counting or use some other method just in case. Those ideas faded when Roanna began to speak.

"The Ancient Knights came to this world to observe and share their knowledge. They were great explorers and fierce warriors. But, most important of all, they were a people of science," Lady Roanna shared.

La'Rue followed the other woman, looking up at the paintings as they walked. "You talk as if they no longer exist," she murmured.

"They exist," Lady Roanna contradicted firmly.

"Where did they come from and where did they go?" La'Rue asked.

Lady Roanna shook her head. "No one knows for sure where they came from or where they went," she confessed, pausing beneath one of the panels. "The records they shared and left behind were entrusted to my people before they departed. They gave us little of their own history beyond their limited time here in our galaxy and their knowledge of the gateways which allowed them to journey between the other galaxies. What you see here are the few chronicles that they shared with us and which we now protect. We were the last ones they visited before they left our galaxy."

La'Rue stared up at the three dimensional holographic cylindrical images displayed in the space above them. One after another, an enlarged spaceship maneuvered into a position just above them and then was replaced by the next in the series. Her hand instinctively moved to the video camera on her jacket and she angled it upward again. The images of the ships were small, barely half the size of her freighter. If they were the actual size of the alien spaceships, they didn't look large enough for deep space travel.

"What is that?" La'Rue asked, pointing up at the image of the gateway.

She could sense the other woman studying her face. "The gateways were created by the Ancient Knights. The last ones to leave said the Knights would always be here during our greatest hour of need," Roanna quietly explained.

La'Rue thought of Sergi, Ash, Josh, and the statue of the woman still being carved. How could the return of four – possibly five Ancient Knights – defeat something as powerful the Legion forces? Dread filled her when she thought of the future of their star system.

"The woman – the sculptors are carving a new statue of a woman. Is she here?" La'Rue asked, looking at Roanna.

"Why do you search for an Ancient Knight, La'Rue? Do you seek power, profit, or – hope?" Roanna inquired.

La'Rue didn't look away from the inquisitive eyes searching her face. If the other woman was capable of reading her mind, she would know why La'Rue was here, but she was about to answer anyway when the sound of a horn suddenly reverberated through the silence, sounding the alarm.

Turning to look through the huge front doors, she felt the ground tremble under her feet. Her gaze flew back to Roanna. The other woman's expression remained calm, but the serene look in her eyes was no longer there.

"What is going on?" La'Rue demanded, her hand moving to the pistol by her side.

Roanna spoke in a sharp tone to several women who came hurrying forward. "Send out the order to release the bridges," she commanded before turning to look at La'Rue. "Legion Battle Cruisers have entered our airspace and are attacking."

"Sergi!" she breathed, turning in the direction of the massive doors.

The ground shook under their feet again. La'Rue bent her knees for balance, her heart in her throat. She held out her arms to steady herself. Turning away, she darted for the massive doors that were slowly beginning to close.

She twisted, passing through the narrowing space between the doors and out onto the landing. The sky above was filled with Legion fighters. Her gaze jerked down to the floating islands far in the distance. The bridges connecting them were falling away. Horrified, La'Rue rapidly descended the stairs and took off at a fast run toward the only bridge connecting this large island with the one where she had left Sergi and her freighter.

"Sergi, the Legion is here. The sky is filled with them. You have to get out. You have to hide," she breathlessly ordered as she ran.

She was almost to the bridge when a Legion troop carrier rose up from beneath the edge of the island and lowered a ramp. Black clad soldiers began filing out. La'Rue didn't stop. She ran as fast as she could past them onto the bridge. Behind her, she could hear the soldiers' shouts for her to stop.

A cry escaped her when laser fire burst around her. She ducked and continued to run. She was less than twenty feet from the other island when the bridge suddenly disappeared from beneath her feet. A scream ripped from her throat as she felt her body falling.

Her hands shot out and she frantically grabbed for any type of hold. Her body twisted and her back hit the bridge as it bounced against the side of the island. She flipped in midair, and halfway through the turn, her hands touched one of the guide ropes that made up the railings of the bridge. She grabbed the rope, crying out again when the thick woven strands burned the palms of her sliding hands. Her legs swung down and she anchored her legs around the ropes until she slowed to a stop.

La'Rue buried her face against the rope for a moment as she tried to quiet her racing heart. Fear for Sergi and the realization that she was still in danger forced her to look up. She had to get to the top.

"Sergi, you have to hide," she whispered, reaching over her head to grab a plank of the bridge, using it like a ladder. She began the short but precarious climb to the top. "Sergi, can you hear me?"

La'Rue paused to check the comlink attached to her ear. Her bloody fingers traced along her earlobe. The comlink was gone. She clung to the bridge and felt for the video camera attached to the front of her jacket. It was missing as well. Both must have fallen off when the bridge collapsed under her feet.

"He knows. H would have warned him," she whispered to comfort herself, continuing to climb.

La'Rue finally reached the top. She struggled to pull herself over the edge. Rolling to the side, she watched in disbelief as Roanna's floating island slowly descended toward the ocean below. The Legion's troop carrier and the Legion forces that had landed on the island were being tumbled over the edge, driven back by the counter attack of Roanna's forces. The moment the bottom of the island touched the water, a glowing sphere surrounded it. The protective shield encased the Cathedral's island. The history of the Ancient Knights and the inhabitants of the island were protected against further Legion attack. The island slowly began to sink and disappear beneath the ocean's surface.

Rising from the ground, La'Rue turned to run to her freighter when she felt the ground under her feet begin to shake. Her stomach dropped as she felt the movement of the island. She had only taken a few steps before a sleek fighter appeared. The fighter rotated in place, facing her before it landed between herself and her freighter.

Her heart dropped when the platform lowered mere seconds later and a tall man strode down it, his troops filing out after him. La'Rue stumbled backwards, but there was nowhere for her to go. Legion soldiers were forming a living wall on each side of her and the edge of the island was behind her.

La'Rue's gaze flickered over the face of the Legion Officer walking toward her. She knew who he was – everyone in the galaxy knew who General Coleridge Landais was and what he was capable of doing. Fear for Sergi threatened to choke her. Her eyes immediately moved to her freighter before moving back to the general.

She straightened and waited, trembling when he slowed to a stop in front of her. Her bloody hands twitched and impulsively moved toward the blasters at her hips. She stiffened when she felt two sets of hands reach out and grab her upper arms – preventing her from drawing her weapons.

"Sir, this island is beginning to sink," one of the younger officers said.

"Who are you and what are you doing here?" General Landais demanded.

La'Rue swallowed and lifted her chin. "La'Rue Gant, captain of the *Star Runner*. I am an independent freighter pilot," she replied, sticking to the truth without elaborating.

"What have you seen?" Landais demanded.

She raised an eyebrow at him. "Besides the Legion attacking a peaceful planet? Nothing. I arrived less than an hour ago," she replied.

Pain exploded through her right cheek. The unexpected blow would have sent her to the ground if the soldiers on each side of her hadn't still been gripping her arms. She touched her tongue to her split lip and tasted blood. She turned her head to look back at Landais through narrowed eyes.

"Sir! We found something," a soldier said, hurrying forward.

La'Rue's eyes widened when she saw the soldier walking toward her carrying an item that she had all but forgotten about – Sergi's spacesuit. The fear she had been feeling increased to pure terror. *They didn't find Sergi,* she told herself. *Breathe. They searched the freighter, and found the suit, but not Sergi.* It wasn't really helping to lessen her terror.

"Where is the Ancient Knight?" he demanded, his expression hard.

"I only found that suit. The pod was empty when I located it on Turbinta," she truthfully responded.

Landais raised his hand to strike her again, but stopped. His cold eyes narrowed and his expression grew thoughtful. She was surprised when he suddenly turned on his heel.

"Take her to my Battle Cruiser – and destroy her freighter," he ordered.

La'Rue's eyes widened in shock. "No! You can't!" she shouted, fighting to break free. "Sergi!"

Landais paused and turned to look back at her, a smug expression on his face. La'Rue wished she could gouge the man's eyes out.

"So, another one has arrived," Landais said. He turned to look at the young officer following closely behind him. "Have the freighter taken to the ship as well. I want it thoroughly searched. I don't care if you have to take it apart piece by piece. Find the Ancient Knight," he instructed.

"Yes, General Landais," the officer replied.

Tears burned La'Rue's eyes, but she refused to give in to them. She wouldn't show the bastard any weakness. Instead, she would try to find a way to escape – hopefully before Landais discovered where Sergi was hiding.

La'Rue stumbled forward when the soldier on her left pushed her. She had no way of knowing if Sergi had even heard her message or if he was hiding on board in one of the secret compartments. With the right detection equipment, it wouldn't take the Legion search crew long to find them. That was why she had never been into running illegal cargo. There were just too many risks involved.

A soldier stepped forward and removed her laser pistols before he stepped back and nodded. La'Rue stumbled a bit when the soldier on her left pushed her again. The soldier on her right side gripped and steadied her. She angrily jerked her arm free. She turned to glare at the man only to have her heart skip a beat when she locked gazes with a pair of very familiar blue eyes. He grabbed her arm again and gently squeezed it before motioning for her to enter the troop transport.

La'Rue stumbled up the ramp and onto the ship. Sergi maintained his guarding position beside her. She sank down on the seat and fumbled for the restraining straps when the young officer who'd disarmed her before stopped in front of her two guards.

"Take her to the main detention block after we board the General's Battle Cruiser," the officer ordered.

Sergi bowed his head in acknowledgement while the soldier on her other side answered.

"Yes, sir," the soldier replied as he turned to snap a restraining wrist cuff around each of her wrists, linking them in front of her.

La'Rue sat back and leaned her head against the bulkhead. She was terrified to look at Sergi. Instead, she sat quietly, drawing comfort from the way his leg pressed ever so slightly against hers. Her fingers fisted against her ravaged palms when the troop transport began to rise off the sinking island.

She stared at the row of soldiers across from her. Sergi was dressed identically to them. Each wore the black Legion colors and full body protective gear. Their black helmets covered their heads while a face shield covered them from nose to chin. Only their eyes were visible. While Sergi's eyes were unusual, there was a chance he could be mistaken for another species – as long as he didn't take off his helmet.

What are we going to do? she couldn't help but wonder.

CHAPTER TWENTY

*T*he troop transport landed amid a long row of Legion transports. It wasn't until the bay doors had been sealed that the interior light flashed from red to green. Several soldiers opened the hatches and they began to file out. The soldier on the other side of La'Rue waited until the others had disembarked before he moved forward. Sergi followed suit, and filed after the other soldier as he led La'Rue out.

He followed the man out of the transport bay and into a long corridor. The other soldier maintained the lead with La'Rue in the middle and Sergi trailing in the rear. They had only walked a few hundred feet when they came to a four-way intersection. They were waiting for a formation of soldiers from another troop transport to pass.

The sound of an angry voice drew his attention. A soft curse swept through his mind when he saw a group of soldiers surrounding two figures. The angry voice came from General Coleridge Landais. He was glaring at the tall, dark haired man standing next to a woman he knew all too well – Julia Marksdale.

"You disappoint me, Roan. Andri feared you might betray us. I told him if you did, then I would take care of you myself," Coleridge was saying.

The man named Roan remained tight-lipped. Sergi didn't miss the way he stood close next to Julia. There was a protectiveness to his stance that went beyond normal duty. If he had any doubt that there was something going on between the man and Julia, it vanished when General Landais struck the younger man.

"Stop! There is no need for violence," Julia snapped, stepping between General Landais and Roan.

"Julia," Roan warned, wrapping his arms around her and pulling her back against his body.

Sergi didn't miss the suddenly considering expression on Coleridge's face as he stared at Julia and Roan. He had seen the same expression far too many times before on some of the most brutal men in power back on Earth. Coleridge would use Julia for his own purposes and the Legion's.

"Take them away," Coleridge coldly instructed.

Making a split second decision, Sergi lifted his hand and removed the tracking device he had planted on La'Rue earlier. He had been able to use it to help him locate her after the video camera failed. Now, he would use it again – to track Julia.

He waited until the second group of guards proceeded closer to them. Just as they were about to pass by them, he stepped to the side of La'Rue. She shot him a confused look at first before understanding dawned on her. He needed a distraction.

"I told you to quit pushing me! I can walk on my own," La'Rue growled, pushing the soldier in front of her into the path of Julia and Roan.

Sergi stepped forward as if to grab La'Rue. Instead, he brushed against Julia. He clipped the tracking device to the underside of her shirt that was hanging loose before he stepped in front of La'Rue and guided her away from the other guards. He winked at her to let her know that he thought she was amazing.

He moved behind her once again, placing his hand on her shoulder as if he was restraining her. His gaze briefly connected with Julia's

startled eyes. A confused frown swept over her face when she looked
at La'Rue before she lifted her eyes to look at him again. Her lips
parted in a soft gasp as recognition hit her.

"Move out," a soldier ordered behind them, roughly shoving both
Julia and Roan.

Sergi noted that the soldier purposely kept a wary distance
between Roan and himself. He didn't know who this Roan was, but it
was obvious the soldiers were leery of him. His eyes followed Julia as
she was marched away in the opposite direction he was going with
La'Rue.

A short time later, he was standing just inside of La'Rue's detention cell behind the lead guard. He had two options at the moment. He
could knock the soldier out and free La'Rue only to get them both
captured. Or, he could leave her here, find out where Julia was and
work out a plan for them all to escape this ship – preferably without
getting them all blown up in the process.

"This is for pushing me, Tesla trash," the guard said, raising his
hand to strike La'Rue.

Sergi might have gone with the second option if the guard hadn't
physically threatened La'Rue. Now there was only the first and now
lethal option for him. He wrapped his fingers around the man's
forearm and twisted it behind the man's back. Turning him, he
slammed the guard's forehead into the wall. The guard struggled to
break free, kicking out at Sergi.

Sergi wrapped his other arm around the guard's neck. Applying
controlled pressure, he held on to the guard until he lost consciousness and grew limp. He released the man, letting him fall to the floor.
Once he made sure the man was unconscious, he removed his helmet.

"Why did you do that? Now General Landais will know you are on
board," La'Rue whispered, glancing at the open cell door with a
worried frown.

"Help me get his clothes off. We'll put him in the bed. You dress as
a soldier in his uniform. We need to find Julia, disable this Battle
Cruiser, and get the hell off of it without getting ourselves blown up

or killed," Sergi said, pulling the key from the guard's belt and releasing the wrist restraints securing her.

"What if someone comes in?" La'Rue worried aloud, biting her lip as she knelt next to the guard and began stripping him of his uniform. "What if he wakes up?"

"I'll make sure that he doesn't," Sergi said.

"How... Oh... Maybe there is another way," she muttered.

Sergi could tell when she bowed her head that she was trying not to think of the intention behind his words. He hadn't wanted to kill the man in front of La'Rue. She might be used to the violence and she was perfectly capable of protecting herself, but Sergi still felt a need to shield her from the darker side of reality. As far as Sergi was concerned, the soldier had forfeited any chance of living when he had raised his hand to strike La'Rue.

"Get dressed, *dusha moya*, I would like to get out of here before anyone else comes in," he encouraged.

La'Rue nodded at him and quickly pulled on the uniform. He noticed that she kept on her own black boots. They were similar enough not to draw too much attention. The guard's boots would have been far too large for her.

"Step outside, La'Rue. I'll be right there," Sergi said, lifting his hand and gently caressing her bruised cheek.

La'Rue smiled at him even as she aimed the laser rifle downward. She pulled the trigger, striking the guard in the chest who had stealthily begun to rise behind Sergi. Turning to look over his shoulder, Sergi watched as the dead man slid down to the floor once more, then looked back at her. He shook his head and gave her a crooked smile.

"You have captured my heart between your blood-thirsty little hands," he admitted with a wry grin.

"Trust me - my hands aren't nearly as blood-thirsty as Kella's, so you'd better be thankful. How are we going to find your friend?" she asked, sliding the helmet over her head.

Sergi's grin widened. "The same way I found you. I removed the tracking device I attached to you earlier and placed it on Julia. I just need to contact H to help guide us," he replied.

"H! General Landais probably has the teams tearing my freighter apart as we speak," she groaned.

Sergi shook his head. "I've been listening. It would appear your freighter has disappeared from the landing bay it was stored in," he said.

"H activated the digital camouflage paint," La'Rue murmured with glee. I love that little robot. As long as they don't bump into the ship, it should reflect the surrounding area."

Sergi nodded. "None of the soldiers want to be the one to tell General Landais that the freighter has gone missing. I guess he has a habit of killing the messenger," he said, looking her over before he nodded in satisfaction. "Let's go. H, I need you to show us the way."

Sergi pulled the small locator device from his pocket and looked at it. A holographic image appeared. Three levels up there was another set of detention blocks. He memorized the diagram and searched for the best route to get there. It looked like they didn't have much choice – they would have to act like they were a part of the General's crew.

"Are you ready for this?" he asked, turning to look at her.

"You go. I've got your back," she said, lifting up the laser rifle.

Sergi grinned and pulled on his helmet. Scanning the outside corridor, he stepped outside the detention cell. La'Rue followed him, sliding the key across the pad to lock the door on the now dead occupant.

～

Roan Landais grunted as another blow hit him in the stomach. The next blow to his jaw sent him to one knee. He bowed his head and spit out the blood.

"I should slit your throat for your betrayal," Coleridge coldly stated, circling around his son.

Roan didn't respond. He knew his father well enough to know that the man wasn't looking for a response. This was about control, power and intimidation. He wanted Roan to feel fear and to cower.

"No words?" Coleridge menacingly chuckled. "You had no words when I slit Calstar's throat, either." He mocked his son.

Roan kept his head bowed, his eyes focused on the black boots walking around him. His fingers curled into fists as he swallowed back his angry retort. He felt a brief wave of grief at the death of his grandfather. He quickly pushed the feeling away. Now was not the time to be distracted by mournful emotions. His father would sense it and use it against him.

Pain exploded through his ribs when his father kicked him. The toe of the polished black boot caught him between two ribs near his left lung. The force of the blow knocked him sideways and took his breath away. His hands clenched behind his back and he forced himself to continue rolling with the momentum until he was back on his feet.

"Where did they come from, Roan?" Coleridge demanded. "How many more are there?"

Roan lifted his head and stared back at his father, his face an expressionless mask. He could see the rage in his father's eyes building until the other man finally snapped. His father reached for the staff hanging at his side. The staff was a symbol of the Knights of the Gallant – one of honor – not of the evil and hatred that stared back at him now.

Roan's body stiffened in surprise. His legs trembled as intense pain swept through him. He looked down to see one end of the staff glowing as it speared into his side. His lips parted on a silent groan when his father twisted it.

"You still have nothing to say? I am almost proud of you, Roan. I wonder if your Ancient Knight will be as defiantly silent as you when I do the same thing to her," his father murmured near his ear.

Roan's jaw tightened, and his lips pressed into a hard, straight line. He wanted to protest, he wanted to rant at his father, but he was afraid if he parted his lips and said anything that he might lose control. His vision blurred when his father twisted the glowing shaft once more before he wrenched it out. Roan could feel the heated surfaces cauterizing the wound as it slid from his flesh.

Beads of sweat glistened on his brow. His father stepped back and motioned for the officer standing by the door to open it. Roan remained frozen in place and upright.

"When you hear the screams, I want you to remember your mother," his father taunted before he turned on his heel and walked out of the maximum security detention cell. The door slammed.

Roan's knees gave out the moment the doors slid shut. He sank to the floor before falling to the side as the darkness began to overtake him. He fought to remain conscious. Forcing his fingers to relax, he felt along the inside of his shirt sleeve for the small master key he had programmed, secreted there and always kept close to hand.

He worked it free. Carefully manipulating the narrow card, it took several tries before he was able to release his wrist restraints. Pulling his arms around, he rolled onto his back and took several deep and painful breaths.

CHAPTER TWENTY-ONE

*S*ergi motioned to La'Rue to fall into step behind an eight-member formation. They marched in time with the group before peeling off and turning in another direction. They had managed to make it to the third level unnoticed. Now, all they needed to do was find out exactly where Julia was being held.

He was about to stop and access H again when he saw General Landais step out of a cell almost in front of them. A wave of cold rage washed through him when he saw the blood on the other man's hands. He also recognized the silver inlaid rod the man was holding – it was a staff of the Knight of the Gallant Order.

Sergi had heard enough from Josh, Ash, and Hutu to know what the staff meant to those looking up to the Knights of the Gallant Order. It was a symbol of good, justice, and hope. Such a staff did not belong in the hands of a ruthless, cold-blooded tyrant.

Coleridge stopped outside of the door next to the one he had just exited. Sergi watched as the man retracted the staff, then attached it at his side before he looked over to where they were standing. Coleridge motioned for Sergi and La'Rue to approach. "You two will accompany me." He turned to the officer standing behind him, not even waiting for a response from them. "I want a report on the freighter. Find out where the other Ancient Knight is located. I want him in custody before we depart Plateau's orbit. Once he is secured, set charges to destroy any remaining floating islands and deploy underwater charges. I want this planet wiped clean of every living soul," Coleridge ordered.

"Yes, General Landais," the officer said with a respectful bow of his head before he turned on his heel and strode away.

Sergi kept his eyes lowered as he approached Coleridge. If his expression and coloring didn't raise warnings that something was amiss then not much else would besides him taking off his helmet and shouting 'Surprise!' at the top of his voice. For a split second, Sergi was actually tempted to do just that.

He needn't have worried. Coleridge had already dismissed the two of them as being mere insignificant subordinates. Sergi patiently waited while Coleridge adjusted the cuffs of his uniform before lifting his hand with the key to the scanner outside the door. Sergi watched as the doors slid open.

Julia serenely sat on the end of the single bunk in the room. She rose to her feet, her wary gaze following Coleridge as he entered. Sergi heard her soft hiss when she noticed the blood on his hands and the sleeve of his jacket.

"What have you done to Roan?" she hotly demanded.

"My son knew better than to betray me. He will die by my hand for his deceit," Coleridge replied.

"Betrayal? What are you talking about?" Julia demanded with an icy look of disapproval as she tilted her head back very slightly and looked down her nose at Coleridge.

Sergi had to admit, Julia did not look in the least bit intimidated by the General. She had that cool, rock-hard mask on her face that he remembered her wearing whenever some government official threatened to close down the Gliese 581g project. She couldn't cross her arms, but she didn't need to at the moment. Her expression and no-nonsense tone of voice demonstrated very effectively that she wasn't going to cower before the man standing in front of her.

"I want to know everything you told my son," Coleridge ordered, ignoring her question.

Julia lifted a delicate arching eyebrow. "My name is Dr. Julia Marksdale. I am a Mission Specialist for the Project Gliese 581g interplanetary exploration team. That, sir, is the limit of the information I gave your son and the limit of the information I will give you," she replied in an icy tone.

"I want to know how you got here, where you came from, and if there are any others coming," Coleridge growled.

Sergi suspected that Julia's cool, calm demeanor was beginning to ruffle the General. It was obvious the man was used to intimidating others and not having the tables turned. Unfortunately, Sergi wasn't sure if Julia was aware of the precariousness of the situation.

"We arrived on a spaceship. That is the typical mode of transportation for interplanetary travel and explorations. In order to explain where I came from, I must know where I am in relation to my home world. Since that is not information I currently have at my disposal, the question of where I came from can't be calculated. As to your final question, the answer is yes. There are others coming," she answered. Julia's gaze briefly flickered over Coleridge's shoulder toward Sergi. Calmly she returned her indifferent eyes to the General's face. "In fact, I believe they may have already arrived," she continued with a sweet, serene smile.

Sergi saw Coleridge frown. The other man partially turned his head to look over his shoulder at him. Their stares locked for a fraction of a second. Sergi saw the moment when the realization hit the General that he wasn't a Legion soldier and sank in. Coleridge's hand had begun moving to his side, reaching for his weapon.

Sergi had already raised the laser rifle in his hand. He smiled when he saw Coleridge's eyes widen in shock. A loud groan slipped from the General's lips and he collapsed to his knees, his hands clutching his privates protectively.

It took a second for Sergi to understand exactly what had just happened. He looked over in time to see Julia step back and lower her booted foot to the floor. Her lips were in a tight frown and her eyes flashed with anger.

She leaned forward and grabbed the front of Coleridge's uniform to keep him from falling face first onto the floor. Sergi heard La'Rue's soft snicker. He definitely needed to remember never to antagonize the quiet, almost mousey science nerd.

"A man should never treat his son the way you have. Now, what have you done to Roan?" Julia hissed, bending forward so that she was in Coleridge's face.

"I… will… kill… you," Coleridge painfully hissed.

"Good luck trying," Julia said, pushing Coleridge away from her and looking up at Sergi.

Sergi struck the butt of his laser rifle against Coleridge's temple. The other man had once again been reaching for his laser pistol at his side. The General fell sideways in an unconscious heap. A deep gash spilled blood down onto the floor and it began to pool around the man's head.

"You blew my cover," Sergi informed Julia as he bent to pull the laser pistol out of Coleridge's hand.

Julia raised an eyebrow. "He had blood on his hands and shirt. I had no desire for him to add *my* blood to them," she retorted, holding out her wrists. "Could you please remove these?"

"I'll unhook them, but I'll need you to keep them around your wrists," Sergi stated, kneeling to pat down Coleridge to see if the man had anything that they could use – like a master key to get off the damn ship.

"I'll release them," A smiling La'Rue offered, stepping forward with the key she had taken from the other guard. "I'm La'Rue. That was a really effective kick, by the way."

"Julia Marksdale. Thank you. Mei taught me that move," Julia confessed before she looked at Sergi with a slightly unsteady smile. "Is she alive? Did… Did Ash and Josh make it?"

Sergi's expression softened. "Ash and Josh are alive and well. Josh is helping to lead the war effort against the Legion. Mei survived. Ash and Kella have gone after her," he said.

"What is the plan to get out of here?" Julia asked, looking down at the man lying unconscious at her feet with a look of utter disgust. "We have to find Roan. We can't leave him here."

La'Rue shook her head. "*The* General Roan Landais? There is no way we are helping him. He is just as bad as his father. Let them kill each other," she said with a shudder.

Sergi saw the stubborn look come back into Julia's eyes. He'd seen it a hundred times when they were training and during the course of their journey. When Julia made up her mind, there would be no changing it – no matter how dangerous their situation might be.

"I won't leave him. His grandfather saved my life. The last thing Calstar asked of me was that I help Roan," Julia insisted, looking back at Sergi. "I promised him, Sergi."

"I'm pretty sure he is next door," Sergi conceded with a sigh.

La'Rue turned to glare at him. "You do know that the man she wants us to help is General Roan Landais, who is a general of the Legion. There are only two other men that I know of who are feared as much as he is – and they are both related to him," she argued.

"She made a promise, *dusha moya*. How can I tell her no?" Sergi asked, looking at her with a mixture of pleading and teasing.

"Argh! I hate it when you look at me like that! If he so much as twitches wrong, I'll put a disintegration disk on him," La'Rue hotly vowed.

"And I will press the activation unit's button," Sergi reassured her.

In the next instant, La'Rue raised up the laser pistol at her side, aimed and fired a shot into Coleridge's chest. She glared at Julia when the other woman hissed in surprise. Sergi couldn't help but think that La'Rue was the most beautiful woman in the universe and the perfect woman for him.

"Let's get out of here," La'Rue said, just as the door opened behind them.

Sergi and La'Rue both turned and raised their weapons to fire. La'Rue's loud curse mixed with Julia's. He reached forward and grabbed the bloodied man barely able to stand in the doorway. He grunted under the man's weight.

"We need to get off this ship," the man said, looking blankly down at his father. "What happened to him?"

"I kicked him in the balls, Sergi knocked him in the head, and La'Rue shot him," Julia succinctly clarified, stepping up to wrap her arm around Roan Landais' waist.

"Sergi? La'Rue?" Roan muttered, looking at Sergi with a frown.

"It is a long story. I suggest I tell it to you once we are off of this ship. You wouldn't perchance have any suggestions as to how we can do that, would you?" Sergi inquired.

"As a matter of fact, I do," Roan replied through clenched teeth. "I just need someone to access the main computer frame."

CHAPTER TWENTY-TWO

*L*a'Rue gritted her teeth to keep from cursing. If they were smart, they would have left Roan Landais dead on the floor next to his father. Instead, she was returning to the room with a maintenance cart so that they could transport his body in it.

Fortunately, lady luck was currently being nice and staying on their side. The large maintenance cart had been left down the corridor. La'Rue had answered the terse questions from the single guard at the area's central control room. She explained that General Landais had requested that some soiled materials be removed.

"The Ancient Knight soiled the bedding," she stated, unable to think of anything else.

"Get it cleaned up. I don't want to have to do it," the guard had growled.

La'Rue muttered under her breath as she guided the cart back to the detention cell. She looked around before opening the door and entering the room. A glance around showed her that Roan was now lying on the bed with Julia leaning over him, carefully wrapping the wound on his side.

"We need to get a move on. The guard will be changing soon. Right now, the one manning the post there is too stupid and too lazy to be bothered with checking what is going on. We might not be so lucky with the next one," she warned.

"This is the best I can do until we can find some medical supplies," Julia said, rising to her feet and helping Roan stand up.

"Do you have a lock on my freighter?" La'Rue asked, walking over to help Julia guide Roan to the cart.

Sergi nodded, pocketing the device. "Let me help you," he softly ordered when Roan released a low hiss of pain.

"I can do this," Roan said with a determined shake of his head.

La'Rue watched as the Legion General climbed into the maintenance cart and folded himself into its confines. She had to admit that she was impressed that he had not only accomplished it, but had done so without making a sound.

A second later, Sergi was helping Julia into the cart as well. Once Julia and Roan were inside, La'Rue closed the top. Opening the door, she looked out both directions before she guided the cart through the door and down the corridor. Sergi followed behind her a short distance away.

"Did you get it cleaned up?" the guard demanded, looking up from the screen he was watching.

"Yes. The General ordered us to take it immediately to the disposal unit in case of contamination," she said. "He is concerned there might be alien parasites in the Knight's discharge."

The guard blanched and motioned for them to move on. "Get it out of here. If the General is concerned about it, then I sure don't want to have to deal with it," the guard growled.

La'Rue turned away and rolled her eyes. It was a good thing she had killed the General. Otherwise there was an excellent chance that this guy would end up floating in space – without wearing a spacesuit. It would probably still happen when Andri found out that his favorite General had been killed and his other almost favorite one had disappeared.

That's if we get out of here alive so I can enjoy it, she ruefully thought as they exited the detention block and turned in the opposite direction to the disposal units.

~

The journey to the bay where La'Rue's freighter was located felt like it took them forever. There had only been one slight delay which Sergi had effectively dealt with in a nonchalant manner. The service panel was going to start stinking in a few days.

"H, open the lower hatch," Sergi quietly ordered.

The lower hatch separated before the platform was lowered. He helped Julia out of the cart before they both helped a very pale Roan out of its confines and over the edge. The moment the cart was empty, La'Rue guided it to the far end of the bay. Hurrying back, she stepped onto the platform and pressed the controller button.

Within minutes, they had Roan in La'Rue's small, but fairly well equipped medical room. Sergi helped Roan lay back on the bed. Julia immediately began cutting his shirt away from the wound. La'Rue handed Julia an unfamiliar to her medical device. Julia looked back at La'Rue with a confused expression.

"Maybe I should do this," La'Rue reluctantly offered. "We need to know how to get off this ship without getting blown up or having a thousand fighters using us for target practice. General Landais appears to be the only one who knows how to accomplish that at the moment."

Roan turned his head to look up at her. He winced as he tried to reach into the pocket of his trousers. An amused, pain-filled smile curved his face when Julia gently slapped his hand away and reached her own hand into his pocket.

"You are good at slapping my hand away," he teased in a strained voice.

"Shut up," Julia instructed at the same time as La'Rue looked at Roan with an expression of distaste.

"That is just so wrong on way too many levels to mention. He's flirting while lying here about to bleed out and we could be captured again at any moment," she muttered with a shake of her head.

"Where does this need to go?" Sergi asked, stepping closer to the bed and taking the disk that Julia had pulled free.

Roan looked at Sergi. "One of my former crew members was able to shut down my Battle Cruiser with the programming on that disk. I've added my authorization to it. I doubt Coleridge would have thought to have restricted my access yet. This needs to be inserted into the main computer panel. Once installed, it will initiate a complete shutdown of all systems, including environmental. That will force the crew to evacuate into designated life support areas until all of the ship's systems reset. This should give us enough time to get through the rings and make a jump. The fighter bays will be locked down," Roan explained in a voice laced with exhaustion.

"How do we get it down there?" La'Rue asked, glancing at Roan's pale face etched with pain.

She applied a pain inhibitor. Almost immediately, Roan's body relaxed. She cleansed the wound before applying the tissue regenerator over it. The nanobots would work on cleaning and repairing any damaged organs and tissue. It was an older model unit, but still worked – not that she had used it all that often.

"I will take it," Sergi said.

La'Rue's head jerked up. "No! It is only a matter of time before they discover General Landais' body and the ship will go into lock down," she snapped.

"I will go," Roan said, holding the tissue regenerator to his side as he struggled to sit up.

"No, you will not. You'd collapse before you made it half way down the corridor," Julia retorted, pushing against his shoulder and forcing him back down on the bed. "Sergi is very good at what he does."

La'Rue saw a wary expression come into Sergi's eyes. Julia was looking at Sergi with a slight smile and an amused expression. La'Rue decided right then and there that she would have liked Julia even if the other woman hadn't kicked Coleridge Landais in the balls.

"H can go. He can get into places most people can't," La'Rue suggested.

Roan frowned. "Who is H?"

La'Rue grinned. "Only the smartest service robot in the entire galaxy," she boasted.

Sergi nodded. "I will second that," he agreed, curling his fingers around the chip.

La'Rue looked at Julia. "Make sure the General here doesn't move or touch anything. We'll be back," she ordered.

"She is almost as bossy as you are," he muttered to Julia.

"I'll take that as a compliment," Julia dryly replied.

La'Rue turned and started for the door, following Sergi. Behind her, she heard Roan Landais release a frustrated grunt. Exiting the room, she hoped they weren't making a mistake by taking the Legion General with them.

~

Pain radiated through Coleridge's head and chest. His hand rose to the area just over his heart. He could feel the scorched cloth there. Fortunately, the blast – even at such close range – had not penetrated the protective shield he wore under his uniform. He couldn't say as much for his head.

Rolling to his side, he pushed up off the floor. He touched his throbbing temple. His fingers probed around the deep gash. He looked at their blood covered tips before he scanned the room.

The image of vivid blue eyes swept through his mind. One of the guards had been the other Ancient Knight – the one from the freighter. He would kill the man and both women. Rising to his feet, he felt for his comlink. It was missing, along with all of his weapons and his security key.

He stumbled to the door. Without the key, he was locked inside. Lifting his hand, he brought his fist up against the door of the detention cell. It took nearly a dozen poundings on it before the door opened. The guard looked back at him in shock.

"Gen… General Landais," the man stuttered, stepping back when Coleridge stepped out of the cell.

"Where did they go?" Coleridge demanded.

The guard looked confused. "Who, sir?" the man asked, looking at him with a blank expression.

The rage that Coleridge was feeling grew at the guard's inept response. He grabbed the guard by the front of his uniform and drew him closer. His other hand reached for the guard's weapon.

"There were two guards. Where did they go?" Coleridge demanded in a hard, low voice.

The guard pointed toward the exit. "They... They took the... the soiled materials to the disposal unit," the man replied.

"Give me your comlink and security card," Coleridge ordered.

He took the items from the guard's trembling fingers before he pressed the weapon he had also taken to the guard's side and pulled the trigger. Stepping over the dead guard, he held the pistol ready as he swiped the security key over the control panel mounted on the wall by Roan's cell door.

The first thing Coleridge saw was the discarded wrist restraints that had been on Roan. A quick scan of the small cell showed it was empty. Turning, Coleridge exited the cell. His hand lifted the comlink to his mouth.

"Level Five alert. There are two escaped prisoners from the maximum security detention cells. One of the prisoners is General Roan Landais. Have every soldier remove their helmet. There are two members of the Rebellion on board. Check the lower detention cells for the freighter captain," Coleridge ordered as he strode out of the detention block toward the bridge.

Coleridge stepped onto the bridge at the same time as the first alarms began to sound. He turned to face the man striding toward him. He scanned the bridge. His officers were scrambling to contain the situation.

"Status report, Commander Manta," Coleridge demanded.

"The systems are shutting down, General Landais. There appears to be a full system override bypassing the security protocols. Each system is shutting down in a random order," Commander Manta replied.

"What of the freighter captain?" Coleridge asked.

"Gone, sir, along with the freighter, although there is no record of it having left our ship," Commander Manta replied.

Coleridge's mind raced through the possible scenarios. "If there are no records that the freighter has left then I suggest that you have a team search for it," he replied through gritted teeth.

"Yes, General Landais," Commander Manta replied.

"Shut down the alarms and find a way to stop the ship from being disabled," Coleridge growled to the men and women on the bridge.

Coleridge turned and strode for his office adjacent to the bridge. He dismissed the Medical Officer who had appeared as he was about to enter his office. Instead, he took the medical kit from the man and continued through the open doorway.

The door closed behind him. Coleridge walked over to his desk and tossed the medical kit on it before turning to pour himself a drink. Returning to his desk, he picked up the medical kit and walked into his cleansing room.

In a few minutes, he had cleaned the blood off of his hands and face, doctored his wounds, and changed into a clean uniform. He frowned, and his lips tightened when the lights began to flicker. Tossing the used medical items and his ruined uniform into the disposal unit in the wall, he exited the cleansing room.

"Computer, bring up the ship's status," he ordered.

"System shut down imminent," the computer responded.

Coleridge was scanning the log of the systems shutting down when there was a chime at the door. Looking up, he gave a sharp command to enter. Commander Manta stepped into the room.

"One of the technicians has discovered the cause of the issue. She is currently repairing the damage," Commander Manta informed him.

"And the freighter?" Coleridge asked.

Commander Manta's mouth tightened. "The landing bay where it was placed has been opened. We believe the freighter has some type of concealing shield. We are tracking the engine's heat signature left behind. It has turned back toward the planet," he explained.

"Order the other Battle Cruisers to deploy their fighters. Destroy the freighter – and the Plateauans," Coleridge ordered.

"I'll order the attack immediately, General Landais," Commander Manta responded with a stiff bow of his head before he backed out of the room.

Coleridge started to turn away when a notification sounded on his computer. He glanced at the screen. Andri's image appeared. Irritation flared inside him. He flexed his fingers. The last thing he wanted to deal with now was his half-brother's arrogance.

Turning on his heel, he left the room and stepped onto the bridge. Minutes later, he was disembarking the lift onto the fighter bay level below. It was time to show his son what it felt like to be on the opposite side of the Legion – and to feel the full force of its devastation.

CHAPTER TWENTY-THREE

"*W*here did you get this?" Roan asked, picking up the staff that Sergi had placed on a cabinet near a panel he had opened.

Sergi warily watched as Roan turned the staff in his hands. He watched the other man run the tips of his fingers over the design. Roan finally looked up at him when he didn't immediately answer.

"I took it off of your father," Sergi admitted.

Roan frowned. "Do you know what this is?" he asked.

Sergi nodded and turned his attention back to the control panel. La'Rue had asked him to make sure that everything was lit up, just in case one of the Legion soldiers had disabled the weapons system's main power controls. He checked each row and saw that the green light was on next to the indicator for the small cannons that had been retrofitted while they were on the moon base.

"Yes, I know, but do you?" Sergi countered, stepping back and closing the panel. He turned to look at Roan. "This weapon, it holds a lot of meaning, *da?* It was not given to use as a symbol of suppression, but as one of hope and protection."

Roan's mouth tightened before he slid the weapon into the pocket of his jacket. Sergi could tell there would be no more discussion about it with the man. He thought about requesting the return of the staff, but his gut told him that it had found its rightful place.

"What type of weapons do you have on board?" Roan asked, nodding toward the panel behind him.

"The freighter was retrofitted with several auto-cannons. There wasn't much time to add more. We wanted to intercept you in case you found Julia," Sergi replied.

"What about shields?" Roan asked.

Sergi raised an eyebrow. "This is not a fighter or a Battle Cruiser. It has shields. Our biggest asset is our ability to hide in plain sight. La'Rue developed a special paint that, when combined with the shielding, bends the light around the ship making it virtually invisible to the viewer," he explained.

Roan frowned. "That would work on the planet or in space as long as the ship's engines weren't emitting any heat signatures. Otherwise, scanners would be able to track the freighter through its propulsion system," he reasoned.

Sergi nodded in agreement. "Which is why we are searching for a place to hide. There is no way we could out-distance the fighters or even the slower Battle Cruisers," he admitted.

Roan lifted a hand and ran it across his bruised jaw. Sergi knew what the other man was thinking – a few bruises would be the least of their concerns. Both men turned when they heard La'Rue call out to the men. Sergi could tell from her voice that time had run out for them.

"We have company," La'Rue said in an urgent tone.

"I need to take over. If we are in a battle against Legion fighters, we'll need more than a freighter captain at the helm," Roan growled.

"La'Rue isn't your typical freighter captain," Sergi reassured him as they strode down the corridor.

~

La'Rue glanced over her shoulder when Sergi and Roan stepped into the narrow confines of the freighter's cockpit. She returned her attention to the screen where the few dots identifying the locations of the Legion fighters had grown to a swarm of them. There was nowhere to hide.

"Let me take over," Roan ordered.

La'Rue shot the Legion General a heated glare. "My ship, my command," she hotly stated. "H! I need Crock's maps now!"

Roan slid into the co-pilot's seat. La'Rue could sense Sergi sliding into the seat behind her while Julia quietly sat in the navigator's seat watching HL-9 with fascination as the little robot accessed the database and processed millions of star charts and planetary maps looking for the one La'Rue needed.

La'Rue was about to snap at the little robot again when the required map appeared. She breathed a sigh of relief. The frozen islands were locked in ice. La'Rue knew where they were, she just didn't know how to navigate through them.

"La'Rue, this is my world. I know how to navigate through the frozen islands. Your map is outdated," Roan quietly informed her.

La'Rue glanced at the man sitting next to her before looking back at all of the Legion fighters closing in on them. She released a frustrated breath. Unfastening her harness, she slid out of her seat and looked pointedly at him.

"Don't damage my ship," she growled before she turned and looked at Sergi. "I'll take the top pulse gun, you take the bottom."

Sergi grinned at her. "I love it when you are on top, *dusha moya*," he teased, trying to ease her stress.

Julia released a delicate cough and looked at La'Rue with a strained smile of amusement. "And you thought Roan's comment was too much?" she murmured with a raised eyebrow as La'Rue moved past her.

La'Rue rolled her eyes and took off running down the corridor. She grabbed the ladder as high as she could reach and began to climb. Sergi brushed his hand across her lower back as he swept by. His intended message was clear – be careful.

She pushed away her fear. There was no way they were going to survive this even if they made it to the floating ice islands. The area was uninhabited as far as she knew. All she had to go by was what Crock had told her. Since the man had been delivering to Plateau for nearly a century, she figured he knew what he was talking about.

La'Rue slid into the swiveling gun chair and powered it on. The freighter had originally come with two pulse cannons. They fired powerful shots but were only good at close distances. The newer auto-cannons that had been installed were made to keep your enemy at a respectful distance.

She felt the moment the cannons locked on to targets and began to fire. The fighters were following their heat trail. This was another reason she had wanted to reach the frozen islands. The intense cold there would help conceal them.

"Sergi, can you hear me?" La'Rue asked, turning around and looking at the screen in front of her as it locked onto and displayed the approaching fighters.

"I hear you," Sergi replied.

She swallowed. The sound of his voice soothed her. Releasing a sigh, she allowed the warmth of his voice to surround her.

"I love you," she quietly murmured. "If anything happens…. I want you to know that I love you."

The silence in the comlink was deafening. She finally heard him draw in a deep breath. When he spoke, there was a fierce determination and resolve in his voice that made her feel like they might actually have a chance of making it out of this alive.

"Remind me to whip your ass later for waiting until I couldn't hold you to tell me this, *dusha moya*," he replied in a gruff tone.

"I will," she softly replied.

"We will make it through this, La'Rue. I haven't come all this way only to lose the one woman who has accomplished a task I thought impossible," Sergi said.

"What task is that?" she asked, feeling her stomach tighten as the cannons began to fire on the approaching fighters.

"You made me fall in love with you," he responded, opening fire as one of the fighters made it past the auto-cannons firing range. "One."

"One… Ah, you think to win this, do you?" La'Rue retorted,

focusing as two more fighters broke through the cannon's firing range as well.

She fired, hitting one and sending it spiraling downward before swiveling around and firing on the other. It exploded as one of the pulses caught the left wing. She released a long breath.

"Two," she stated.

La'Rue knew this wasn't a game, but Sergi had helped her regain her center – her focus. Her eyes widened when she saw the huge Battle Cruiser appear in the distance. Even if they were able to find a place to hide, the firepower of the Battle Cruiser would reduce all of the frozen floating islands to icy shards.

Her heart pounded as another Battle Cruiser appeared, then a third. Hundreds of fighters poured from the massive ships. The freighter had reached the first series of frozen islands.

Roan wove his way through the frozen towers of water rising up to hold the islands in place. Several of the fighters following them were not as agile and crashed into the icy columns. La'Rue watched as large sections of the ice broke away and fell, forcing the fighters to veer off.

Brilliant blue crystals suddenly surrounded them as they streaked through one of the ice tunnels. Sergi fired on two fighters that entered the tunnel behind them. Just as they emerged from the other side, La'Rue fired at their exit point, collapsing the tunnel so no other fighters could follow them.

Roan guided them above and below ice bridges and through tunnels. La'Rue and Sergi fired on the fighters that came too close but there were too many for their two weapons. She was jerked forward when one of the Battle Cruisers fired on them, striking one of the freighter's rear engines.

The freighter began to rotate as it lost power. A cry ripped from La'Rue when her ship crashed through the side of a frozen cliff and began to plummet. Fear coursed through her when she saw the ocean filled with ice floes growing closer.

"H, I need you to override the safety and give full power to the auxiliary thrusters now!" La'Rue cried as she held onto the cannon's grips.

La'Rue was forced back into her seat as Roan pulled back. The freighter swept under the lip of one floating island before Roan steered it higher. They were still losing power. In the background, La'Rue could hear the sounds of alarms going off and the power was flickering. The scraping of ice on metal screeched through the ship. She could see the billowing smoke coming from the damaged engine.

"Brace for impact," Roan warned in the comlink.

"No!" La'Rue hissed.

She gripped the sides of the cannon's controls, holding on as the freighter fell from the sky and skidded across the icy surface of one of the islands before the nose rose up to face the sky when the ship came to an embankment. The ship teetered at a precarious angle with the nose finally hanging over the edge of the island.

Dread filled La'Rue when she saw the fighters swing back around for another strike run. She braced herself when she saw three of them taking aim in their direction. The *Star Runner* was defenseless.

She started to turn her head, expecting to feel the intense heat of laser fire, when with no warning the three fighters suddenly exploded. Confusion swept through her when she saw small, agile fighters emerging from below them. They swept up from the ocean's depths, locking onto the Legion forces with a deadly intensity and lethal skill.

Hope and adrenaline rose inside her at the realization that they weren't fighting this battle alone. Her heart raced as she realized that they needed to do what they could to protect themselves. Releasing her harness, she swung out of the seat and slid down the ladder, using the hand railings instead of the ladder's rungs. She turned and started running toward the engine room.

"H, I need you to do your magic, little guy. We need power diverted to the shields and the cannons. Shut off anything else that isn't absolutely necessary," La'Rue shouted as she ran.

She knew the little robot would already be working on shutting down any fires that had been caused when they were hit. Her hand shot out to grab the doorframe as she rounded the corner. A relieved hiss escaped her when she saw Sergi already working on the damaged power panel.

"You're safe. The bottom turret...?" she gasped.

Sergi shook his head. "...Is buried in the ice and snow," he replied.

"Someone is assisting us," she informed him, kneeling beside him.

She pulled out the damaged circuit board, wincing when the heat of the board burned her fingers. She tossed it aside and pulled out two more. Rising to her feet, she pulled out several replacement boards from a supply cabinet. She handed them to Sergi. He had handed over the panel he was working on to H.

La'Rue stumbled when the *Star Runner* shuddered from a blast. She gripped the side of the circuit panel. A frown creased her brow when she saw her mother's staff lying beside Sergi. It had been over a year since she had used the powerful weapon.

She swallowed and reached down to pick up the staff. Tears burned her eyes as she wrapped her fingers around the symbol of the Gallant Order. For the first time, she felt like she was meant to use the staff.

Straightening, she started to turn away. She stopped when she felt Sergi's strong fingers wrap around her wrist. He looked up at her with an intense expression.

"What are you doing?" he demanded.

La'Rue gave him a shaky smile. "What I was meant to do.... You need time to repair the damage. Get the shields and cannons back online," she instructed.

"La'Rue," Sergi started to protest before his gaze moved to the door where Roan and Julia now stood.

"She is correct. Repair the shields and bring the cannons back online. La'Rue and I can help protect the freighter," Roan said, gripping his father's staff in his hand.

"With those?" Sergi demanded in a skeptical tone.

"Yes," La'Rue and Roan both replied at the same time.

La'Rue bent and brushed a brief, hard kiss across Sergi's lips before she turned and hurried out of the room. Deep in her heart, she knew that no matter what happened, Sergi and Julia needed to survive. With the help of their unexpected allies and the Ancient Knights of the Gallant Order, there was hope that they might just make it out of this alive.

～

"Do you know how to use the staff?" La'Rue asked as she and Roan emerged out onto the top of the freighter.

Roan held the staff out in front of himself and extended the rod. Twirling it, he aimed it at an approaching Legion fighter that was firing on their allies and released a powerful burst from the tip. The orb-shaped ball of energy cut through the center of the fighter from stem to stern and it then spiraled out of the sky and disappeared beneath them.

"Yes," he replied, aiming at another Legion fighter.

La'Rue swallowed. Extending her staff as well, she focused on remembering what her mother had taught her before she was murdered. She and Roan moved with the fluid grace of dancers as they smoothly maneuvered in an effort to protect the freighter. All around them the sky was filled with fighters from the Legion and those of their allies.

"Who is helping us? I've never seen fighters like this before," La'Rue shouted, watching in amazement as the smaller, more agile fighters streaked overhead.

"Plateauans," Roan replied, striking another Legion fighter that was coming in low. "Many are unaware that the Plateauans are fierce fighters and have an advanced military defense system."

La'Rue wanted to ask him how he knew, but decided this was probably a discussion better suited for another time. She turned when she saw a movement out of her peripheral vision. Her eyes widened when she saw a Legion fighter rise above the edge of the cliff.

Her lips parted in disbelief when she saw General Coleridge Landais in the cockpit. The sight of the Legion general, still alive, shook her. The bastard was supposed to be dead! Lifting her chin, she stared back at him in defiance. If there was a next time she would aim for his head! Even better yet, she would aim between his eyes!

Below her, she felt the vibration of the *Star Runner* as the ship came back online. Near the front of the freighter, the pulse cannon turret rotated to face the Legion General's fighter. The freighters shields were back online as well.

She watched as the fighter rose higher in the air. Her first thought was that the Legion general was giving up. It wasn't until the silhouette of a large Battle Cruiser covered the sun that she realized that even with the shields, the *Star Runner* was still very vulnerable.

"Look out!" she yelled when she saw the Battle Cruiser's cannons turning toward them.

Without thinking, La'Rue surged and wrapped her arm around Roan's waist. The force of her tackle knocked both of them off balance and they slid down the curved top section of the freighter. A cry of horror escaped her when she saw Roan disappearing over the side.

She twisted and frantically reached out in an effort to slow her descent as she neared the edge of the freighter. Her fingers curled around one of the outer maintenance grips as her legs went over the side. She swung dizzily for a moment before she released her grip and fell just as Julia opened fire on the Battle Cruiser.

La'Rue mentally braced for her impact with the frozen ground. She was surprised when her fall was cushioned by a pair of strong arms. The force still sent them both sprawling on the slick surface.

She rolled to the side and looked over at Roan. He was already rising to his feet. Her head turned in the direction that he was staring. One of the Battle Cruisers was breaking apart and falling into the ocean below. Additional ships were converging on the Legion forces. Her eyes widened when she saw one of them was the *Long Haul,* which was one of Crock's freighters.

She started to rise to her feet when several strong blasts made the ground under them violently tremble. The force of the blasts knocked Roan back off his feet. Watching in confusion, it took a moment for her to understand what was happening. The Battle Cruiser wasn't firing on the *Star Runner*; it was firing on the section of frozen ground in front of the freighter. The Legion's motive was clear – total destruction of the freighter and those aboard it. If they couldn't get through the shields, they would destroy the ground beneath it and send it plummeting to the ocean below.

"No!" La'Rue screamed as the ground began to break away and tilt under them.

"Come on," Roan yelled.

Roan grabbed her hand and pulled her to her feet. She fought to break free, but he refused to release her. In horror, she watched as the freighter tilted and began to slide. Julia continued to blast away at the Battle Cruiser but the pulses couldn't penetrate the warship's shields. La'Rue's breath was knocked out of her when Roan pushed her beneath an icy overhang. Together, they watched as the ground finally broke away from under the freighter and caused it to slide over the side.

"No! Sergi!" La'Rue cried, reaching out a hand in denial.

CHAPTER TWENTY-FOUR

"*S*ergi, I think you should hurry," Julia calmly stated in the comlink.

"Perfection takes time," he responded, slipping the circuit boards into the panel.

"Imperfection has its place as well, especially when there is a very large enemy spaceship heading our way," Julia retorted.

"System is rebooting," he replied in a tone that belied the tension of the moment.

"It's about damn time," Julia muttered in his ear.

Sergi chuckled. He knew Julia was stressed when she started cursing. The woman was still as cool as a cucumber.

"H, bring the engines online," Sergi ordered, before pressing his comlink. "La'Rue, I need you and Roan back on the freighter. The shields are online."

He impatiently waited for a response as he left the engine room and headed for the bridge. Above him, he could hear Julia opening fire on the Battle Cruiser. He slid into the pilot's seat and began checking the systems.

"La'Rue, I need Roan and you back inside," he grimly ordered again.

"Sergi, Roan and La'Rue have gone over the side of the ship. I don't see them," Julia informed him, her voice filled with angst.

Sergi's fingers flew over the scanner controls the moment they came back online. He pulled up a visual of their two heat signatures near the back of the freighter. There was no way to fire up the engines without killing them. He was about to rise from his seat when the ground under them violently shook.

Looking out of the front screen, he saw the Battle Cruiser was firing at the side of the island beneath them. If the ground gave way, the freighter would fall to the ocean below. Caught between the choice of killing La'Rue and Roan or saving himself and Julia, Sergi's mind could only flash through all of his options.

"Are the engine's online?" Julia asked.

"Yes, but I can't engage them without killing La'Rue and Roan," he replied.

He gritted his teeth as the freighter began to tilt. His eyes flashed to the two heat signatures. They were moving away. If he timed it just right and had enough momentum....

"The math says it is possible," Julia murmured in his ear, coming to the same conclusion he had.

A wry smile of determination curved Sergi's lips. "Hang on. This is going to be a bumpy ride," he warned.

Julia's soft snort echoed through the comlink. "You missed the Gliese 581 going through the gateway and breaking apart. This is going to be a piece of cake in comparison," she informed him.

Sergi shook his head. If this was going to be a piece of cake, he was glad he had been unconscious for the first event. He ground his teeth together, sat back and fastened the harness on the captain's seat, and waited. Another shattering blast shook the freighter before a loud snap resonated through the metal hull. He felt the freighter tilt before it began to slide on the slick surface of the ice-covered island.

His eyes narrowed on the ocean below as the ship fell. With swift, practiced moves, he fired the engines. The added kick pressed him back in his seat. He heard Julia's low moan and knew she could feel the G's pushing against herself as well. His eyes flew to the instrument panel. Counting down, he pulled back on the stick, leveling out the *Star Runner*. The bottom of the freighter skipped like a flat rock along the surface of the ocean before rising above it again.

"Woohoo!" Julia's excited cry echoed throughout the ship, almost deafening him.

"Ash has nothing on me," Sergi bragged as the freighter gained altitude.

Once he was high enough, he began the curve to the left to return to the frozen island that they had just left and where La'Rue and Roan were stranded and defenseless. His heart pounded when he saw the battle filling up the sky. What made his blood run cold was the sight of three Legion fighters approaching and two of them landing on their island.

~

"Collapse the shelf above them," Coleridge ordered from his vantage above the island.

He watched as the two fighters accompanying him opened fire on the ice shelf beneath which his son and the woman were standing. Shards of ice and rock rained down around the two of them. He watched in satisfaction as the two disappeared under the debris.

"I want their two staffs," he ordered once the firing had ceased.

He watched as the two fighters landed and the pilots disembarked their spacecraft. They ran over to the avalanche of debris. His mouth tightened when he saw a glow of red right before one of the pilots flew backwards, obviously dead. As much as he wanted the two staffs – and his son's knowledge of how he knew to reprogram the one that had belonged to himself – the situation was fast becoming too dangerous for the General.

His hand moved, locking his fighter's weapons controls onto the pile of debris. He paused when an alarm sounded. He cursed when he saw that another ship had locked onto his craft. Pulling back on the controls, he veered to the right as several powerful bursts from a pulse cannon struck where he had just been. He spun out of control for a moment as he fought to override the fighter's automatic defense system. That was when he caught sight of the freighter that he thought had been destroyed.

"General Landais, additional rebel ships have appeared. We are the last surviving Battle Cruiser, sir. If we do not retreat now, we will all die," Commander Manta informed him in his comlink.

Coleridge's mouth tightened as a surge of hatred washed through him. "Give the order to retreat. Have a squadron of fighters escort the Battle Cruiser out of the planet's orbit," he ordered, turning his own fighter back toward the Battle Cruiser.

"Yes, General," Manta calmly replied.

~

Sergi circled around the island. Below him, he could see two Legion fighters – and two dead Legion soldiers. His stomach clenched when he saw Roan clearing away a section of debris. There was no sign of La'Rue.

"Sergi, it looks like the Legion is retreating," Julia said. "I see Roan, but I don't see La'Rue," she quietly added.

"I don't see her either," he replied, focusing on landing the freighter.

Sergi landed the Star Runner as close as he could near Roan. . In seconds, he was running down the corridor. He crossed the larger cargo bay and slammed his palm against the panel to open the platform. He jumped from the opening to the ground as soon as there was enough clearance. Running across the frozen ground, he didn't slow until he reached Roan.

"Where is she?" he demanded.

"We were separated when they started firing on us," Roan grimly replied.

Neither of them spoke while they continued to dig away at the debris. Time slowed as Sergi's desperation grew. He knew that survival could potentially come down to seconds for the woman he had fallen in love with. Pushing a large block of ice to the side, his heart pounded when he saw the tips of La'Rue's fingers.

"Roan, I found her," Sergi urgently called.

It took both of them to move another huge block of ice that had fallen over her, wedging her between two large boulders. It was that bridging slab of ice that had saved her from being crushed beneath all the other debris. He worked on clearing the chunks of ice from her chest while Roan freed her legs.

Sergi could feel his fingers tremble when he touched them to her neck. Her skin felt like ice. Unsure if he felt a pulse, he leaned his head down and pressed his cheek against her chest. He felt the faint, telltale movement. Sitting back, he gently ran his hands down over her head, neck, shoulders, and chest; checking for injuries.

"I don't think her legs are broken," Roan said.

Sergi looked at the blood coating the palm of his hand where he had run it over her head. She had a head injury, but he couldn't tell how severe it was. He carefully slid his arms beneath her shoulders and knees before slowly rising to his feet.

"She has medical equipment on the freighter. Do you know how to use it?" Sergi asked as he turned away.

"Yes," Roan replied, bending to pick up La'Rue's staff.

Sergi turned and carefully worked his way over the debris field. Roan steadied him when he started to lose his balance on some loose ice. He nodded his appreciation.

Julia must have seen them coming from the upper turret because she met them at the platform. Sergi ignored the Plateauan fighters still flying overhead. He strode up the platform past Julia, across the cargo bay and to the small room used for medical services. He started to turn for a thermal blanket. But, Julia was already standing silently behind him, holding out one of the thin blankets.

"I'm concerned about the gash behind her left ear," Sergi said, gently turning La'Rue's head to the side.

"Let me clean the wound," Julia said, stepping forward.

"I will run the scans to make sure there is no internal swelling," Roan added.

Sergi nodded and stepped back. While he had medical training, it was nowhere near as advanced as that of Julia. He turned when he heard an alarm. Roan paused, holding the scanner in his hand and looked at him.

"I will see what is happening," Sergi reluctantly said, turning to leave the room.

He strode down the corridor to the cockpit. A quick look at the scanner's display showed him that a larger ship was approaching. He slid into the cockpit and readied the auto-cannons. They were down to fifty percent power. The shields were down to twenty.

"*Star Runner* this is the *Tracer*," a deep voice greeted.

Sergi released a long relieved breath. "Hutu, this is Sergi. We are in need of emergency medical assistance," he said.

"Affirmative, Sergi. A medical team is being deployed," Hutu informed him.

Sergi closed his eyes, bent his head, and did something he hadn't done since he was a child – he prayed.

CHAPTER TWENTY-FIVE

Plateau:

S ergi looked up from the report he'd been reviewing when he heard a soft knock on the door. He placed the report down on the bedside table and rose from the chair he had drawn up next to the bed. A quick glance at La'Rue's peaceful face told him she was still asleep. The doctors onboard the larger Gallant warship had told him that they had given La'Rue a powerful sedative to allow her body time to heal fully.

He walked over to the door and opened it. A smile softened the frown on his face. Opening the door farther, he motioned for Julia to enter. She stepped inside, her eyes immediately going to the bed.

"Is she...?" she started to ask with a worried expression.

Sergi smiled. "The doctors from Hutu's warship and here on Plateau have assured me that she will be fine. There was some swelling, but they said all the scans came back showing no brain damage," he murmured. "Would you like a drink?"

Julia shook her head and looked around. She lifted a hand toward the open balcony door. He nodded and followed her when she stepped outside. They both walked over to the railing to look out across the incredible view.

"It is beautiful here," Julia commented before she stopped and began to worry her bottom lip.

"What is it? Have Ash and Kella reported in yet?" Sergi demanded, turning to lean against the railing so he was facing her.

Julia shook her head. "No, nothing yet," she replied in a faint, distracted voice.

"What is bothering you?" he gently probed.

She lifted a hand and waved it outward. "This... That.... Everything," she admitted, turning to look at him with a troubled expression. "When my father... when my father first photographed the gateway I never expected anything like this. This world, the technology, waking up and...."

"Waking up in an alien world in the middle of a civil war and being mistaken for some prophesied knight?" he finished with a sardonic smile.

Julia nodded. "Hutu has imprisoned Roan," she confided, looking up at him.

Sergi lifted an eyebrow. "Roan is a Legion general," he reminded her.

"I know," she replied with a loud sigh, turning to look out at the view again. "It's just... complicated."

"For the safety of the Gallant Order, it is probably for the best, at least temporarily" Sergi suggested.

Julia shrugged her delicate shoulders. "Did the doctors say how long La'Rue would sleep?" she asked, changing the subject.

"A day or two, then they would check on her again if she does not wake up on her own," he replied.

She nodded and turned back to face the bedroom. "I'm glad you and Ash and Josh made it. I hope Ash and Kella can find Mei.

I... I almost forgot to tell you that I spoke with Roanna. She is the leader of the Plateauans. She said there was the possibility that there might still be another functioning gateway in existence. She is going to research their archives. If there is, there might be a way to return to Earth," she said.

Sergi nodded, but didn't say anything. He already knew deep down that he would never return to Earth, even if there was a way to do so. His life was here now, in this world with his La'Rue. He fit in here.

"Roanna wants to meet with us when La'Rue wakes. She says it is important," Julia quietly added as she opened the door.

"Once La'Rue wakes, I will meet with Roanna," he promised. "And, Julia, ..."

Julia turned to look at him. He could see the worry in her eyes. He could also see the concern.

"If you need help, let me know," he added with a wink.

A smile played at the corner of her mouth. "I will. Thank you, Sergi," Julia quietly replied.

"Anytime, my friend, anytime," he said.

Sergi watched as Julia walked down the corridor. He closed the door when she turned the corner. Turning back around, a tender, relieved smile curved his lips.

"You have awakened, my sleeping beauty," he murmured with a growing smile.

"So, are we busting out the Legion general?" La'Rue asked.

Sergi threw his head back and laughed. Walking over to the bed, he climbed onto it and pulled La'Rue into his arms. He held her tightly against his body and pressed a kiss to the top of her head. A shudder ran through him when she ran her hand over his arm and rested her cheek against his chest.

"Remind me to whip your ass later for scaring me," he murmured.

La'Rue chuckled and rubbed her cheek against him. "Only if I get to whip yours first for doing the same," she retorted.

"Deal," he murmured, closing his eyes in contentment.

~

Three days later, Sergi walked beside La'Rue, Julia, and Hutu up to the tall, imposing cathedral built to record the history of the star systems.

They paused when Hutu came to a stop and stared up at the statue of Jemar de Rola and his young son, Jesup.

Sergi could sense Hutu's deep grief at the senseless loss of life. They began walking again when Roanna appeared at the top of the steps. Hutu bowed deeply to the tall, regal woman. Sergi bowed his head as well.

"Rise great Knight of the Gallant," Roanna requested. Her tone was welcoming to the dark red skinned warrior.

Roanna turned her attention to Sergi, La'Rue, and Julia. She beckoned them to step closer.

"I am so glad to see you are well, child," Roanna said to La'Rue.

"Thank you. I'm sorry about your grandson being locked up," she said, unable to think of anything else to say.

Roanna chuckled ruefully. "Yes, I have expressed my disappointment as well," she replied, shooting a look at Hutu before she focused again on La'Rue.

"Your mother was a much valued member of the Knights of the Gallant Order. I know that you will be as well," Roanna said.

Sergi wrapped his arm around La'Rue's waist when she quietly thanked Roanna and stepped back. Roanna turned her attention to Julia next. He frowned when Roanna raised her hand as if to touch Julia's hair only to skim her hand over the air a few inches from Julia.

"You are a very special woman, Julia Marksdale. You remind me of my daughter," Roanna quietly murmured.

Julia's eyes filled with tears. "I'm so sorry for what happened to your husband, Roanna. I never meant any harm to come to him," she responded in a voice filled with tears and grief.

Roanna shook her head and took a deep breath, her own eyes filled with the unfathomable grief that could only come from losing the source of a lifetime of love. "Calstar's time to journey on had come. He would wish you to have this, Ancient Knight. This belonged to my husband and would have passed down to our daughter if she had chosen to accept it. Now, it belongs to you," Roanna said, holding out a silver cylinder.

Sergi's eyes widened when he realized that Roanna was giving

Julia a staff of the Gallant Order. Julia looked down at the cylinder in confusion before she looked up at Roanna's twinkling eyes.

"I know someone who knows how to use it and would love to show you," the older woman said with a surprisingly mischievous wink.

Julia's lips twitched. "I'll remember that," she promised, stepping back when Roanna turned to look at Sergi.

"For you, Ancient Knight," Roanna said in a formal tone. "I give to you my staff in gratitude for your help in saving my grandson's life. The Ancient Knights of the Gallant live, and with them lives the hope for a new world."

Roanna turned to face Hutu once more. "We Plateauans will stand by the Order of the Gallant. You have my pledge, General Hutu."

"Thank you, Roanna. The Gallant Order needs the support, strength and technology of the Plateauan people," Hutu stated, bowing his head in respect once more.

"They also need the knowledge and insight my grandson can provide, General Hutu. I suggest you take that into consideration as well," Roanna quietly replied before she turned and calmly walked away.

"I agree," Sergi told Hutu with a grin.

"So do I," La'Rue said, lifting her chin and looking at Hutu.

"I do, too," Julia added with a sigh. "So, will you release Roan now?"

Hutu crossed his massive arms and returned Julia's heated look. "No," he responded with a stubborn grunt.

"You know we'll just have to break him out," La'Rue said, looking at Hutu with a grin.

"Oh, I like that idea," Julia commented, looking at the staff in her hands with a frown. "I wonder if I should have told Roanna that I'm not a very good soldier."

Sergi snorted. "After the way you put Coleridge Landais on the ground, I would disagree with that statement," he muttered in disagreement.

Hutu turned to Julia and frowned. "You put General Landais on the ground?" he exclaimed with a tone of disbelief.

Julia looked at Hutu. "He was being a perfect ass," she replied with an inelegant sniff and a shrug of her shoulders.

Sergi's lips twitched when he saw the huge Torrian's mouth drop open. Julia gave Sergi a surreptitious wink before she turned and started to walk away. Sergi chuckled when Hutu took off after the very prim and proper Dr. Julia Marksdale. He couldn't help but wonder what other things Mei had taught Julia during the eighteen months they were journeying in space.

"I need to work on my freighter," La'Rue said, watching the other two walk away.

"Roanna has had a crew working on it day and night since it was brought here. I have a feeling that there may be some ancient technology involved," he said, wrapping his arm around her waist.

"Sergi, what do you think will happen now?" she quietly asked.

He stared out across the bridge attaching them to the other floating islands which extended far in the distance. He could see people, young and old, peacefully going about their daily lives. He wasn't sure what tomorrow would bring, but he knew that he would do everything in his power to use his skills not only to survive, but to forge a different life in this strange, but amazing new world.

"I don't know, *dusha moya,*" he finally admitted, looking down at her with a warm, tender expression. He lifted her hand to his lips and pressed a kiss to her still healing palm. "But whatever happens, we'll find out together."

EPILOGUE

Legion Battle Cruiser: Deep Space between Plateau and Tesla Terra

"*I* told you what would happen if you failed me, Coleridge," Andri said with a savage expression.

Coleridge returned his half-brother's heated look with an icy one of his own. He had not been able to avoid dealing with Andri any longer. Sitting back in his seat, he remained silent as his brother continued to disparage him and express his utter dissatisfaction at this latest outcome.

"You are weak. You should have killed Roan when you first sensed that he was questioning our plans. If he joins the rebels, we will have a fierce opponent who knows more about the Legion than anyone. He must be stopped, at any cost," Andri snapped.

"I am well aware of what Roan is capable of doing, Andri. I also know his weaknesses. I have not failed you or the Legion's cause. Roan will pay for his treason and I will bring you an Ancient Knight. This is a setback, brother, not a defeat," Coleridge countered smoothly.

"It had better not be, *half-brother*," Andri replied, emphasizing the last word before he ended the transmission.

Coleridge rose from his seat. Walking over to the window, he stood gazing out, lost in thought. He turned when the door chimed.

"Enter," he ordered.

"You requested my presence, sir," Commander Manta said, standing at attention.

"Yes, Commander. I read through your bio. You were raised on Turbinta," Coleridge stated.

He didn't miss the way Manta's mouth tightened before he answered.

"Yes, General Landais. I would like to point out that I was never officially trained with a Turbintan Master," Manta clarified in return.

Coleridge walked over to the man who he had unexpectedly promoted. He studied the man's calm expression and the faint markings trailing from the man's forehead.

"Which parent came from Tesla Terra?" he inquired.

"My mother, sir," Manta answered. "My father was a Turbintan."

Coleridge walked around his desk. "I have a special mission for you. It will require your unofficial training on Turbinta to complete," he stated in a cold voice.

Manta looked at him now with an intense, but curious expression. A satisfied smile curved Coleridge's lips. To fight deceit, you sometimes had to use deceit. He was not above using an assassin.

To be continued:
Honor Bound: Project Gliese 581g Book 4....

When the Legion forces strike back at the Gallant Order, Julia Marksdale finds herself caught in a cat and mouse game between two lethal Legion generals.

READ ON FOR SAMPLES!

MAGIC, NEW WORLDS, AND EPIC LOVE IN
THE MANY SERIES OF S.E. SMITH…

SAMPLE OF THE SEA WITCH'S REDEMPTION

Synopsis:

She expected to die saving her world...

Gabe Lightfoot and his best friend, Kane Field, have stood side by side through thick and thin. Brothers by circumstance, they have seen the darker side of life, and lived to remember it. When Gabe rescues a wounded woman in the waters off the coast of Oregon, they have no idea what's in store for them...

Read on for three full chapters of The Sea Witch's Redemption!

Prologue

Centuries Ago:

Magna lay on the soft sand in the secluded cove that she, along with her cousin, and their best friend had found and claimed as their private fortress when they were younger. She released a contented sigh and stared up at the stars. It was truly a magical night. A warm breeze swirled around her, and she dug her fingers into the sand.

"Do you ever wonder if there is anyone else in the world besides us, Orion?" she asked, letting the sand trickle through her fingers

"I don't know. I suppose so," he murmured.

Orion gazed morosely out over the water. She turned her head to look at his frowning face.

"Lighten up, cousin. You are thinking too hard about the future again," she teased, tossing a handful of sand onto his leg. "Accept that you'll be king of all of this and be done with it. There is nothing else you can do," she advised with a wave of her hands.

"I hope it is not for a very long time," he said with a grimace.

Magna sat up. "What, is there more going on in that head of yours? Are you upset because Kapian couldn't join us tonight?" she asked.

Orion shook his head and looked down at the sand. He picked up a handful and let it filter through his fingers before doing it again. She waited, barely containing a huff of impatience.

Finally, he sighed and spoke. "Kapian went with his father to the Isle of the Monsters," he said in a distracted voice.

"The Isle of the Monsters! Oh, I would love to go there. We should have followed them. I heard the Empress has these wonderful birds that are made of lightning, and beasts so huge that they make even the Giants appear tiny in comparison. I think we should go there tonight," she breathed, thinking of all the amazing creatures she had heard about while growing up.

Orion chuckled and shook his head. "Why am I not surprised you'd say that?" he retorted before he sobered.

Magna twisted and scowled at her cousin. "Why not? If we left now we could be there by tomorrow night. Our stags are the fastest in the ocean! I bet we could beat Kapian there. Can you imagine his expression when he sees us?" she said in excitement.

She stood and twirled around to look at Orion. Biting her lip, she gazed at him with a pleading expression that usually worked. Her smile faded when she saw the glum look on his face.

"I can't go," he said, rising to his feet to stand next to her.

"What's wrong? You've been all moody tonight," she complained.

Orion was silent for a moment before he shrugged. "Father and Mother have chosen my bride. I'm to be married," he said.

"Married! But...," she started to protest before her voice faded as the realization of what he had said sunk in. "Can't you tell them you aren't ready? There are so many things we planned to do still," she murmured, gazing up at him in dismay.

"Those were childish dreams. It is time to grow up. We each have our responsibilities. Kapian told me yesterday that his father reminded him that I would one day be king. Servants and guards are not the friends of a king. They are there to serve him," Orion stated in a tight voice.

Magna snorted. "Kapian's father has a seaworm stuck up his butt. Just because you are a king does not mean you are no longer a person! Even a king needs friends. Besides, Kapian and I know too much about you to act like we never saw you covered in Sea Hares or helped you escape from Coralus when he insisted on extra training lessons, but you wanted to ride Sea Fire instead. Your father and mother are great rulers, Orion, but you will be an even better one because you have a genuine connection with your people," she declared with a wave of her hands.

Personally, she wanted more from life than being tied down with the weighty expectations of others. She loved exploring the vast world they lived in. Her plans were to visit every kingdom and meet the people who lived there. She wanted to learn everything that she could about the wonders of their world until she felt like her brain would explode from all the knowledge.

Then, I will find new worlds to explore, she thought with excitement.

She wanted to fly like the dragons, do magic like her mother's people, live in the clouds with the Elementals, and swim to the bottom of the oceans as free as the sea dragons. She was in love with the independence, the differences between the people, and the unexpected treasures that she found when she visited each place.

Orion chuckled. "How did you get to be so smart?" he teased, bringing her back to the present.

She tossed her long black braid over her shoulder, looked up at him, and grinned. "Why from my cousin, the future King of the Sea People, of course," she retorted just before a light in the sky caught her attention.

She parted her lips in awe. Orion took his cue from her and looked up. A bright flash of light was cutting across the dark sky. They both turned, following the path it made across the sky until it disappeared into the sea with a tremendous splash, not far from the cove.

"I call it! It's mine," she yelled, playfully pushing him down onto the soft sand before she laughingly raced for the water.

"Not if I find it first," Orion yelled after her, rising to his feet as he was overcome by her excitement and the challenge of finding the meteorite first.

Magna raced him to the water. With a loud whistle, she called to her sea dragon, Raine. Diving into the waves, she swam as fast as she could out into the water. Raine swam up under her once the water was deep enough. She grabbed the reins and glanced over her shoulder. Orion was a good two hundred feet behind her.

"Go, Raine!" she encouraged, clinging like a second skin to her sea dragon.

Magna loved the heady feel of the race. She really didn't care who found the meteorite first – or even if they found it. It was the thrill of the adventure, the fun of riding as fast as they could through the ocean, and the joy of not worrying about things like getting married or becoming a warrior like Orion and Kapian.

Several miles out to sea, the ocean floor dropped from a sheer cliff into a deep canyon. Orion, Kapian, and she had explored the long narrow canyon a few times out of curiosity. Raine swept down along the cliff, turning in a tight spiral that left Magna laughing and slightly dizzy. Orion charged after her, swiftly closing the distance between them.

"Magna, wait up!" Orion called.

She glanced over her shoulder when she heard him. "I called it, Orion!" Magna replied. "This is my treasure."

She turned back and focused on guiding Raine through the long, narrow crevices that ran along the ocean floor. They weaved through tall ghostly lava vents left over from the volcanoes that had risen up out of the sea to create the islands that would become the Seven Kingdoms. She swayed from side to side in unison with Raine as the sea dragon rounded the columns.

Up ahead, Magna could see a red glow illuminating the darkness. She knew that the canyon dropped again into an even deeper ravine. She had explored the deeper sections once before, but had found them dull and boring. There was not much down there except dark gray sand and volcanic rock.

"Magna, wait!" Orion demanded behind her.

Magna turned to see Orion reining in his sea dragon. She slowed Raine and patted the side of the young sea dragon's elegant neck when it fought against her hold. She turned on her saddle and grinned at Orion. If he thought that she was going to be tricked into letting him race ahead of her, she and the young sea dragon would show him.

"It isn't much farther," Magna replied with a smile. "I can feel it, Orion."

Orion shook his head and frowned. "I don't like this, Magna. Something is wrong," he said, glancing around at the tall, rugged cliffs not far from the drop-off. "The water doesn't feel right."

Magna shook her head and chuckled. Her eyes danced with merriment. She waved her hand through the water surrounding them. It felt the same to her.

"You aren't afraid, are you?" she teased. "The water hasn't changed."

Orion shook his head again and pulled back on the reins of his sea dragon. "No, there is something very different about it," he said in a slow measured voice. "We should go back."

Magna's face crumpled with disappointment, and she glanced back over her shoulder toward the dark crevice with a look of longing. While she wanted to see if they could find the meteorite, she knew that if Orion said the water felt different, then there was something wrong. Pushing aside her disappointment, she reluctantly nodded.

"Okay," she muttered with a sigh of regret. "But, I still call it, even if we never found it."

Orion laughed. "I'll give you this one," he agreed with a grin. "I'm still ahead though."

Magna rolled her eyes. She was about to argue with Orion when a dark shadow rose up from the depths beneath him. Her eyes widened when she saw the mass of dark tentacles reaching for him. Without thinking, she kicked Raine's sides and rushed toward him in a race to get to Orion before the black mass did.

"Orion, look out!" Magna cried in horror.

Orion yanked the reins in surprise to avoid colliding with Magna's mount. The move startled his stag, and it bucked. Magna watched in horror as Orion flew over the neck of his sea dragon. His head struck a section of the rock face, and his body went limp. Terrified, she moved on instinct. She grabbed Orion around the waist as he began to sink and pulled him over the saddle in front of her.

"Go, Raine, go!" Magna urged as the tentacles began to close in around them. "Go!"

The young sea dragon, weighted down by two riders, fought in vain to rise above the reach of the creature coming up out of the abyss. Raine cried out in pain when one of the black tentacles grazed her hindquarters, leaving behind a long welt. The frightened sea dragon kicked back, but the ugly tentacles continued to reach for her.

Magna realized that if she didn't immediately do something, they would all be lost. Sliding off of Raine, she slapped the sea dragon on her hindquarters. The sea dragon bolted upward and away.

A strangled scream of pain and terror slipped from her lips when a tentacle wrapped around her slender ankle. Searing pain exploded through her and began spreading up her leg. She struggled to break free, but more of the creature's tentacles wrapped around her, pulling her struggling body down into the abyss.

She reached up, grappling for a hold on the rock wall of one of the lava vents. Her palms were shredded by the sharp rocks. Blood from her torn flesh mixed with the water. Anguish filled her when she realized that there was no way she would be able to break free. The grasp around the lower half of her body was slowly moving upward, consuming her.

"No!" she choked.

Despair filled her as she watched Raine disappear with Orion, still unconscious, on her back. The black sludge was rising higher and higher. She felt like she was on fire instead of surrounded by water. Fear gave way to a certain knowledge that all her dreams would never be realized, because she was about to die.

"Help me," she whispered, stretching her lacerated hands upward in a silent plea even as her vision began to blur.

Magna twisted and was pulled deeper into the abyss. Shivers wracked her body. The water had never sent a chill through her before. As one of the sea people on her father's side, the oceans were her home. Now, the frigid temperature of the water seeped into her bones. Whatever held her in its grasp was sliding beneath her skin, scorching the very core of her bones with a fiery cold. The pain burning through her was overwhelming. Her heart thudded violently as she desperately tried one last time to break free.

Please, do not let me die like this, she silently begged as her mind became cloudy and disoriented.

You will not die, a hollow voice whispered through her mind. *We need you. We need your world and you will give it to us.*

For a moment, Magna saw what the creature was and what it wanted. It would use her to take over not only the sea people but all of the kingdoms. It would spread like a deadly virus; taking, using, and destroying everything in its path until there was nothing left. The alien creature would feed on the misery of every species here. Only when it had used up all of its resources would it move on to other worlds.

"Never," Magna whispered. "I will... stop you. I bind you to me. Neither you nor any of your kind may live inside another. Let this spell unite us and give only me the power to set you free."

The spell she wove was powerful, born from fear and the determination to protect those who she loved. If the creature thought to destroy her, it would also destroy itself. She bound the alien to herself, trapping it inside her own body. She could feel the creature's shock and rage at the unfamiliar magic that slid through her and wrapped around it.

Magna's lips parted as agony ripped through her. As the spell continued to wrap around the creature, it tried to withdraw from her. Rage poured through the alien when the spell prevented it from leaving her body.

The creature's tentacles shot outward in an effort to catch up with Raine when it realized what Magna had done. It thought to seek out Orion, to use his body as well. Barely conscious, she felt the recoil as it was jerked back toward her. The spell had held.

A sense of relief swept through her even as she felt the cold surround her heart. With one last effort at self-preservation, she tucked a small part of herself away. To protect that part of herself in a place where the creature could not find her, she used a touch of the ancient magic she had learned from her mother. She would bide her time, and when the creature was least expecting it, she would kill it.

Even if it means destroying myself, she vowed before she slipped away, and the creature took control.

Chapter 1

Present day – Isle of Magic:

Relief filled Magna. It was a feeling she had not felt in so long that she almost didn't recognize the emotion at first. Relief and a sense of peace – another sensation that she had not felt in over a century. Today, she – and the Seven Kingdoms – would finally be free. She had to believe that they would be, because this last shred of hope was all that was keeping her sane. The Goddess would give her the strength she needed, and they would all be free.

Her failures and successes – some new, some old, and some previously forgotten – flooded her until she felt like she was reliving them over and over again. Her heart ached when she thought of how Orion's father had been forced to banish her to the depths of the ocean over a century ago, but it had gotten the alien entity isolated.

She had hoped that given enough time, it would die, and she would be free of its evil grasp, but that wasn't what had happened. Instead, the creature had tirelessly plotted the destruction of her world.

When the Isle of the Sea Serpent was no longer easily accessible, the creature had searched her memories until it discovered her fascination with her mother's home, the Isle of Magic. Tapping into her magical skills, it had forced her to return to the beautiful isle and betray her mother's people.

The creature had wanted her to kill everyone who resisted. Instead, she had turned them to stone, convincing the creature this was a crueler punishment than death.

When the creature had used her to weave a spell that took the magic from the Isle of Magic's residents every night, intending to harvest their magic for its own use, she had twisted the words at the last second to include herself – and by extension the alien – among those who would be powerless at night. Enraged by her blunder, the creature had come close to killing her. The only thing that saved her life was the alien's need for her body.

Over and over again throughout the years, she had tried to take her own life or give others an opportunity to kill her. Each time, the creature had prevented her from destroying them both. Their lives were melded – it could not leave this world, nor could it exist without her.

But finally, her diligence and patience would pay off. Outside of the throne room, she could hear the battle raging. A malicious smile curved her black lips. She ran a trembling hand down her white gown. Deep inside, she could feel the alien's growing frustration and rage.

The creature, in its thirst for power, had spread itself too thin, just as she had hoped it would. The attacks by the combined forces of Drago, Orion, and the other rulers of the Seven Kingdoms were weakening it, and the alien was beginning to realize that it was in mortal danger.

Magna took a deep breath. She would know when the time was right to strike the final, deadly blow. Almost a century of imprisonment had passed before she'd conceived of a way to defeat the parasitic creature possessing her body. The planning had taken time, and she'd had to wait in the shadows of her mind, carefully manipulating the creature until the pieces fell into place.

She had lost count of the times she had been forced to commit atrocities against the peoples of her world. Her acts of defiance had to be subtle, but they had preserved a small amount of hope that one day she could reverse her spells and free those she had turned to stone.

As the years passed, though, harboring the creature's dark essence had drained her. Now, her body was frail from the constant stress of fighting the creature, but she fought to retain enough strength to ensure that her spell would be powerful enough to succeed. This would be her one and only chance to destroy the creature. If she failed, the Seven Kingdoms would be doomed.

Taking another deep breath, she mentally considered her plan. In order for everything to work, four things had to occur. The first three had been the most difficult to set up, but it was the last one that was the most important.

The first thing she needed was the magic of dragon-fire. Guilt-ridden grief struck her at the high cost to the Kingdom of the Dragons. The alien inside her had rightly feared that the dragons had the most potential to destroy it, and so a whole species was taken out of the war, all except one dragon.

Dragon-fire burned hotter than a normal flame, and none was more intense than that of Drago, the Dragon King – especially now, fueled by his all-consuming need for revenge. That was why she had refused to turn him to stone so many years ago.

The creature had railed against her, inflicting excruciating pain on her after she had briefly taken control and escaped into the sea. During it all, Magna had desperately tried to convince the alien entity that leaving Drago alone was the smart choice. She had told the creature that only the natural death of Drago would void the spells and wards protecting the famed power of the dragons – the Dragon's

Heart. She'd told it the King of the Dragons would suffer greater pain if they did not turn him to stone. He would retreat into his unbearably empty kingdom and die of loneliness and grief. When the spells lifted, she reasoned, she would safely be able to retrieve the Goddess's gift to the dragons.

The creature had finally relented, but only because it could sense the tremendous pain and the piercing silence that had followed when Drago had retreated to his lair. She'd gotten lucky that Drago really hadn't died of loneliness and grief.

She needed Drago's aid to weaken and destroy the tentacles the alien had posted along the surrounding wall and huge portions of the palace itself, while she focused on the parasitic host that was her master. Only a fire created by a dragon's magic could injure the alien creature.

Second, she needed the power of Orion's trident. The electrical energy contained within the trident would disrupt the creature's ability to communicate with, not only her, but also with the unnatural creatures it had created from itself with the help of her magic, like the Hellhounds and the living vines.

The third element she needed was a weapon not of her world. This had been the trickiest part of her plan. She had opened a portal between the Seven Kingdoms and another world using a spell she had discovered in King Oray's library. The portal had allowed the arrival of Carly Tate which had resulted in a series of events that had led to today's final battle.

The final element was the spell she had carefully crafted. The alien had to have a host to thrive. The only way to kill it was to release the bonds she had crafted so long ago, allowing the creature to leave her body. Currently it was incapable of leaving her body – unless she died, and then, she feared, the creature would merely find another host.

Timing was everything. She needed to release her bond on the creature inside her and utter the spell to kill it while the alien was still within a few feet of herself. At the same time, she needed the others to attack the alien, disrupting its powers and distracting it, while continuing to prevent the creature from finding another host. She had to do this while giving everyone else in the room enough time to escape. Anyone remaining with her and the alien would perish from the power of the spell.

There were so many factors which could go wrong that she was beginning to have serious doubts about being successful. She ruthlessly pushed them away. Each horrible thing she had been forced to do, each day of torture she had endured since that night so long ago, and each desperate ploy had led to today. She refused to give up and concede defeat.

She didn't wince when the doors to the throne room exploded inward, the burning body of a Hellhound collapsing under the scorching heat. From where she stood in the shadows behind the throne, she saw two figures cautiously enter the room. She recognized the woman as a witch from the Isle of Magic, but it was the man with her who drew her attention. He was from the other world, the one that Carly Tate had come from, and the one who would unwittingly help her machinations succeed.

She lifted her chin and breathed deeply in an effort to quiet her eagerness. Orion and Drago were not far behind the man and witch. Inside her, she could feel the creature trying to command its minions to coalesce in the throne room. There were few remaining. Vast sections of its vines stationed outside and most of the Hellhounds had already been destroyed. The creature's extensions who persisted inside the palace came closer to the throne room, covering the ceiling with a thin film of black ooze.

Prepare to attack, the malicious voice whispered in her head.

I am ready, she dutifully replied.

You will unleash all of your power on them. Our combined strength will not be defeated, the alien vowed. *Without their leaders, the Kingdoms will be ours. It is time to destroy them all!*

Yes, Magna agreed.

Do not fail me this time or the pain you feel will be unlike any I have given you before, the alien warned.

I will not fail, Magna quietly vowed.

The creature sensed the resolve inside her, unaware of the true reason behind it. The alien's arrogance was a tumor, rapidly growing out of its own control, much like its tentacles. Keeping a tight grip on her own emotions, she patiently watched and waited for her opportunity. Her eyes drifted to the throne where King Oray, the King of the Isle of Magic, sat. His body was unnaturally stiff and frail; the spell he had cast to protect himself and the kingdom was slowly draining the life from him. Once again, a shaft of remorse swept through her at the pain and suffering she had been forced to cause.

Taking a deep breath, she waited until the witch and man neared the throne before she stepped out from behind it. She inwardly grimaced at the high-pitched laugh that escaped her and echoed throughout the room. Sliding one hand along the back of the throne, she drew a long, curved dagger from the sheath strapped to her waist.

The witch was the first to straighten when she saw her. Magna caught and held the woman's intense gaze.

"Release him, Sea Witch," the female demanded, her face and voice filled with fury. Magna's head tilted to the side and a sardonic smile twisted her lips in a silent reply. "We are not alone. The Sea King and Drago have joined with my people to stop you."

"I tremble at the mere thought," Magna drawled sarcastically, looking at the woman with utter disdain.

She turned her head slightly to the side so that the witch couldn't see the flash of grief in her eyes. She focused her attention on the bent form of King Oray. He looked ashen and listless. His continued fight against the alien had drained him of most of his power. It was time to free him and the others as well.

It shouldn't be too difficult to convince the others to attack me, she thought with morbid self-loathing.

Taking a deep breath, she returned her gaze to the woman and raised the curved dagger. With a quick motion of her hand, she cut a thin, shallow line across the king's throat. The alien inside her grew excited by her bold move. A soft hiss slipped from her parted lips when the creature surged forward for the next action.

Not yet, she murmured.

Kill him! He will be the first to die. I no longer need him, the alien entity ordered.

If I kill him, the others will have no reason to come closer. We must wait until they are all close enough before we strike, she insisted, keeping the swirling mass along the ceiling in her peripheral vision.

Magna released another shrill laugh before she addressed the witch. "The Sea King is bound by the laws of his people. He is weak and unable to harm me," she goaded with a shrug of one slender shoulder.

"He might be, but I'm not," a loud voice retorted from the entrance to the throne room.

Her eyes shifted to the doorway. Inside, she felt the alien recoil. She could almost taste the creature's fear and craving for the over-whelming power of the dragon. She took in Drago's massive form with a surge of satisfaction and anticipation.

Drago stood in the center of the now destroyed door frame, his face and body taut with rage. Magna bit her lip. The alien inside her was still too strong for her to release her bonds. Before Drago's fire could be effective enough, she needed the last element of her plan – Orion and his trident.

"It is time to die, Sea Witch! I have waited far too long for this moment. You should be thankful that I will make it swift. I would love nothing more than to make you feel a measure of the agony that you have caused others," Drago sneered as he stepped into the room.

His eyes blazed with a ghost of his dragon-fire. Vengeance burned so brightly within him that his chest glowed a dark, blood red through the fabric of his shirt. His features were hard, and his long black hair flowed around him as he strode toward her. The intent was clear in his eyes – death.

Out of the corner of her eye, she saw the movement of long threads of the black, thorny tentacles reaching downward to wrap around Drago. Her hand reached out in warning, and a cry slipped from her lips.

"Watch out!" she cried.

You defy me! the creature hissed inside her.

It was time. She could not wait any longer.

"Goddess, please... give me the strength I need to finish this," she whispered.

Her eyes teared with the sudden intense pain that swept through her. Fire burned through her veins. Her lips parted in a scream of agony when another intense wave hit her, but she swallowed it. She had to do what she could to distract the alien so that Drago or one of the others could strike at her.

A shuddering breath hissed from her. "Yesssss! You will never be able to defeat Drago and Orion," she whispered to the being inside her as she fought for control.

I will destroy them all. Then, I will take care of you, the creature inside her hissed in fury.

"I... will not... allow you to harm... them," she vowed.

She fought, but the creature forced the hand holding the knife to rise. She knew exactly what it was intending to do – kill King Oray. She wrapped her other hand around the wrist of the hand holding the knife, pushing against the movement with both hands.

"No!" she screamed, her body twisting away from the King.

The alien creature sent shards of electrical charges through her body, and her body bowed, her heart stuttering. She straightened like a puppet on a string and the knife again headed for the king's throat. At the same time, the sound of an explosion resonated throughout the chamber. Magna felt a mind-shattering pain rip through her left shoulder. The knife fell to the floor as the force of the blow violently jerked her body backward, forced to turn from the impact on her shoulder, and she collapsed onto the floor.

She lay dazed on the cold stone near the throne. She could feel the warmth of her blood seeping through her clothing and beginning to pool under her. As she panted, the alien strained to free itself from her body, and she instinctively tightened her hold on the spell binding it close to her, but the alien surged through the spell-less path which had been created with the weapon's gaping wound.

She issued a long, pain-filled gasp and her body arched as the dark entity poured out of her body through the wound in her shoulder. A shudder ran through her and she watched as the black cloud rose above her in a swirling mass. She sank back to the floor as the last of the entity vacated her body. A strange feeling, as if there were a huge, cavernous void inside of her, left her feeling momentarily confused and weak.

The feeling was quickly replaced with one that was all too familiar – fear. It burned through her, leaving her fingers and toes numb with it and her lungs constricted when she realized that the alien was now searching for a new host. It was too soon for it to be unbound; Orion hadn't yet hit her with the Trident's power. The alien was still fully in control of all of its own power.

The creature turned its attention to King Oray. Lifting her right hand, she whispered the spell that had bound them. Her body jerked when the spell hooked the entity, compelling it away from the frail King.

On the other side of the throne, she heard her cousin's voice. Tears filled her eyes at the sound of it. There was so much she wanted to tell him. She would give anything to be able to beg for his forgiveness for everything that she had been unwillingly forced to do.

"Fire on it," Orion shouted.

Release me, the alien hissed, wrathfully twisting and turning as Orion and Drago attacked it. *I will destroy you!*

Magna ignored the threat, knowing that she would be the one doing the destroying. She held the slender thread of connection between herself and the alien that had controlled her for the last two centuries with an iron will born of hope, desperation, and grief.

Closing her eyes, she focused on that link, slowly wrapping a second spell around it. The spells would hold the alien suspended in place above the throne, preventing it from moving away from her while also stopping it from returning to her body. A shudder ran through her when she felt the touch of a warm hand under her chin. She opened her eyes and stared up at the man who had injured her with his strange weapon. Tears slowly trailed down from the corners of her eyes at his look of concern.

"Go!" she ordered, licking her dry lips. "You have to... go," she repeated, forcing the whispered words past the tight lump in her throat.

The man shook his head. "Not without you," he replied in a grim tone.

He started to slide his arm around her shoulder and lift her. Her face contorted at the intense pain threatening to drown her in its fierce waves. Her right hand reached up to push against the man's shoulder. She shook her head in regret.

"What is your name?" she asked, needing to know.

The man gave her a startled look. "Mike Hallbrook. I have to get you out of here," he replied with a frown.

Her gaze moved to the ceiling above them again. He turned his head to see what she was looking at. Now was the time to strike. The creature was being torn apart by Drago's dragon-fire and the disrupting bolts of power from the tridents of Orion and his men. She would kill the alien creature once and for all.

"No," she said with a slight shake of her head when he started to lift her again. "No, I know how to... how to kill it now. Go! What I have to do will kill you all if you don't. Go, Mike Hallbrook. Save my king and the Isles. Take the others with you. There is no hope for me. I would be sentenced to death anyway. Let me at least have some purpose to my life," she pleaded in a tired voice.

She watched Mike's eyes darken with indecision. Fear and determination gave her the strength she needed to push him to the side. She unsteadily rose to her feet. Taking a deep breath, she pulled on the last dwindling ounce of her strength and lifted her head. She ignored the agonizing pain in her shoulder as she raised her arms above her head and began chanting in a clear voice filled with determination.

Magic flooded her body, and she could feel the energy from the Isle of Magic seep into her, giving her the added strength she needed to cast the final blow that would free them all. Bright red blood ran down from her shoulder, staining the front of her white gown. She ignored everything but the magic of the spell building inside her and the black swarm of the alien near the ceiling.

I will not fail, she vowed to herself.

In the background, she could hear the urgent sound of Mike yelling for Drago and Orion to retreat. Mike had King Oray over his shoulder and was hurrying toward the burnt-out entrance of the throne room. Drago and Orion stopped their attacks to leave with him, and the alien refocused all its remaining strength to fighting against her hold.

"Let the light of truth guide me and be my sword," she chanted.

Bright light flared out from around her as the spell she cast ignited the air in the room. Surging waves of power rolled through the room like a thick fog, sucking the air out of it. She could hear the sizzle of the alien's body as the power swept over it, igniting its body with the bright light.

The creature struck out at her, but the blinding power of the light radiating from her prevented it from reaching her. Magna felt her body rising above the stone floor. Closing her eyes, she thought of the vast ocean that was her home and wished its cool liquid was surrounding her, extinguishing the flames that were scorching her tired body. As the air around her blazed with power, she felt her body being ripped apart until the void of blackness finally gave her relief.

It is over, she thought. *I am free.*

Chapter 2

Off the coast of Yachats, Oregon:

Gabe Lightcloud powered his thirty-two-foot trawler along the rocky coast. He took a deep breath of the crisp salty air. Today had been a good day.

He glanced at the time on the depth finder. *No wonder my stomach is protesting,* he thought. It was nearly seven o'clock in the evening. Turning the wheel, he started the long trip back to the docks. He had left the house just before sunrise and had spent most of the day doing catch and release for the U.S. Fish and Wildlife Service. A new program at the University of Oregon had given him an opportunity to combine work with research. The University of Oregon's grant was part of an on-going research program backed by the USFWS to study the migratory patterns of Chinook Salmon.

As far as Gabe was concerned, he'd been assigned the fun part of the research – tagging, releasing, and not having to deal with people. He enjoyed the peace and quiet of working offshore. The sound of the motor, the waves slapping against the hull of his boat, and the high-pitched cries of seagulls hoping for an easy meal were his companions. He preferred them above anything else. He rolled his shoulders, glad he had finished his last catch for the day.

He hadn't had anything to eat except an egg sandwich and a thermos of coffee this morning. He grinned as he stared out at the water. A nice shrimp dinner sounded pretty good right about now. If he couldn't snag any, he'd settle for a nice grilled halibut. His mouth started watering at the thought of them cooking on the grill. Either one would be a welcome treat and was just what he needed to quiet his rebelling stomach. Hell, he might even be nice and see if Kane wanted to come over to watch the football game.

He turned the wheel when he saw a school of fish on the depth finder and pushed the throttle to neutral. Stepping out of the wheelhouse, he released the lock on the winch and lowered the net into the water. He made sure it wasn't tangled before he turned back to the helm. Checking the settings on the depth finder, he searched the bottom for any structures that might be an issue before he pushed the throttle forward. He decided he'd troll for half an hour before pulling everything in and heading back home.

The time was almost up when he felt a slight drag on the boat. He turned in time to see the buoy attached to the net violently dip below the surface. He quickly pushed the throttle back into neutral. He muttered a curse and sighed in frustration. He should have quit while he was ahead. If the net was caught on the bottom or worse, tangled around some floating garbage, it could mean a long night, which meant it would be even longer before he had anything to eat.

Gabe grabbed the net and began pulling it in. The one thing that bugged him more than anything else was when people decided to use the ocean as their own private garbage dump. He was always finding shit that someone had thrown out.

He frowned when he felt the net shift. Afraid it might have caught on something, he looked over the side, but didn't see any sign that it was snagged. He hoped it wasn't, because the net was a pain in the ass to patch. Shifting the winch into gear again, he continued reeling in the net. Then he heard a moan.

"What the hell?" he muttered, pressing the stop button on the winch control. "Shit!"

Muttering under his breath, he decided he must have snagged some unsuspecting seal pup. He grabbed the net and continued pulling it in by hand. His eyes widened in shock when he saw a person caught in the net. Moving swiftly, he finished pulling the net in. He lowered it and his unexpected catch to the deck of the rocking boat. Grabbing the side of the net, he released it from the rigging and knelt next to the still, cold body.

"Damn it," Gabe muttered under his breath. "I don't need a dead body on my boat."

He gently rolled the body over, pulled away the netting tangled around it, and gasped when he saw that it belonged to a woman. Yanking off his gloves, he carefully brushed the long tangle of midnight hair back from her pale face. He touched the icy skin of her neck, feeling for a pulse, and pulled back in surprise when she shuddered and moaned.

He gently touched her cheek again, smoothing back a long strand of hair. She was deathly pale with dark shadows under her eyes. His shocked brain also noted that she was beautiful in a weird, exotic way.

"Hey, lady," Gabe said in a rough voice. "Can you hear me?"

He watched in fascination as her lush, black eyelashes fluttered for a moment before she opened her eyes. He gazed down into crystal-clear green eyes. He couldn't help but wonder who in the hell she was and why she was miles off the Pacific Coast in freezing water. He was just about to ask her when she rolled to her side and threw up all over his rubber boots.

"Ah, hell," he muttered, looking down at the heaving figure.

∼

Half an Hour Earlier:

Magna softly moaned as the pain from her shoulder pulled her to consciousness for a brief moment. The pain was the first thing telling her that she hadn't died from her Starburst spell. The gentle sway of her body surrounded by water and the feeling of weightlessness was the second thing.

For a brief moment, she wondered if the Goddess had granted her a measure of compassion. That thought quickly fled when she tried to move and was in too much pain and too exhausted to do it. The current flowed around her, sweeping her along the rocky bottom, and she was powerless to prevent herself from bumping against the rocks, causing even more excruciating pain to radiate through her. The spell had taken every ounce of energy she had left.

Eventually, an upwelling current caused her to rise, mercifully giving her a measure of relief. As she floated along, Magna didn't bother opening her eyes. She preferred not knowing where she was for fear of waking up and discovering it was all an illusion and she was once more a captive inside her own body. She wanted to hold onto the feel of the water surrounding her, even if it came with pain.

She listlessly floated for what seemed like an eternity before something wrapped around her. The weight of the coarse threads pushed her back down to the bottom. She tried to lift her hand and push it away, but it was useless. She was too weak. She gave up, and let it take her. Deciding that her dream was coming to another agonizing end, she gave in to the darkness.

She awoke again when she was lifted out of the soothing comfort of the water. She wanted to scream in protest, but the scream came out as a soft moan. As she was lowered onto a hard surface, a stray tear slipped from the corner of her eye and grief filled her. All hope was gone. She couldn't fight the creature any longer. The only way she could still be alive was if she had failed. Nausea rose in her throat when the cold air connected with the wound in her shoulder. A protest formed on her lips when she was suddenly rolled onto her back.

A shudder swept through her when a warm hand pressed against her neck. Her eyes fluttered open and she found herself staring up into a pair of unfamiliar brown eyes. The combination of pain and the movement of her body was too much for her rebellious stomach. Rolling to the side, she ejected the last remnants of the dead creature from her stomach all over the man's scuffed up white boots.

She dropped her head to the side when she was done. She was too weak and tired to bother lifting it. Instead, she closed her eyes and shuddered again as the darkness rose up to claim her. She hoped this time it was for good. She really was too tired to fight any longer.

~

Gabe contemplated the woman lying on the deck of his boat as he knelt next to her limp body. There was a little more color in her face now that she'd thrown up. Muttering a series of expletives under his breath, he gently scooped her up in his arms and rose to his feet. He squinted, and carefully searched the water nearby before looking up to scan the horizon. There wasn't another boat in sight. He looked toward the rocky coast. Hell, he was at least a mile offshore. There was no way the woman swam that distance, especially wearing an evening gown.

He looked down at her again and froze. The gown on her left shoulder was bright red with fresh blood. He tightened his lips into a firm line and he walked toward the lower galley and cabin area.

Awkwardly navigating the stairs, he breathed a sigh of relief when the woman didn't react as he shifted her around to fit through the doorway. He walked over to his bunk and gently laid her down, then turned on the light above his bed. He gripped the material on her shoulder and ripped it open. His eyes widened, and he paled when he saw the evidence hidden beneath the silky material.

"Shot?" he hissed, glancing back up at her pale face. "Lady, what the hell happened to you? Why would anyone shoot you and dump your ass in the Pacific?"

He gently lifted her enough to see the other side of her shoulder. There was no exit wound. Gabe stood up and pulled open the cabinet above the bed. He pulled out the first aid kit and sat back down. Setting the kit down on the bed, he opened it and pulled out some gauze bandage and tape. There wasn't much he could do for her on the boat. It wasn't the cleanest place in the world and he didn't have the medical expertise to remove a bullet. He would patch her up as best he could and radio for assistance.

He quickly dried the area, covered the wound with the clean gauze, and taped it down. He looked at the relaxed lines of the woman's face. She hadn't moved an inch during his clumsy patch job. Unable to resist, he reached out and turned her face toward him. Her features were arresting. She didn't look like she was of European descent, but she didn't look like she had any Asian ancestry either. His fingers ran down her pale cheek.

A slight, rusty smile curved his lips before a frown creased his brow when he noticed a thin line along the right side of her pale neck. It started just behind her ear and curved down about two inches. Another line of faint but colorful tattoos ran down beside it. He reached out to touch the marks but quickly pulled back when he felt the smooth, glossy texture of each design. They reminded him of…

"Scales?" he muttered with a disbelieving shake of his head. "What the hell is going on?"

Standing, he quickly deposited the scraps from the bandage into the trash. He returned the first aid kit to the cabinet before he grabbed a thin blanket and covered her with it. He frowned and ran a hand through his hair, trying to think if there was anything else he should do before he returned to the upper deck.

He decided he had done the best he could for the moment. Glancing down one last time to make sure the woman was still unconscious, he turned on his heel and strode back up the stairs. It looked like it was going to be a long night. He grimaced when his stomach growled in protest again. Dinner would have to be pushed back until his unexpected guest was safely delivered into the hands of the proper authorities.

Gabe quickly secured the net and made sure the deck, and his boots, were cleared and cleaned before he stepped through the passage to the bridge. He pushed the throttle forward, slowly picking up speed, and headed for home again. He reached for the mic on his radio, then paused. With a low growl of frustration, he pulled his hand back and ran it through his disheveled hair before he reached for his cell phone instead.

His gaze flickered from the sea in front of him to the phone. He released the breath he hadn't realized he'd been holding. He had three bars. Pressing the phone icon, he punched in the number he knew by heart.

"This is Kane," a distracted voice said on the other end.

"I need help," Gabe bit out in a sharp voice.

There was a slight pause before Kane spoke again. "How bad?" Kane asked.

"Gunshot to the left shoulder," Gabe replied.

This time the pause was filled with a low hiss. "Who'd you piss off this time?" Kane asked sharply. "You know I'm supposed to report anything like this."

"Yeah, I know," Gabe said in a low voice. "It's not me this time. Just be at my house in an hour. I'll be coming in from the dock."

"I'll be there," Kane responded in a tense voice. "You sure you don't want to come to the clinic?"

Gabe's lips twisted in a sardonic grin. "Naw," he said. "Then you'd really feel like you had to report it."

The sound of a frustrated sigh made Gabe thankful he wasn't onshore yet. Kane wasn't above bending the rules or looking the other way when he felt it was necessary, but Gabe wouldn't ask his friend to jeopardize his practice or his medical license by having to cover for him there. Now, coming to his house… What happened there, stayed there.

"One of these days I'm going to ignore it when you call," Kane threatened. "I'll be at the dock."

"Thanks, man," Gabe replied in a soft voice. "Something tells me that this should be kept quiet."

"You can explain when we're together," Kane retorted.

"Right now, there's not much to explain," Gabe admitted. "I'll be coming around the point in about forty minutes."

Gabe clicked the phone off and slid it back into his pocket. Exactly forty minutes later, he automatically swung wide into the mouth of the narrow inlet and slowly pulled back on the throttle so he wouldn't create a wake. Frustration ate at him, and his fingers twitched in impatience on the throttle. He knew the feeling of restlessness and unease was due to his unexpected passenger.

"I hope to hell this doesn't become more complicated," he grunted as he navigated the narrow, winding passage to the dock below his house.

The Sea Witch's Redemption

SAMPLE OF DUST: BEFORE AND AFTER

2016 Gold Winner of the Wishing Shelf Book Awards!

Synopsis:

Dust wakes to discover the world as he knew it is gone after fragments of a comet hit the Earth. It isn't the only thing that has changed, though, so has Dust...

Read on for more than a full chapter of Dust: Before and After!

Chapter 1
Before and After

Dust woke from his sleep, blinking up at the dark gray skies. He could see the swirl of acidic clouds through the hole in the ceiling. It took a moment for his body to catch up with his mind.

He often forgot to focus on it. Since the morning he woke up alone in a collapsed building that had once been his home, he realized that things would never be the same. Before, he was just a fourteen year old boy who loved playing video games and hated going to school. A year had passed since the day the comet hit the Earth. A year since the strange cloud had washed through the small town where he had lived *Before*. That is what he called his life... Before. Now, he was in the After.

His body wrenched as it came back to its solid form. He was used to the feeling now and thought no more about his unusual ability to dissolve into the shadows. Rising up off the floor, he stretched and twisted. Glancing around, he walked over to the bent metal cabinet where he had hidden his knapsack. It contained one pair of jeans, one shirt, a clean pair of underwear and socks, and a bottle of water.

With a wave of his hand, the debris in front of the cabinet rose up into the air and moved. He opened the door and pulled out the dark green knapsack he had found in one of his many excursions over the past year. Slinging the strap over his shoulder, he turned and quietly left the building.

Dust paused on the sidewalk outside the small convenience store where he had taken refuge. His disheveled brown hair stuck out in all directions. Glancing around, his dark brown eyes paused on a moving shadow between two abandoned cars halfway down the street. The sense of danger rose in his gut. His gaze narrowed on the three shadowy forms that slowly stepped out from between them.

Devil dogs.

He didn't know if that was what they were really called, but that was the name he had given them. They were like him... different.

Turning, he slipped the straps over his shoulders so he could run faster. It was time to move on. Where there were three of the creatures, there could be more. Dust felt the adrenaline surge through him as he took off at a steady pace, glancing back and forth as he ran through the center of the small town he had arrived in late the night before. He had hoped to find food. The changes to his body demanded that he eat more often.

Food wasn't always the easiest thing to find. The lack of it was what had finally forced him to leave the small town where he had lived with his family during the time Before. As the sole survivor, he had foraged for every piece of food he could find during the past year until he could find no more.

Dust didn't bother turning to see where the creatures were. He knew they would follow him. They were hungry. He knew, because he felt the same hunger. There would be a fight, of that he had no doubt. Up ahead was the shell of a two-story building. With a wave of his hand, the door was ripped off its hinges and it flew out behind him. He heard a snarl and a thud. They were closer than he'd realized.

Sprinting across the sidewalk, he disappeared into the shadows and allowed his body to dissolve. It would be difficult to keep his shadow form for long. He desperately needed food if he was going to continue using the amount of energy that he needed to maintain this form. Scooping up a metal pipe as he flew by, he turned just as the first shape came through the door behind him. The end of the pipe caught the creature in the chest, impaling it and driving him back against the wall. His body solidified at the force and the wind was knocked from him as he slammed into the wall.

The creature's glowing red eyes flashed and its jaws snapped, but he could already see the light fading. He immediately recognized that the creatures must be starving to attack him so boldly. Not only that, they couldn't hold their shadow form any longer than he could. He pressed the metal rod down to the floor and forced the metal tip further through the beast and twisted it. The creature's loud snarls turned to a scream before silence engulfed the room. Dust didn't wait. There were at least two left, possibly more.

Ripping the pipe out of the creature, he turned toward the open stairwell. The faint sound of glass crunching under heavy feet pulled his gaze to the ceiling. He could hear one of them. It must have gone through an upper level window. Dust's jaw tightened. He would have to kill all of them or the creatures would follow him and he would never find food or rest. His fingers wrapped around the cool metal and he started up the steps, taking them in a slow, steady climb. He was almost to the top when the huge black creature appeared at the top of the stairs.

Dust glanced over his shoulder when he heard a second snarl

behind him. He was stuck between the two beasts. Glancing back and forth, he realized that they had set up a trap for him. A shiver ran through him. He started when the one above him suddenly jumped. Focusing, he used more of his precious energy. The creature flashed through his body, sending a wave of nausea through him. His body once more solidified and he thrust upward, pushing the rod through its soft underbelly while it was still in the air. He allowed the weight of the creature to twist him around. The force of the movement and his gradually weakening strength tore the metal pipe from his hands as it crashed into the beast moving up the stairs at the same time.

Stumbling back against the wall, he watched as the dying creature struck its companion. He gripped the stairwell and pulled himself up. He needed to find another weapon before the last beast regained its footing. His legs shook as he half crawled, half climbed the stairs. He barely had time to roll to the side before the third creature came up through the narrow opening and turned. Dust rolled to his stomach, his gaze froze on the heaving chest and foaming jaws. His arms trembled and he knew he didn't have the strength to dissolve.

He pushed upward in a slow, steady movement, never taking his eyes off the beast. He was almost to his feet when it sprang. Jumping, he twisted to the side and rolled. Almost immediately he was back on his feet and twisting around. The beast had slid into a large wooden desk. The force of its body hitting the desk shattered one of the legs and the heavy piece of furniture collapsed on top of it. He took advantage of the reprieve, darting down the staircase. He jumped over the dead creature at the bottom, tearing out the metal pipe protruding from its chest. Running, he burst back outside.

A loud crash resounded behind him. Dust didn't pause. Spying an abandoned SUV with its door partially open across the street, he pushed every ounce of energy he had left inside him to his quivering legs. He reached out and grabbed the door handle, pulling it open far enough to squeeze through. He barely had time to pull it closed before the beast hit the door with enough force to knock the SUV onto two wheels. The force of the blow knocked Dust across the console and into the passenger seat. He quickly pulled his legs up when the glass on the driver's door shattered.

Dust fumbled for the handle behind him as the beast thrust its long black head inside, its jaws snapping viciously at his legs. Blood dripped on the fine leather interior from where the ragged glass cut into the beast's neck. That didn't stop it. If anything, the creature became more enraged, clawing at the glass and pulling it away so it could try to wiggle into the vehicle. Dust kicked out, striking the canine-like snout. It jerked its head back, giving him just enough room to grab the door handle. He fell out the other side, landing heavily on his back. Kicking his foot out again, he slammed the door just as the creature jumped into the driver's seat.

Rolling stiffly onto his hands and knees, he gripped the metal rod in his hand and rose to his feet. Glancing back at the snarling beast, he took off running. It was only a matter of seconds before he heard the sound of breaking glass again. Ducking under a torn awning, he darted through the open door of another building. It didn't take long for him to realize his mistake. The back section of the building was blocked by fallen debris. The only thing separating him from death was a tall refrigerated display case and the metal pipe in his hand. Turning, he backed up as the dark shadow paused in the entrance.

"Don't move until I tell you," a soft voice said behind him.

Chapter 2
Someone Else Lives

Dust froze, his eyes locked on the blazing red eyes of the devil dog even as he wanted to turn to the sound of the voice. It was the first voice other than his own that he'd heard in over a year. Afraid he was dreaming, he stood ready, holding the bloody pipe in front of him.

The beast took another step and snarled. White foam dripped from its mouth and its yellow teeth snapped as it moved through the doorway. Dust knew it was about to attack. The sound of the voice yelling for him to move echoed through the air at the same time as a thin shaft flew past his right shoulder.

He jumped to the side, sliding under a table that was bolted to the floor. His back hit the wall and he jerked his legs out of the way as the beast's thick, black body slid across the few feet of cleared space on the dirty tile. He stared in shock at the two thick shafts of wood sticking out of its throat and upper chest. The beast's red eyes were blank and its jaw hung open as it pulled in its last breath of air.

Dust slowly scooted out from under the table, keeping his eyes on the creature just in case. He was rising to his feet when a movement behind the counter caught his attention. Turning, he held the dark gray pipe out in front of him. Two figures, one slightly taller than the other rose from behind an old display. Swallowing, Dust stared at the two dirty faces looking back at him with a combination of curiosity and fear. It took a moment for him to realize that the tall person was pointing one of the long arrows at him.

Dust waited, staring at the girl. He saw her swallow, but she didn't lower the bow in her hands. The small boy next to her scooted slightly behind her when Dust glanced at him. His gaze returned to the girl's face. He curled his fingers into a tight fist as a wave of dizziness washed through him. The hunger was beginning to become unbearable. He needed something to eat.

"Who are you?" Dust asked in a rusty voice, his eyes locked on the face of the young girl who seemed to be close to his own age.

Dust swayed as he waited for the girl to respond. He saw her swallow again and nervously bite her bottom lip. She still didn't lower the bow in her hands, even though he had dropped the pipe to his side. The small boy next to her stared back at Dust with a wide-eyed, curious expression. Dust kept his gaze fixed on the girl's face.

Dust: Before and After

ADDITIONAL BOOKS AND INFORMATION

If you loved this story by me (S.E. Smith) please leave a review! You can also take a look at additional books and sign up for my newsletter to hear about my latest releases at:

http://sesmithfl.com
http://sesmithya.com

or keep in touch using the following links:

http://sesmithfl.com/?s=newsletter
https://www.facebook.com/se.smith.5
https://twitter.com/sesmithfl
http://www.pinterest.com/sesmithfl/
http://sesmithfl.com/blog/
http://www.sesmithromance.com/forum/

The Full Booklist

Science Fiction / Romance

Cosmos' Gateway Series
Tilly Gets Her Man (Prequel)
Tink's Neverland (Book 1)
Hannah's Warrior (Book 2)
Tansy's Titan (Book 3)
Cosmos' Promise (Book 4)
Merrick's Maiden (Book 5)
Core's Attack (Book 6)
Saving Runt (Book 7)

Curizan Warrior Series
Ha'ven's Song (Book 1)

Dragon Lords of Valdier Series
Abducting Abby (Book 1)
Capturing Cara (Book 2)
Tracking Trisha (Book 3)
Dragon Lords of Valdier Boxset Books 1-3
Ambushing Ariel (Book 4)
For the Love of Tia Novella (Book 4.1)
Cornering Carmen (Book 5)
Paul's Pursuit (Book 6)
Twin Dragons (Book 7)
Jaguin's Love (Book 8)
The Old Dragon of the Mountain's Christmas (Book 9)
Pearl's Dragon Novella (Book 10)
Twin Dragons' Destiny (Book 11)

Marastin Dow Warriors Series
A Warrior's Heart Novella

Dragonlings of Valdier Novellas
A Dragonling's Easter
A Dragonling's Haunted Halloween
A Dragonling's Magical Christmas

Night of the Demented Symbiots (Halloween 2)
The Dragonlings' Very Special Valentine
The Dragonlings and the Magic Four-Leaf Clover

Lords of Kassis Series
River's Run (Book 1)
Star's Storm (Book 2)
Jo's Journey (Book 3)
Rescuing Mattie Novella (Book 3.1)
Ristéard's Unwilling Empress (Book 4)

Sarafin Warriors Series
Choosing Riley (Book 1)
Viper's Defiant Mate (Book 2)

The Alliance Series
Hunter's Claim (Book 1)
Razor's Traitorous Heart (Book 2)
Dagger's Hope (Book 3)
The Alliance Boxset Books 1-3
Challenging Saber (Book 4)
Destin's Hold (Book 5)
Edge of Insanity (Book 6)

Zion Warriors Series
Gracie's Touch (Book 1)
Krac's Firebrand (Book 2)

Magic, New Mexico Series
Touch of Frost (Book 1)

Paranormal / Fantasy / Romance

Magic, New Mexico Series
Taking on Tory (Book 2)

Alexandru's Kiss (Book 3)

Spirit Pass Series
Indiana Wild (Book 1)
Spirit Warrior (Book 2)

Second Chance Series
Lily's Cowboys (Book 1)
Touching Rune (Book 2)

More Than Human Series
Ella and the Beast (Book 1)

The Seven Kingdoms
The Dragon's Treasure (Book 1)
The Sea King's Lady (Book 2)
A Witch's Touch (Book 3)
The Sea Witch's Redemption (Book 4)

The Fairy Tale Series
The Beast Prince Novella
*Free Audiobook of The Beast Prince is available:
https://soundcloud.com/sesmithfl/sets/the-beast-prince-the-fairy-tale-series

Epic Science Fiction / Action Adventure

Project Gliese 581G Series
Command Decision (Book 1)
First Awakenings (Book 2)
Survival Skills (Book 3)

New Adult

Breaking Free Series

Capture of the Defiance (Book 2)

Young Adult

Breaking Free Series
Voyage of the Defiance (Book 1)

The Dust Series
Dust: Before and After (Book 1)
Dust: A New World Order (Book 2)

Recommended Reading Order Lists:

http://sesmithfl.com/reading-list-by-events/
http://sesmithfl.com/reading-list-by-series/

ABOUT THE AUTHOR

S.E. Smith is a *New York Times, USA TODAY, International, and Award-Winning* Bestselling author of science fiction, romance, fantasy, paranormal, and contemporary works for adults, young adults, and children. She enjoys writing a wide variety of genres that pull her readers into worlds that take them away.

31901063202032